Hawley Smart

A Racing Rubber

A Novel

Hawley Smart

A Racing Rubber
A Novel

ISBN/EAN: 9783337032760

Printed in Europe, USA, Canada, Australia, Japan

Cover: Foto ©Andreas Hilbeck / pixelio.de

More available books at **www.hansebooks.com**

A RACING RUBBER

A Novel.

BY

HAWLEY SMART,

AUTHOR OF

"BREEZIE LANGTON," "BOUND TO WIN,"
"THE OUTSIDER," "BEATRICE AND BENEDICK,"
&c., &c.

IN ONE VOLUME.

LONDON:

F. V. WHITE & CO.,
14, BEDFORD STREET, STRAND, W.C.
1895.

PREFACE.

" 'Tis done; and old Time is the winner,
I held him a race to the last,
But the sands must run fainter and thinner,
And the notches all count to the past."
—WHYTE MELVILLE.

IN these latter days, when the extreme sensitive-
ness of the Nonconformist Conscience would seem
to imply that horse-racing is in itself a crime, it
appears that some explanation is needed in offering
to the public a story, which, as the title implies, does
on the face of it deal almost exclusively with that
ancient and classic sport so dear—from all time—
to the Northern race.

In consequence of this feeling, I have been
advised to change the name of my husband's last
story—last in the sense, that it was upon its con-
cluding pages that he was actually engaged at the
time of his sudden and unlooked-for death.

But this I have declined to do; because, first,
for no possible advantage to myself would I pre-
sume to change, or in any way touch, the work of
one, whose absolute knowledge of his subjects—a

knowledge not gained by hearsay, but acquired by practical experience of both soldiering and racing— when the latter certainly, stood higher in general estimation than at present, had made him a favourite with the reading public for nearly forty years.

And also because a report having arisen— I know not how—to the effect that I had of late "assisted" in the writing of Captain Hawley Smart's novels, I am advised to take this opportunity of absolutely denying such to have been the case.

Excepting so far as the merely mechanical work of writing from dictation, numbering and arranging of chapters, proof correcting, etc., may be termed "assistance," and which my experience, as my husband's secretary, made it my duty, and —although now a most sorrowful one—even my pleasure to undertake alone, now he can no longer direct me, I have in no way ventured to touch this or any other of his novels. I offer this story therefore as it was left me by him, and in the full hope that it will meet with the appreciation of those, whose opinion he valued most, and whose good-will and friendship, now he is no more—I, as his widow, cherish more dearly, and more gratefully than ever I did in my happier and more prosperous days as his wife and helper.

Neither in the present instance, nor in any

future dealing which may possibly arise with regard to the MSS. left in my hands, should I be so
foolish as to interfere in any way. One might
have supposed that, even to those least versed
in the mysteries of racing, it would have been
tolerably apparent that for a woman, or an outsider of any kind to meddle with the technicalities
of the turf, still more to attempt to write a novel
on the same, must be to come to immediate and
ignominious grief. And this is my best refutation
of so foolish a statement.

It was probably more to Captain Hawley Smart's
accurate knowledge of the ins and outs of racing
and military matters—a knowledge by no means
invariably shared by some of those who fearlessly tackle these subjects—than to his other
literary merits (of which it is not for me to speak)
that he owed his great popularity in these—his
special lines.

That he *wrote of what he knew;* had studied
racing from those palmy days of '49 and '50,
when Sir Joseph Hawley's two-year-olds almost
swept the board; had learnt at least practical
soldiering in the trenches before Sebastopol;
and again in India in '57 and '58, gave an
actuality, a *vraisemblance,* to his writing, which
was from the first duly recognized by the public
(and who so good a judge?), for as everyone knows.

nothing in great or small matters is so convincing as sincerity and truth.

For racing itself, and its moral effects as a national amusement, there is indeed much to be said both ways; happily there are yet many to defend it. And while it enjoys as it does the patronage of, amongst others, the Prince of Wales and the Prime Minister, one can but hope that it will survive the storm of abuse that has been showered upon it of late. It is certainly unfortunate that betting should be inseparable from it. Yet even Mr. Hawke and the Dissenters will perhaps allow that there are two ways of treating most subjects, and that until human nature be other than it now is, there are few professions—even religion and politics —not capable of degradation by ignoble use, and false pretences.

So much the more honour then to one, who, loving the sport himself, conscientiously gave his best work to its delineation in his books. And who to the last—for he died in harness, and whilst admittedly at his best—dealt always with his subject, not from the point of view of a gambler, or bookmaker, but always from that of a sportsman and a gentleman.

A. H. S.

Jersey, Sept. 19*th*, '94.

CONTENTS.

A RACING RUBBER.

A RACING RUBBER.

CHAPTER I.

PROMISING YOUNG ONES.

"IT's a pretty ride, no doubt, and as far as getting an appetite for dinner goes, all very well, but whether this paragon of yours is worth coming all this way to see, Tom, I rather doubt."

"Now, Mr. Praze," returned his companion, who looked like what he was, a well-to-do young farmer, " you know very well I don't talk at random, and I tell you again, this foal is worth your looking at. The old man don't know what he is, or he'd never neglect the poor little beggar in the way he does. He took him, and the half-bred one that's running with him, in payment of a bad debt."

" It don't much matter how old What's-his-name— Darley, isn't it ?—got him. The question is, whether I think him a good-looking foal when I see him. He don't go in for horse-breeding, this Mr. Darley ? "

" Not a bit of it," replied Tom Bramber, " he's about as hard and close-fisted an old curmudgeon as there is in the county. He farms about a couple of hundred acres, and as for horses, he has only those necessary to work his land, and none to spare

1

either. Not a cheerful house, Mr. Praze, nor yet
a very cheerful old fellow in it. I should think
those children of his have a rough time of it now
and again, for they're a precious pair of pickles, and
I shouldn't think old Darley was the man to stand
larks."

They had left the breezy Hampshire Downs behind them by this, and were wending their way
through a more enclosed country. What Mr.
James Praze might be exactly, was hard to determine, but there was one thing about which there
could be no manner of doubt, that, let his vocation
be what it might, it was in some way connected
with horses. The neat boot, the cut of the trouser,
the single-breasted coat of Oxford grey, and the
man's easy seat in the saddle, all shewed it, though
in what particular capacity he dealt with them,
one might not be able to say.

"We've not much further to go now," said
Bramber, " and remember we shall have come two-
thirds of the distance. My place lies off to the
right here, and we've no call to retrace our steps."

Suddenly screams from the adjoining field fell upon
their ears; not of terror, but of mingled applause
and laughter, and a tremendous yell close at hand
caused them to check their horses sharply. It was
well that they were going at a foot's pace, for in
another instant, a ragged boy sitting bare-backed
on a clever-looking pony, came flying over the fence
on their right hand, the pair landing in a somewhat
confused heap, on the bank of the opposite hedge.

Had they been only going a little quicker, the chances are the young urchin would have landed on the top of them. For a moment the two men were too much astonished and too concerned at what looked like a severe "crumpler," to speak, but no sooner did the boy and his fellow-culprit pick themselves up, and it had become evident that they were none the worse for their exploit, than Mr. Praze demanded angrily what the devil the young gentleman meant by endangering people's lives in that fashion? Didn't he know that nobody but a thorough tailor would have jumped into a lane like that, unless hounds were running? What the etc., etc., did he mean by it?

"Please, sir, I couldn't help it, and I ain't a tailor," replied the boy indignantly. "I couldn't hold him with this old snaffle, and he got clean away with me. When I found I couldn't stop him, there was nothing but to send him at it, best pace, and chance what came of it."

"It's young Jim Darley," said Bramber, in a low tone; "and I'm blest if he hasn't got Silcox's pet pony. Hulloa, Master Jim," he continued, addressing the lad, "I'd no idea you and Mr. Silcox were such friends. It isn't everybody he'd lend that pony to. How are his knees after that tumble?"

The boy's face fell, and a look of intense relief came over his face as, after a rapid survey of his steed's legs, he ascertained that the skin was unbroken.

"Please, sir," he rejoined, "his knees are all

1 *

right, and—and Mr. Silcox didn't exactly lend me the pony——"

"And if he didn't, I should like to know what you're doing with him?" said Bramber.

"Well, sir," replied the boy, "it was in this way. Mr. Silcox's ten-acre runs up to our forty-acre, and the fence isn't in very good repair. It's father's, you see, and he won't have it done up, and the pony got straying down there." And then, seeing the broad grin on Bramber's face, regaining his habitual confidence, which the fall and the subsequent detection of his crime had temporarily shaken, he added: "And I thought he wanted a gallop."

"You young scamp," rejoined Bramber laughing, "You've stolen Mr. Silcox's pony, and precious near broke its neck. What do you expect will happen to you if he finds it out?"

"I shall get a jolly good hiding from either him or father," said the boy, without hesitation. "And I only hope it will be from him."

At this juncture, Mr. Praze became conscious that there was another spectator of the scene. Gazing over the hedge and evidently much interested in her brother's fate, was a very pretty girl about sixteen years of age. She was apparently quite satisfied with the turn the affair had taken, for, upon seeing she was discovered, she called out:

"Are you all right, Jim?" To which the culprit nodded in the affirmative.

"Well, young 'un," said Tom Bramber, "it's not

my business, and I'm not going to say anything to either Mr. Silcox or your father, but you take my advice and just you put that pony back where you took him from as quick as you can."

"And remember," said Mr. Praze, "next time you jump into a lane, to think of other people's necks, whatever you do about your own. And here," he added, taking a note-book from his breast pocket and rapidly scribbling in it, " a young scamp like you is certain to make your home too hot to hold you before long. When you do you can write to me. There's the address," and throwing the leaf to Jim Darley, Mr. Praze gave him a friendly nod and trotted on.

"That was the girl," said Bramber ; "and she's just about as wild as she is pretty. Both of them, I should think, as likely to go to the bad as any two children in England. It's a thousand pities. There's good stuff in them, and they are quick-witted besides, but with that stern, miserly old father of theirs they'll never have a chance."

It was too true. "Those Darleys" had already attained an evil reputation in the neighbourhood. As may be gathered from Bramber's remarks, old Darley himself wasn't likely to be a popular man in any parish in which he might reside. There was nothing to be alleged actually against him ; if he was hard and parsimonious, he was also just, and paid his way honestly enough. A keen hand at a bargain, no doubt, but then that was all in the way of business, and it was not that was the cause of

his unpopularity. A surly man, well-known to be a
thorough despot in his own family, and showing no
disposition whatever to ask the stranger within his
gates ; a man not to be melted by any tale of
distress, who held emphatically that charity began
at home, and that when people fell upon evil days,
they had only their own want of thrift and
indolence to thank for it. As for Mrs. Darley,
she was a worn, faded-looking woman, suffering
severely from suppressed loquacity. She had been
intended for a cheery gossiping little soul, but was
now thoroughly cowed by her husband's morose
temper. It is difficult no doubt to curb a woman's
tongue, but garrulity must be to some extent
quenched, when responded to by a stern command
to " hold your prate," or " give over cackling."
Mr. Darley was emphatically master in his own
house, and his wife would sooner have bitten her
tongue out, than roused the simoom of his wrath.
As for the children, though small for their age,
they were both good-looking. They were fond of
their mother, but feared, and at times may be said
to have even hated, their father. Quick, clever and
hot-tempered, they might have been done anything
with by kind treatment, but once put their blood
up, and they had wills of their own, and vehemently refused to do anything they disliked. With
their teachers, strange to say, they were rather
favourites, they learnt easily and well, and had a
natural passion for reading. Kate, too, was gifted
with a vivid imagination, and built up airy castles,

in which she invariably figured as a great lady, while the more prosaic Jim, though occasionally persuaded to regard himself as a "lord of high degree," more often persisted in assuming the humbler *rôle* of huntsman, more especially if he could lay hands on any four-footed animal on which to perform the part, and they said in the parish that there was nothing Jim Darley wouldn't try to ride, and the more wicked they were the better he liked them. Cows the imp had been heard to speak disparagingly of; but there was a donkey that had dismissed him as well as most of his companions, for which he had a great respect. Kate and her brother indeed were in the front of most of the mischief in the village. Their associates admired them for their audacity, and though their hot tempers led them into continual quarrels, yet upon the whole they were popular with their schoolfellows.

By the time Mr. Praze had extracted this much information from Bramber, they had arrived at their destination, and opening the gate of a small paddock, Tom led the way inside, and walked his horse leisurely across to where a rough and ragged foal was struggling hard to pick up a scanty living.

"That's him," said Tom; "old Darley don't waste much corn upon him, you may take your oath. That half-bred colt there," and Tom pointed with his hunting crop to the other end of the field, "is master of him."

"Is he?" said Mr. Praze, throwing his eyes

once more critically over the object of Tom's recommendation.

" Yes, and bullies him proper," rejoined Bramber laughing. " You see the grass is a good bit better at that end of the paddock than it is here, and that half-bred beggar won't let him come down there, and you may depend upon it what little corn old Darley may give 'em, he takes good care this one shan't put his nose into it."

" He's not a bad shaped one; but it's rather buying a pig in a poke you know. I suppose you're quite sure about his pedigree ? "

" Quite, he's by Barbarossa out of a Sultan mare."

" And what do you suppose the old man will be asking for him ? "

" He took the couple," rejoined Tom, " in quittance of a debt for a hundred pounds from a young fellow who was broke, and it is possible that he would sooner have that hundred than the colts, but anyhow a little advance upon that, I have no doubt he would jump at."

" Well, it's not a very ruinous price," returned Mr. Praze; " but it's chancy work buying foals."

" Well, Mr. Praze, he'll mend of that mighty soon, he'll be a yearling remember in about two months' time. And I'm sure buying them is quite as big a lottery. Just think of all those you saw sold at Newmarket last week. Look at the prices they fetched, and you know as well I do how precious few of them will turn out worth the money that's been given for them. It's not the young ones that fetch the most money that distinguish themselves on the race-course. I've a great fancy for the blood myself, and if you buy him, you will never repent it. Why before you've had him three months you won't know him."

"I say, Tom," replied his companion laughing, "what commission's old Darley going to give you for bonnetting up his foal in this way?"

Bramber joined in the laugh. "Ah, never mind," he said, "you mean taking him I see, and in that case you had better leave it to me. If a stranger goes to him about that foal, Darley will jump to the conclusion at once that he's worth money and double his price. I can get him cheaper for you than you can for yourself."

"All right, Tom, I'll take him, and I'll leave the business in your hands. And now we had better push on to your place. I must be back in Town to-night, I want to catch the seven-o'clock train."

"Lots of time," replied Bramber as he led the way back into the lane. "And don't forget me in the buy, remember."

Mr. Praze looked at him enquiringly.

"I want to go halves in the colt with you" continued Tom, "I'm game to pay half his expenses, and take my share of what he picks up."

"All right," replied the trainer, "you shall, on the one condition that I have the sole management of him."

CHAPTER II.

THE BIG FROST.

IT was a frost, a terribly hard frost, not one of those black, sunless abominations which wrap the whole country in gloom, and scatter influenza, bronchitis and all the ills that flesh is heir to, in their train, but a bright, hard, old-fashioned frost, which made pulses tingle even if it nipped noses, and produced undue exhilaration of spirit amongst all young people. Down in the Fen country skates were ringing, and the notabilities of those parts were striving their best to break the record and skate the mile in some seconds less than it had ever been done heretofore. Flooded fields were rife in that country, the farmers hadn't seen their land for weeks, and as one of these cheerful agriculturists said it was a comfort to see the spring wheat doing so nicely under the ice. The London Parks were thronged, and the Regent's Park particularly attracted crowds, not only to witness the graceful gyrations of the Skating Club and their imitators, but also for the purpose of joining themselves in the fun. Down in the Shires hunters were eating their heads off, while their masters had flocked after their wont to London, when such a *contretemps* besets them. And in those small country towns where, as Whyte Melville sings—

"The business of life is to hunt every day,"

it is astonishing what boredom descends upon men when the weather puts a stop to their favourite diversion. One can kill a good deal of time at the whist table, but whist from noon to midnight is apt to pall after two or three days. Small wonder that the continued frost sends their visitors trooping back to the metropolis. Down at Newmarket all training operations are comparatively at a standstill, and horses are restricted to walking exercise on the straw beds, and cognoscenti remarks that the Lincolnshire Handicap will result, as it not unfrequently does, in the survival of the fittest, meaning thereby that the horse brought to the post in the best condition will probably win, although he may have his superiors behind him.

Lounging outside the gate of a large stable yard, surrounded by loose boxes, is Mr. James Praze, in earnest confabulation with Tom Bramber.

" I don't say it wasn't a good buy," said the former quietly. " He's growing into a very nice horse, and there ought to be a good race in him when his time comes."

" He's a real beauty," cried Bramber enthusiastically. " When his time comes," he continued impatiently, " Of course you know best, but how you could pass by *all* those great two-year-old stakes beats me. Why there's some thousands he might have won if you'd only let him try."

Mr. Praze looked at his companion with a pitying eye.

" Tom," he said, " if ever you take to training,

bear in mind the secret of success lies, as in many other things, in patience. To hurry a great big topped colt like that would be probably to break him down, and the chances are he'd never be worth a roll of ginger-bread."

"But his legs are clean enough," replied Bramber.

"Yes," rejoined the trainer, "but look how tender I've been with him. Patience, I tell you, and he'll do us a good turn yet. As far as I've ventured to try him I've found him all we could hope for."

"It's more than two years ago since I bought him for you."

"Yes," rejoined Praze, "and who could have supposed that he would turn into the great slashing horse he has? Never fear, Tom, he'll have lots of chances this year. He's entered for plenty of good stakes. If he turn out only as good as I fancy him——"

Here the boxes in the stable-yard opened, and some six or eight boys, who had been busy dressing down their horses, trooped through the gate-way of the yard on their way to breakfast.

"Here you, Darley," suddenly exclaimed Mr. Praze, "come here. Don't let me catch you fiddling with your ash plant again as you were this morning. I don't give a chance to a boy of mine to wear silk till he's learnt to keep his whip still. It'll be quite time for you to try *that* two or three years hence, when you've learnt how to use it."

"I was obliged to hit my horse this morning, sir, he showed temper."

"No he didn't," rejoined the trainer, " but you did. Can't you understand that he's a young skittish scary thing? Something startled him this morning and instead of coaxing him, and speaking gently to him, and so giving him confidence, you lost your temper and hit him. There, that's enough, don't forget."

"How does your sister get on, Jim?" said Bramber as he nodded good-humouredly to the boy.

"She was all right when I heard from her last," replied young Darley, "but I expect she doesn't care about it much. She's rather sharply bitted to what she has been used to."

"Well, the pair of you couldn't expect to run wild for ever," replied Tom, as the boy turned to follow his companions. "How's he doing?" he continued, turning to Praze.

"Well enough," rejoined the trainer; "he's a born horseman and if he can only master his temper will ride some day, but he's an awful hot-tempered little beggar. You see the discipline of my establishment is as strict I take it as any school, and he was a little inclined to kick against it at first, but he very soon found I stood no nonsense. He's awfully ond of his horse, and has any amount of pluck, but his temper sometimes gets the best of him, and he's not to be trusted yet without a sharp eye on him. Ah, I was right about one thing though, this is just the best school he could have come to. His real love of horses and riding will go a long way to keep him

straight." And then the trainer and his guest went
in to breakfast, and had what Mr. Bramber considered a rather unsatisfactory talk about their joint
purchase, insomuch as the impatient Tom could not
induce Mr. Praze to say positively for which of the
great races of the year he contemplated running the
colt.

That jump into the lane of two years ago had been
fraught with considerable importance to the young
Darleys. I may say the young Darleys, because
though at first sight it would seem merely to have
influenced the fortunes of the boy, yet it also in-
directly influenced his sister's career. Tom Bramber
had kept honourable silence with regard to the
felonious appropriation of Silcox's pony, but, to such
a pickle as Jim Darley, that was but a short reprieve.
Some similar escapade speedily brought down upon
him his father's wrath, and the old man was not one
to fall into the mistake of sparing the rod in such
cases. Jim paid the penalty of his transgression with
his usual stoicism, but he had resolved that he would
have no more of it, and a day or two afterwards he
disappeared from his home. It was not likely that
a lad of Darley's would be in possession of much
money, still he borrowed a few shillings from his
sister, and with that and the assistance of his own
legs, made his way to Newmarket. There he
enquired for Mr. James Praze, and had no difficulty
in finding the trainer's dwelling. He was not much
surprised at seeing the lad, but then it took a good
deal to surprise Mr. Praze, moreover he had prog

nosticated that it wouldn't be long before he found his home too hot for him, but when Jim in conclusion asked for work, he replied :

" I don't mind giving you a trial for a month if you like, but it must be all shipshape. We don't take runaway lads here. You must write to your father and let him know where you are, and tell him that if I'm satisfied with you, I'll take you as an apprentice. If he consents to that, you will be bound over to me for five years, and understand that means you can't leave me without my consent, and remember it won't be any use your running away, because no racing stable will employ a runaway apprentice."

Jim Darley who had been wild with the idea ever since he had contemplated what Mr. James Praze of Newmarket might open to him, was only too delighted to do as he was bid. As for Mr. Darley senior, he regarded it as an interposition of Providence on his behalf, that any one should be found willing to take a lad with such a never-to-be-satisfied appetite as Jim's off his hands, and grimly rejoined that he had no doubt his son was going straightway to the father of lies, and that he would get there rather sooner on horseback, while Kate who had abetted her brother in absconding, though grieving sorely at parting with him, saw at once what a chance it was for a boy with his tastes, and highly approved, and so it came about that a few weeks after that memorable ride on Silcox's pony, Jim Darley signed his indentures as apprentice to

Mr. James Praze, for the term of five years, two of which had now elapsed.

Old Darley was the tenant of a Mr. Chacewater, who though not a large landed proprietor owned a comfortable house on a very nice estate on the Wiltshire border, a good old-fashioned country squire, fond of field sports, and spending the greater part of the year in the country, a man who piqued himself on his pigs and had fads about his short-horns, a man who not only farmed well himself, but took care there should be no slovenly farming amongst tenants of his. Mrs. Chacewater too was a kind of Lady Bountiful in the parish. She knew all their own tenants, and their affairs to boot, pretty nearly as well as they did themselves, a good-hearted managing woman, but for all that by no means fussy nor given to interference amongst their people, a popular woman, albeit it was quite recog-nised the Squire's lady could speak her mind, as well as anybody in the parish. They had three children, of whom Reginald the eldest, after dis-tinguishing himself at the University, equally on the cricket field and in the class-rooms, was now called to the Bar in London. The eldest girl was married and in India with her husband, but she had just confided her two children, whom the climate had compelled her to send home, to the care of their grandmother, and casting about for a nursery governess for these, and one who might also be a companion to her younger daughter, Mrs. Chace-water suddenly pitched upon Kate Darley. The girl was too old, she argued, to be running wild as she was in her own home at present. She was just about the same age as Jessie, and she made up her mind that it would be an excellent arrangement all round, good for Kate Darley, a bright, pretty, intelligent girl, in whom she had always taken a great interest, good for her own child Jessie, and it was certainly time those chicks of Anna's were at all events taught to spell. At first Kate was somewhat appalled at the idea and shrank from the inevitable restraint it must put upon her movements, but the loss of Jim had made a terrible gap in her life, and what with her father's morose temper, and her mother's low spirits, she was fain to confess that her home was dull and dreary, so she finally consented to Mrs. Chacewater's proposal, and a few months after Jim's flight, she found herself installed at Chacewater Grange.

There she had passed a very pleasant year, giving much satisfaction to all about her, although she had been occasionally in disgrace, by her inability to control her passionate temper, but if the engaging of Kate had turned out a most successful hit on the part of Mrs. Chacewater, it had been a most excellent thing for the girl herself. One of the things Jessie Chacewater wanted was someone to ride with her, and this to Kate was a supreme delight, and a pleasure in which as yet she had only indulged furtively. Miss Chacewater, though she had had considerable practice, was but a timid horsewoman, while as for Kate, she positively did

2

not know what fear was. Living at the Grange
too, she rapidly acquired a refinement it would have
been impossible for her to have attained in her own
home. Quick and intelligent, and just of an age to
speedily conform to the habits of those with whom
she lived, the tom-boy girl of sixteen, in her eigh-
teenth year was transformed into a vivacious but
perfectly well-mannered young lady. And it was
at this time came a break up of the little family
circle; Mrs. Shackerston, Miss Chacewater that had
been, returned from India, and after paying a visit
to the Grange, she and her husband took a house at
Bath, and the children of course returned to the
care of their own mother. Miss Chacewater, it was
determined, should go to a finishing school in
London, and Jessie, who had become much attached
to her friend, pleaded so hard against their separation, that Mrs. Chacewater finally determined that
Kate should go to the same school in the capacity
of a pupil teacher, and at the Misses Rushey Platt's
Seminary for young ladies, Kate found herself at
the beginning of the big frost.

It was the middle of January, and, with some two
or three exceptions, all the girls were away with
their friends and relations for the Christmas
Vacation. The two or three pupils left were a good
bit younger than Kate. Jessie Chacewater had left
for good, and, much to Kate's dismay, there had
been no invitation for her to stay at the Grange
this year, and Mrs. Chacewater had further inti-
mated that she should have no occasion for her

services in the future. It was rather a dreary look-out that future, for Kate; of course that she should think to pass her life at the Grange was absurd, she had been engaged there mainly as a nursery governess, and her pupils were now departed. They had all been very kind to her, but it was one of those arrangements that in the nature of things was bound to come to an end. It was doubtful whether she could even continue where she was, whether the Misses Rushey Platt would consider her accomplishments sufficient compensation for her board and the instruction which she herself received under their roof. Mrs. Chacewater, she knew, had paid something towards her expenses in the first instance, but she could not expect that would continue. There were only two things open to her, she must either seek another situation or go home, and she shuddered at this latter alternative, unless her services were really needed in case of sickness, or something of that kind. Oh, dear! how dull it was, how sick she was of looking out of the window, she was bored to death, she would go out for a run, no she wouldn't ask permission, of course she ought, it was the rule, but she would just slip out by herself, and say nothing to anyone.

Another five minutes, and Kate had let herself softly out of the house and was speeding away towards Regent's Park. She had made up her mind what she would do with her contraband freedom. She would go and look on at the skating there. She was quite sure that would meet with much dis-

2*

approval from Miss Rushey Platt did she but know it, and although Kate had been for a good two years under discipline, she had not yet lost her zest for stolen pleasures. She soon reached the borders of the lake, which was covered by a crowd of revellers, some disporting themselves in graceful arrowy fashion, others turning and circling, and performing all sorts of complicated figures, in most artistic manner, while others again, after sprawling about the ice in ludicrous style, eventually sat down, with neither dignity nor design. What fun it was, and how fond she had been of skating once, how she should like a spin now; just one good race the length of the lake and back again would brighten her up wonderfully, and here the tempter was by her side, with "Try a pair of skates, my lady. Only just wait while I look out a pair small enough." And one of those artful jackals, that haunt the margin of the ice in the London Parks, and equipped with a windsor chair, a gimlet, and several pairs of skates, lure their fellow creatures to their undoing, placed a chair by Miss Darley's side, and, proffering a pair from his stock, declared they might have been just made for her. Yielding to the temptation, Kate seated herself. Two or three minutes, and the irons were fitted to her feet, and striking boldly out, like the practised skater she was, Miss Darley was lost in the throng.

CHAPTER III.

" SKATING FOR LIFE."

LOOKING out of a window, in a set of rooms in the Temple, at the bare trees and frost-bound earth, was a good-looking young fellow, who seemed by no means to share in the exhilaration caused by the keen weather. Mr. Reginald Chacewater was, at the present moment, revolving how one of those financial crises, common enough in all young gentlemen's lives, was to be met. The spending of half-a-crown out of sixpence a day has always been reputed easy, at all events in the Army, and to young men of good connections is doubtless just as easy outside its ranks. But the much needed alchemist in search of whom our forefathers sank much good gold, has, sad to say, yet to be discovered ; to wit, the man who can *pay* half-a-crown out of sixpence a day. If he had not taken honours, Reginald had distinguished himself at Cambridge. He had passed a very good final examination ; moreover, he had been in the Eleven, and, in the eyes of his father, that probably was a distinction of higher importance. That Reginald should have exceeded his allowance, Mr. Chacewater regarded as all in the natural course of events, that his account for hacks and hunters was portentous, the Squire would have deemed compensated for by the knowledge that Reginald was hard to beat with the " Drag ": in short, Mr. Chacewater was perfectly satisfied with his son's College career, and at the end of it, paid his debts without wincing, and only remarked that now he had had his fling, he should expect him to make his allowance do. Reginald was no gambler, nor was he by any means viciously extravagant, but he had entered into all the amusements of the University with all the zest of his age, and without much consideration as to whether the game was worth the candle. He had excellent abilities, and at times read hard, and had he not devoted so much time to his pleasures, would have doubtless come out high on the lists at the final examinations. As it was, many fathers would have been quite satisfied with his record, and that ' his own should be so was really all that was of much consequence to Reginald. But he had made one great mistake at the finish. When his father called upon him for a schedule of his debts, he was ashamed of the total, and suppressed the bigger half of them.

London is a place in which, although no doubt you may live for very little money, there [is also the temptation to spend a good deal. At all events a young man with a moderate allowance finds it difficult to lay by sufficient to make any perceptible diminution in debts amounting to some hundreds. His Cambridge creditors were getting clamorous, and declared that they would wait no longer, that, unless they had something substantial on account, they should be compelled to take legal proceedings. They were no longer to be satisfied with an odd ten pound note, they ravened for blood, or rather their money; the larger malcontents taking counsel together, came to the conclusion that they had granted credit enough, and that if Mr. Reginald Chacewater were only laid by the heels, or even served with a writ or two, his friends and relations would come to the rescue and make a clean sweep of his encumbrances.

Turning from the window, Reginald glanced at his table, where reposed not only two of these last disturbers of peace and serenity, but divers angry blue-covered letters, all threatening legal proceedings with more or less severity. He was not one of those weak and timid dispositions that think that all is lost the minute they find their bark amidst the breakers. He had plenty of confidence in himself. He was not making much money as yet, but he saw his way. Only give him time, and he was sure he would be able to pay all these cormorants ere long. The said cormorants had .they been consulted would have pointed out that they had given him time and that nothing had come of it. Reginald knew that his father was not a rich man. It was not a large estate, and land was not what land used to be. Moreover, whatever income the land may yield, it exacts from its proprietor a good deal back. A point in which railway shares and stock of all kinds have a decided advantage. Then there was the house and grounds to keep up, and the Squire was not the man to put down a gardener or discharge a stable-boy from motives of economy. In short, Reginald knew his father had many calls upon his purse, and was resolute, as far as he was concerned, to dip into it no further. But then what was he to do? Legally, of course, the Squire was not liable for sixpence, but what was he, Reginald, to do? He knew his father would never allow him to remain in Holloway Prison, and indeed would be dreadfully annoyed that a son of his should suffer the indignity of arrest.

" No," he muttered, " the poor old Dad behaved like a brick when I left Cambridge, and I was a cowardly fool not to make a clean breast of it. I'm getting my oar in fast too, my small stories are readily accepted, and I've got it in me to write a big one too, or a play, who knows? And what money there is in a successful play nobody can guess. Enough to pay all these sharks off, over and over again. I'll not stick the dear old Dad again that's certain, and yet I see no immediate way out of the scrape. To disappear is all very well, but it's only putting off the evil day. I'm sure to be hunted down sooner or later, unless I go abroad, and, I can't help thinking that if I'm to do anything in literature, I ought not to leave London just at present. Well, it's no use staying here, brooding over them won't pay the confounded things, and my brains are all too muddled for work. I'll just go for a real good stretch, and I may as well take my skates. I haven't had a look at the ice, yet, nor had a turn in the 'pattens,' since I left College."

As he passed the porter's lodge he said " good-day " to that janitor, and enquired how he liked the cold weather.

" It suits young men better than us old ones," replied the man, smiling. " You are going to have a turn with the skates I see, sir. I used to be rare fond of it in my younger days."

" Younger days, Cross ? " replied Reginald laughing. " Why you've not quite finished them yet. It is nothing but your confounded laziness keeps you off the ice now."

" Eh, sir," grinned the old man, " you'll learn all about the rheumatics in course of time, and if I'm alive I'd like to take your opinion about it then." But young Chacewater had not waited for a reply to his last remark, and was by this time out of hearing.

The keen bracing air and the exercise soon revived Reginald's spirit. Given health and strength, our scrapes and consequent fits of depression do not weigh heavily on us at five-and-twenty. Although not a bit nearer a solution of his difficulties than he had been when he left his rooms, as he reached the Regent's Park, he had walked himself into the belief that there must be a way out of his troubles, and that he should hit upon it before long, and by the time he had reached the edge of the lake, he had cast his cares on one side, at all events for the present. He stood for a moment gazing at the gay throng, listening to the ring of the irons and shouts of laughter that resounded through the clear frosty air, then seating himself on a chair called to its ragged proprietor to put on his skates for him. While this was being done, the conversation of two men fell upon his ear and arrested his attention. The one who was dressed as a Park-keeper remarked to his companion in earnest tones :

" It will be a good job, Tom, when we've got 'em all off. There's a sudden change in the state of the ice, and a rise in the barometer, that's startled the Humane Society people. It's too late to stop 'em, now, but they wish they had warned people the ice was no longer safe a couple of hours ago. But you see they hadn't a suspicion of it themselves."

" No," replied the other, " nor should I think there's any danger still, I have no doubt, from what I've seen, the frost is about to break up, but such ice as this will be safe enough for a day or two yet."

Reginald Chacewater thoroughly coincided with the last speaker's opinion. There were always alarmists who questioned the safety of the ice whenever people began to disport themselves on it, prophets of evil these, who neither skated nor curled, and who saw danger in all athletic pursuits. Ice of such thickness as a fortnight's sharp frost must have made this, was not likely to give way in a few hours. The Humane Society always cried out before there was any necessity. It was their object to prevent people getting drowned, and there was no

insurance equal to confining them to dry land, and
with those reflections, he struck boldly out, and in
a few minutes had gained the middle of the throng.
For a good hour he had been amusing himself, and
had already forgotten all about that ominous pile of
letters that he had left upon his writing table. Few
exercises are more exhilarating to the initiated than
skating. To those graduating, it is no doubt accompanied by tremors and exasperation, and the most
conceited person breathing must be conscious of not
appearing to advantage, when taking his first lesson
in skating ; but to the passed master it is the poetry
of motion, nothing comes near it, save sleighing with
a free horse during the beginning of the winter in
the snow countries, ere the traffic has knocked holes
in the Heaven-made road. The fun was at its
height, when suddenly a report like a cannon rang
through the still air, immediately followed by
screams of terror, and cries of " To the banks for
your lives, the ice is breaking up." Reginald
paused for a moment, to look back at the panic-
stricken and shrieking crowd. Already they were
falling and tumbling over each other, in the mad
stampede for the land. He saw at a glance that,
once entangled in that throng, there would be
nothing for it but to face the danger, and trust that
the ice might last some little time yet. The
foremost of the throng were already nearing him,
and he was about to take advantage of the start
which his position outside it gave him, and make
for the bank with all speed, when he saw a girl

knocked down by a terror-stricken rough who had
cannoned against her. Quick as thought Reginald
dashed over the space that intervened between him
and the prostrate young lady. It was well he did
so, for entangled in the rush, the girl would have
found some difficulty in recovering her feet without
his assistance. The sharp cracking of the ice,
sounding like pistol shots in every direction, gave
warning that one of the most sudden breaks-up of
a hard frost ever known had come upon them.

Seizing the girl's hand, he exclaimed, " Strike
out the best you can, the sooner we are on land the
better. Check me if I am going too fast for you."

" Thank you, I will do my best," was the brief
reply, and before they had gone a hundred yards,
Reginald found that his task was comparatively an
easy one, and that his companion was a practised
skater. That the ice had given way in many places
behind them they knew, but if it would only hold
good for two or three minutes in front of them,
they would be out of danger. The brief delay had,
it is true, involved them to some extent in the
crowd, but still, thanks to his timely assistance, his
companion had regained her feet so quickly that
they were in the front rank, and not in the thick
of it, and ran little risk now save being knocked
over by some of the panic-stricken roughs who in
such cases have no thought of anyone but themselves. A little more and they had gained the
bank, and Miss Darley, as she gasped her incoherent
thanks, was fain to lean against a tree to recover

from her excitement and exertions. She had been skating not only at the top of her speed, but for her life, a struggle for which is apt to be followed by reaction, however cool one may be at the time. That Reginald had come to her aid at a very critical moment, Kate Darley thoroughly recognised. How helpless a woman is in a crowd she was quite aware and that once off her feet in one dominated by panic, a girl runs grave risk of being trampled to death, is palpable to everyone, to say nothing in this case of the risk of drowning to boot. That the accident was on a large scale and attended with considerable loss of life was clear, and Kate felt that she would have been hardly standing in safety on the bank, had it not been for Reginald Chacewater's assistance. Yes, she recognised him in a moment, but saw at once that he had no knowledge of herself, it was not likely. Kate and her brother had been mere children when Reginald went to college, and since leaving that he had been but little at the Grange. During her sojourn there, he had only visited it once, for a few days, and then probably had taken but little notice of the children's governess. Certain it is that he had no recollection ot her at present, and merely mentally ejaculated, " Deuced good-looking young woman I've helped out of that scrape." Miss Darley resolved to retain her *incognita*. If she recognised him, she would have to tell him who she was. The adventure before long was sure to be talked over at the Grange, and then Kate foresaw the probability of awkward questions being asked, about her fortunate escape, how came she on the ice, who was she with, &c. Ah, who indeed? Then the story was safe to come round to the Misses Rushey Platt, and then suddenly she exclaimed to herself, " Good gracious, I wonder what time it is! It's almost dark. " Hastily divesting herself of her skates, and throwing liberal *largesse* to their proprietor, she once more thanked Reginald for his help, and said she must hurry home, that her friends would be getting anxious.

" More especially," said Reginald, " should any news of this accident reach them before you return. It would be sheer waste of time to discover the friends who were with you; we must only hope that, like ourselves, they reached the shore in safety."

" I am by myself," she replied, " and, though I am anxious to get back, they are not likely to feel alarmed on that account, as no one knows that I had any intention of skating," and she held out her hand to say good bye.

" Odd," thought Reginald, " a pretty, lady-like girl coming up here to skate by herself among such a very mixed crowd as she might be sure of finding in any of the parks."

" I don't think," he replied, laughing, " you can do as yet without your escort. What with people flying from it and people flocking to the scene of the accident, the crowd is, if anything, denser than it was on the ice. Let me see you through it and put you comfortably into a hansom, and then I shall feel that you are really in safety."

Kate gratefully accepted his offer. She was by no means a nervous young woman, but she recognised that to make her way through that hurrying, excited crowd, would be hard work for a lady, and before they were out of the park, she had much reason to be thankful for the support of Reginald's arm. Once there, a cab was soon picked up, and having placed his charge in it, Reginald asked where he should tell the man to drive.

"York Terrace," replied Miss Darley demurely. "I don't know how to thank you sufficiently for your kindness. Thanking anyone for saving one's life is very difficult. All words seem so trite and commonplace."

"You are making much of very little," he replied. "You must allow me to call and satisfy myself that you are none the worse for the perils we have braved together. What number shall I tell him?"

"I am sure you will add to the debt I owe you," replied Kate, "by not making any enquiry about where I live. York Terrace will be quite sufficient. Thanks. Once more, good-bye."

Reginald felt that he could make no further enquiry, and having given the driver the necessary direction, raised his hat and walked leisurely away.

"Quite an adventure," he muttered, "and very near being an awkward one too. We shan't know all about it till to-morrow morning, but I am afraid there were a lot of people drowned. Of course, there were lots of appliances for saving life, and

any amount of assistance at hand, but then there
was the panic, there's no reckoning with that.   As a
theatrical manager once said to me, 'I'd back
my audience to be out of the house in three
minutes on any ordinary night; in case of fire, I
daresay it would take three quarters of an hour.'
What a pretty girl the companion of my race for
life was! How I wonder what she was! She
looked a lady, but skating all by herself up
in that crowd, doesn't look as if she was very
particular.   However, she didn't desire to culti-
vate my acquaintance.   I can't boast of receiving
any encouragement at all events.   Why, if she
had been drowned this afternoon, nobody would
have ever known what became of her.   Good
Heavens, there's an idea; what a dramatic exit
from this world! You were thinking of disappearing
from the ken of your creditors this morning young
man.   Now's your time, here's your opportunity.
I must have a smoke, and think this over," and
lighting a cigar, Reginald proceeded to walk up
and down Portland Place, in which he now found
himself, for the space of at least an hour.

CHAPTER IV.

"'ERUPIT EVASIT,' AS TULLY WOULD PHRASE IT."

NOTHING theoretically sounds so easy for a young
man living in chambers as to efface himself, to
totally disappear.   It is a solution of troubles that
must often occur; to such there is a touch of

melodrama about it, calculated to entrap the imagination of youth, but practically, to vanish, and to
be accredited dead by all your friends and relations,
is fraught with inconceivable difficulties. You are
innocent of all crime; there is no cause for the
police to interest themselves in your proceedings;
and yet you must be friendless indeed, if there is
not a hue and cry raised at your disappearance.
The nomads of the streets, houseless wanderers,
may fade away by the noiseless river, or be found
wrapped in eternal sleep on curb or doorstep, and
there may be none to enquire who it was or what
manner of life had been that which had led to so
sad an ending; but for a young man of position to
be missing is sure to provoke a searching enquiry
as to what has become of him, and people, to say
nothing of the law, are slow to believe in the death
of one whose body has not been discovered. It may
be doubted whether Reginald Chacewater took all
this into consideration, but he was shrewd enough
to see that if he determined to take advantage
of the accident, and be returned as amongst the
missing, that there were a good many precautions
to be taken, and a good many little things to be
thought about. To begin with, money was a necessity. He must have the wherewithal to live, until
he had devised some means of earning his own living.
He had fortunately a considerable sum in his possession at the present moment, but to obtain it it
was necessary to get back to his chambers, and that
without observation. To do this, he must wait till

3

the small hours of the morning, when Cross, the Temple porter, would be in his bed, instead of in the lodge, and he should run little risk of encountering any acquaintance, either in quadrangle or on staircase. The idea fascinated him, and as he threw away his cigar, his mind was made up. He would get something to eat in one of the obscure restaurants of Portland Street, get through the hours as he best could, till it was safe to regain his rooms at the Temple, then get his money, thrust a few things into a handbag, and take one of the first trains out of London in the morning. Where to ? it didn't much matter, as long as it was to some place where he was quite unknown, one was as good as another.

He never reflected on all the sorrow that he must inevitably occasion at the Grange, of the agony it would cause his mother, of the tears that would trickle down the cheeks of his pet sister Jessie, and that the loss of his only son would wring his father's heart in a manner to which the mere irritation of having to pay his debts would have been as nothing. No, I am afraid Reginald simply regarded the whole thing as a stupendous lark. It world be a " tremendous sell " for his creditors, and after a short time when the public had allowed a welcome to a new writer, he would emerge from oblivion, and reappear at the Grange with all his budding laurels thick upon him. He had thought the thing well out, and counted up carefully every point in his game, and Cross the porter could testify to his

having left the Temple with his skates in his hand
and with the avowed intention of using them.
Since the accident he had luckily encountered no
one he knew, as he summed it up to himself; there
was proof of his intention on leaving the Temple;
there was a terrible accident on the ice in the
Regent's Park that afternoon and nothing had been
heard of him since. The sole person who positively
knew anything about him was the girl he had
rescued, and even she could not possibly know who
he was. It was not likely that he should ever see
her again, and if he did, how was she to know that
he was supposed to be drowned? The conjecture
couldn't possibly enter her head. In short, when
Mr. Chacewater, carrying a small handbag, emerged
from the Temple about four in the morning, he
muttered to himself, "Now the world is all before
me; exit Reginald Chacewater, barrister, and enter
—confound it, I must have a name. I never thought
of that. What shall I call myself?" And pondering on this knotty problem, he made the best
of his way to Waterloo Station.

It was late when Miss Darley reached the door of
the Misses Rushey Platt. She had been late when
she left the scene of the accident. It had taken,
moreover, some time, as we know, for herself and
Reginald to make their way through the excited
crowd then thronging the Park; but even after the
cab had safely deposited her in York Terrace, she
walked up and down for some little time, thinking
of the adventure of the afternoon. No sooner was

the door opened, in answer to her knock, than one
glance at the servant-maid's face sufficed to tell
Miss Darley that something unexpected had taken
place. Sarah's face was a mixture of pity and con-
sternation, as of one who pities another, for having
got into a terrible scrape.

" Oh, please, Miss," she exclaimed, without
waiting to be interrogated, " we've been all in
such an awful state about you. The old ladies
are half out of their minds about it ; they
say there's an awful accident up in the ' Regent's,'
and Miss Jemima sent me out to buy an evening paper ; and please, Miss, the laundress's girl,
who came in an hour ago, declares she passed
you walking in the Park ; and that there's lots
of people drowned, and she thought it very likely
you were one of them ; but of course you weren't,
Miss ; but I'm awful glad to see you back all the
same."

" Thank you, Sarah," replied Miss Darley, laughing as she ran up-stairs. As she passed the
drawing-room door, a voice from within called out :
" Is that Miss Darley ? "   And Kate replying in the
affirmative, she was at once told to come in ; and
obeying the request, found herself in the presence
of her two instructresses.

" Thank Heavens, Miss Darley, we see you alive,"
exclaimed Miss Jemima, the younger of the two
ladies. "You have given us both quite a turn. We
had no idea you were out."

" You neglected to acquaint us with your intention in that respect," observed Miss Rushey Platt, with considerable asperity.

" And there's a terrible accident taken place on the ice in the Regent's Park, and there's a foolish girl here from the laundress, who would insist upon it that she'd seen you in the Park this afternoon," continued Miss Jemima. " Of course we know now it was all a mistake, but it made us very anxious."

" My nerves are all in a twitter," said Miss Rushey Platt. " It has given me a shock that I shall not recover from this evening. Your going out without asking permission is indefensible, indeed I may say wicked."

" But I told you I was right, Laura," exclaimed Miss Jemima triumphantly. " I felt sure Miss Darley would never commit such a monstrous impropriety as to go into the Regent's Park by herself, especially crowded with such a very mixed lot of people, as it must have been lately, in consequence of the skating."

But Kate's temper was up, and it was with a rebellious smile she replied :

" The girl was right, I was there ; and, what's more, I skated."

She might have committed an imprudence ; but, had Miss Darley confessed to heinous crime, the two sisters could not have been more dismayed. Words failed them. Miss Rushey Platt's lips syllabled the word " skated," but no sound escaped them, while Miss Jemima, who was of a softer disposition, could hardly refrain from weeping over this obviously impenitent sinner. The idea that one of their young ladies should have been guilty of such a shameful vulgarity was indeed more than the Misses Rushey Platt could bear.

"Go to your room, Miss Darley," exclaimed the elder, at last. "I am quite unfit to speak to you to-night ; but your common sense must tell you that it is impossible for a young lady who displays such an utter disregard of the conventionalities of society to continue to reside under our roof. Now go."

Kate bent her head and disappeared. On arriving in her own room, she closed the door, and breaking into a fit of rippling laughter, murmured to herself —" Well, now I have done it. I have made this place too hot to hold me. They'll never get over it. The idea of one of their young ladies pirouetting amongst the mob will haunt them to their dying day. They forget that I am a daughter of the people, and that the base-born blood in my veins will break out sometimes. Ah," she said, after another merry peal of laughter, " it's all very well, but what's to become of me ? I shall have to leave to-morrow, no doubt. I won't go home ; but where I am to go is a puzzle. It's not likely that the Misses Rushey Platt will give me a recommendation, and it's hardly to be supposed that any family would be willing to accept an interesting stranger in any capacity without some guarantee. How lucky Jim was ! When he fled from the wrath to come, he had that Mr. Praze to go to. What am I to do ? My

slender store won't keep me for very long ; and if I
can't contrive to earn my own living, there will be
nothing for it but to go home, and I *won't* go
home." And while puzzling over this problem,
Kate's healthy young appetite once more re-asserted
its claim. She had had nothing to eat for several
hours, and had had, moreover, an afternoon of un-
wonted exercise. She rang the bell, and desired
Sarah to get her some tea and something to eat.
And while the girl was getting it, she made up her
mind to pack up her trunks and leave the house
quietly without any further interview with the Misses
Rushey Platt.

In pursuance of this determination, she told the
girl, on her return, to call her early the next morning, and then, having finished her preparations for
departure, went to bed. But, though tired, she was
unable to sleep. Whether she was over-tired, or
whether it was the excitement of her escape from
the ice, matters little, but, resolutely though she
wooed it, sleep seemed further from her eyelids
than ever. All the events of the day were whirling
in her brain. Once more she heard the first terrible
crack of the ice; once more the wild cry of—" To
the banks ! " and the shrieks of the knocked down
and terrified women rang in her ears ; once more
she saw the wild rush of the panic-stricken crowd,
and then thought that she was knocked down and
sinking. She was in that slightly feverish state
which is worse than utter wakefulness, when, though
unconscious of sleep, we constantly keep dozing

off for a few minutes at a time, only to awake
with a start from more or less disagreeable dreams.
Through all such phantasies, Reginald Chacewater
was a prominent actor.   Sometimes they were
perishing together, sometimes he was the rescuer;
but whichever way the vision might shape itself,
he figured conspicuously.   And with her wakeful
moments came the more common-place, but equally
unpleasant reflection that a full and high-coloured
report of her misdemeanours would be forwarded to
the Grange.   That anyone could deem there was
any harm in skating itself, she knew she could
afford to laugh at.   She did not even suppose that
the Misses Rushey Platt were so narrow-minded as
that, but for a young lady of eighteen to plunge,
unaccompanied, into the Saturnalia of a London
Ice Carnival was, she knew, a breach of decorum not
easy to justify.   Mrs. Chacewater, though by no
means a stickler for the proprieties, and even one of
the earliest apostles of athletic exercises for girls,
would, she knew, shake her head at it, if she did no
more ; and in the silence of the night-time, Kate
pictured that lady having a great deal more to say
about it than that, while she could fancy Jessie as
much shocked as her present duennas.   Kate had
grown very fond of the Grange family.   Mrs. Chacewater had not only been very kind, but had done a
great deal for her, and Kate winced at the idea of
being held guilty of wrong-doing in that lady's
eyes.

It was a mere mad, girlish escapade, of which no

harm had come, and that was all that could fairly be said about it; but such stories lose nothing in telling; and I am not sure that the committal of actual crime is not easier excused and explained away than a doubtful episode of this kind, which is not justified at the moment. Any way, it never occurred to Kate that the course she proposed was the very worst she could take, as far as putting herself right in the eyes of the Chacewaters went. To leave abruptly without giving any clue to her intentions was an acknowledgment of her offending, and a tacit admission that it was even worse than it had appeared, inasmuch as the culprit had fled sooner than face the consequences of her misdeeds.

However, true to her determination, Kate departed, bag and baggage, early the next morning; and when the Misses Rushey Platt went down to breakfast, it was only to be met with the—to them —astounding tidings that Miss Darley had been gone more than an hour, leaving behind her neither message, letter, nor address.

CHAPTER V.

" A DUAL MYSTERY."

THE daily papers that morning carried terrible tidings into some households, and grave anxiety into others. They were all full of the accident, and contained the names of several of those who had been drawn from the icy waters too late, but who had been already recognised by friends or relations.

Several more were there, not as yet identified; but one singular phase of the disaster had yet to exhibit itself to the public, and was a curious example of the vacillation of humanity. In the course of the next few days, it was marvellous to notice how many of those who had started with the avowed intention of enjoying themselves on the ice, had changed their mind and betaken themselves somewhere else—men who had been mourned for by their families, whose inexplicable absence from home had been attributed to their having perished in the disaster in the Regent's Park, suddenly reappeared; and it may be hoped, in some cases, were able to satisfactorily account for their absence. The reverse was also conspicuous. People whose friends had no suspicion that they intended to skate were numbered amongst the dead, having yielded to the like sudden impulse that had possessed Kate.

The Squire read the account of the catastrophe to his wife and daughter at the breakfast table, who, shocked though they were to hear of such loss of life, little thought that they were personally concerned in it. But the following morning brought a letter from Miss Rushey Platt, which contained an elaborate account of Miss Darley's misdemeanour. The indictment was by no means framed maliciously, but it must be borne in mind that in the eyes of the prim and precise schoolmistress, a breach of the conventionalities was a grave offence; and what she deemed vulgarity, a deadly sin; and Miss Darley had clearly been guilty in these matters

of conduct not befitting a lady. Miss Rushey Platt
again could conscientiously say, that she had always
treated Kate kindly ; although she had entered her
establishment as a pupil-teacher, she had honestly
made no difference between her and the other
young ladies entrusted to her charge ; and, to leave
without saying farewell, to abscond, as Miss Rushey
Platt put it, like "a mutinous maid-servant well-
nigh come to the end of her anarchies," was beneath a girl in Miss Darley's position. Miss Rushey
Platt's narrative therefore painted the delinquent in
very sombre colours, and wound up with fears lest
the unhappy girl might have formed some objec-
tionable acquaintance, and so fallen under evil
influences.

"My knowledge of the world," she continued,
"tells me that no girl brought up under my charge
could have dreamed of perpetrating such a vulgarity
as Miss Darley has been guilty of, unless persuaded
to it by some undesirable acquaintance, and it is
with the deepest regret, my dear Mrs. Chacewater,
that I express my opinion that this undesirable
acquaintance will turn out to be of the Male Sex."

Poor dear Miss Rushey Platt knew about as much
of the world as if she had been brought up in a
convent. If Kate had committed an error in
decamping in the way she did, she had certainly
been right in despairing of making the schoolmistress ever understand the wild impulse that had
seized upon her. That to dissipate a fit of the
blues, a girl could rush off and commit such a

terrible breach of decorum as Kate had done, she
could never have believed. Her story would have
met with little credence from Miss Rushey Platt.
But then there were others to be considered—Mrs.
Chacewater, for instance, who could have thoroughly
understood the uncontrolled desire that a girl,
brought up as Kate had been, might feel when
suffering under a fit of depression, for a good gallop
or its equivalent, looked serious as she asked herself
the question, "What on earth made her run away?
It was a foolish thing, and, without doubt, an un-
justifiable thing of her to go off skating by herself,
but she surely must have known that she had
nothing to fear but a good scolding, and Kate
Darley is not at all the girl to run away from that.
I sincerely hope there are no grounds for this old
woman's suggestion, but Kate's very young, and
what Miss Rushey Platt just hints at is, of course,
possible. I devoutly hope it's not so, for anything
of that sort would probably have a miserable
ending."

Jessie was much surprised and distressed when
she heard from her mother of her friend's disappearance, and in the subsequent conversation that
ensued between them, Mrs. Chacewater convinced
herself that if Kate had a lover, Jessie, at all events,
was not in her confidence.

It may easily be surmised that a very short time
elapsed before Reginald was missed. The alarm
was given in the first instance by Cross, the porter
at the gate, who, as we know, was aware that young

Chacewater had left the Temple with his skates in his hand. All London was ringing with the accounts of the accident, and that Cross should be specially on the *qui vive* to note Reginald's appearance next day was only natural. He never set eyes on him. He had never seen him return from that skating expedition, and then the porter deemed it worth while to mention all this to some of those he knew to be on friendly terms with the young man. It was speedily ascertained that Chacewater's oak was persistently sported, and that knock as you might, drum as you liked on the solid panels, or kick till you were tired, not the slightest response was made from within. One of his intimates put a watch upon the rooms for four-and-twenty hours, and ascertained that no one had either left or entered them during that time. Others, meanwhile, had visited the Royal Humane Society offices to see whether the missing man might be amongst the nameless dead; but no, if Reginald Chacewater had been amongst the victims on that fatal afternoon, it was quite clear that so far his body had not been reclaimed. The Humane Society had little belief that they had not recovered the remains of all those who had perished, but admitted that it was possible there might be a corpse or two entangled amongst the weeds, that had as yet escaped the drags and their appurtenances. All inquiries at his usual haunts failed to elicit the slightest trace of him; at one or two Bohemian clubs of which he had been a constant

frequenter, there was no knowledge of him. Since
the accident, nobody could be found that had seen
him. By this time, a paragraph in the papers had
carried grief and anxiety to the Grange, and
brought the Squire up to London. The hue and
cry was raised for the missing man in all directions,
but in vain; and his friends asked each other the
question, If Reginald is not under the water in the
Regent's Park, what on earth has become of him?
Where has he gone, and why did he go? There
never was a man with less mystery about him. He
was the last fellow in the world to go off without
announcing his departure to his intimates. But he
had said never a word of his intention to anyone.
On the other hand, against the theory that he had
been drowned on that fatal afternoon, it was urged
that, though the sea might not give up its dead, it
could hardly be supposed that such was the case
with the piece of water in the Regent's Park. The
ice was now quite gone, and all those employed in
searching its waters denied the probability of there
being any body still unrecovered. Possibility there
might be, probability there was none. For a week
at least, Herbert Chacewater was untiring in his
search for his son. Not a suggestion was given him
that he did not at once follow up, without regard of
time or expense; but all ended in the same way:
not a trace of the missing man could be found, not
the slightest clue as to what had led to his disappearance. His chambers were broken into; but
this, if anything, only made the affair still more

mysterious. As far as those who searched them could make out, things there all remained as usual. His clothes, portmanteau, etc., were all in their accustomed places; nothing was missing save his skates, which, since the commencement of the frost, two or three of his intimates remembered to have seen lying on one of the upper shelves of the book-case. As one of them said:

"Poor Reginald rather fancied himself in skates, and the last time I saw him, pointed his out saying that he hadn't had a turn on them for the last two years, and must take advantage of the present frost."

Sadly, at length, the Squire came to the conclusion that he could do no more. Reginald had unaccountably disappeared, and what had caused him to do so was beyond conjecture. But Mr. Chacewater was far from convinced that his son was dead. He had gone out to skate, there was no doubt; but not only was there no evidence to show that he was one of the victims of the fatal accident, but there was no evidence to show that he had even been to the Regent's Park at all. He could do no more, and returned to the Grange, with no better tidings than the somewhat negative comfort that, if he did not bring news of his safety, there was as yet no decisive proof of his death.

It can hardly be supposed that the coincidence of the disappearance of Kate Darley and Reginald on the same day failed to escape Mrs. Chacewater, and she racked her brains to think if there could be any possible connection between the two. But no; it was most unlikely. Her son could hardly have seen Miss Darley; and yet it was very singular that they should both be missing on the same day, and presumably have passed that afternoon in skating at the same place. About Kate there was no doubt. She had been seen safe and sound after the accident, and had avowed where she had been and what she had been doing. In Reginald's case it was true this was only supposition. Was it possible that he and Kate had met that afternoon? Could there have been a previous acquaintance between them, unknown even to Jessie as well as the rest of them? And gradually Mrs. Chacewater worked herself round to the conclusion that Miss Rushey Platt was right, that the "undesirable acquaintance" was "of the Male Sex," and her son was the man. If she was right in this theory, then Kate was the key to the enigma. Find Kate and you would have found Reginald. The lady of the Grange was a clever and a prudent woman; they by no means always go together. She resolved to keep her opinion to herself, but quietly to make every effort to discover Miss Darley. She shared her husband's belief that Reginald was not dead, and jumped to the conclusion that was the way to seek him.

Another person to whom the simultaneous disappearance of the twain had been a severe blow was Tom Bramber. About three years older than Reginald, he had known him from boyhood, and, though only the son of one of Mr. Chacewater's

tenants, had been the young Squire's companion
both in cricket and hunting-field. Mr. Chacewater
was a landlord of the old sort, and often asked his
tenants to join him when he shot over their farms,
and many a hard day at the partridges had
Reginald and Tom Bramber put in together. Kate
Darley he had known from a child, but the last two
or three years had transformed her into a very
pretty young woman, and occasioned, as such change
will, considerable alteration in Tom Bramber's sentiments. He thought her just about the prettiest
girl in all the country round. His regular attendance in church was, I am afraid, more to be
attributed to Kate Darley than to those far higher
motives that ought to have influenced him. He
admired her walking, but he worshipped her on
horseback, and vowed that to see Miss Darley ride
when hounds were running, was a sight worth going
miles to look upon, from all of which it may easily
be gathered that Tom Bramber was very much in
love. So far he had had no reason to despair. He
was not only a very suitable, but would undoubtedly
have been pronounced a good match for her by anyone capable of expressing an opinion on the subject;
and now he was haunted by the simultaneous disappearance of the twain, for with all the jealousy of
love, he had come to the same conclusion as Mrs.
Chacewater, that the pair had gone off together.
That this should make Tom Bramber miserable was
a matter of course. He loved the girl, and would
have been only too proud to make her his wife.

4

Would Mr. Reginald, ignoring the difference of their positions, deal as honestly with her as that? It was bad enough to lose her, but he could bear it better if he only knew that she was married. He had even less grounds than Mrs. Chacewater for his suspicions. Reginald's visits to the Grange had been so rare since he left Cambridge, that it would have puzzled Tom to say positively that the young Squire had ever seen Kate since she had grown up. Mrs. Darley wept when the news reached her, but the old man heard it with sullen indifference. It was not a subject upon which his acquaintance ventured to comment, and though, perhaps, except Tom Bramber, nobody suspected the young Squire of having anything to do with Kate's disappearance, yet when a young woman is rumoured to be missing from her home or situation in country parishes, gossip is wont to put but one construction upon it.

In due course it was made known to Jim Darley that his sister had vanished, fled, nobody knew where, and nobody knew why; but if they didn't know, they could surmise; nor was Jim's informant altogether reticent about the imaginings of the village. The lad was devotedly attached to his sister. She stood in his regard higher than even "King of the Huns" himself, and such a horse as that Jim would have staked his existence had never been foaled. He was furious at the innuendoes of his native place. He scouted the idea of his sister doing anything wrong; and again and again the boy shook his head ruefully as he asked himself the question, What did she run away for? Kate, too, who had never feared anything in her life. He couldn't understand it. He chafed and worried dreadfully over the whole business, but he stood loyally to his belief in his sister, and only thought sadly that the scrape must have been indeed a bad one, the consequences of which Kate shrank from facing.

CHAPTER VI.

"KING OF THE HUNS."

IN the early spring time, it began to be buzzed about that there was a dangerous outsider for the Derby at Newmarket, in the stable of Mr. James Praze. Professional turfites had little belief in such stories. "Was there ever a year," they asked, "when there wasn't a dangerous outsider, for the race in question?" And when their opponents triumphantly cited the well-known instances which proved their case, the cynics replied by pointing out the much more numerous occasions upon which these black swans had turned out to be geese of the most ordinary description, and then naturally came that most conclusive of all arguments to an Englishman, a bet, and the pencilling of the long odds against "King of the Huns." The horse had never yet made his appearance in public, albeit the subject of some little talk in racing circles. His name had been whispered occasionally in club smoking-rooms by

4*

those men who invariably do know what will win the
Derby weeks before the event; still report varied
much about him—he was a rank impostor, he was
touched in his wind. Why if he was all right had
they not run him as a two-year-old? Then again
he was entered in the name of a Mr. Bramber. Who
on earth was Mr. Bramber? Did anyone before
ever hear of Mr. Bramber as an owner of race-
horses? And against all this, the supporters of the
" King " could only reply by looking very wise, and
recommending his detractors just to wait and see.

At any other time Tom Bramber would have been
wild with excitement about the approaching début
of " King of the Huns," for the fastidious Mr.
Praze had at last admitted that the colt was about
ready to run, and, further, gone the length of expressing an opinion that he would bustle up some of
them. Which, being interpreted, meant that his
opponents would find the beating of him no easy
task ; but now Tom was too wretched about this
love affair of his to think much about anything
else. A straightforward honest young fellow in all
the throes of his first attachment, and now the
object of his devotion had been stolen from him by
a man who, though above him in station, he had
looked upon as a friend. If when he next heard of
her it should be as a happy wife, then he felt that
he could get over it in time, but if the suspicion
that haunted him should prove true, and she should
turn out to be living in shame with Reginald, then
Tom vowed there should be a bitter reckoning

between him and the young Squire. What he would do, in what way he would strike at this false friend, he had at present no conception, but only let him once be assured that his fears were too true, and Kate's dishonour should be avenged, he was determined.

Day by day the name of "King of the Huns" becomes more current amongst those who discourse on racing. It figures now pretty frequently in the quotations at Tattersall's, and people who, like Acres, have a craving for a long shot, question the bookmakers about what they will lay against " King of the Huns," and, the price being still liberal, venture their modest stake accordingly. It is rumoured now that he will make his first appearance in the Two Thousand Guineas, and those who a few weeks back pooh-poohed his pretensions, are more guarded in their language, as it becomes apparent he will be speedily put to the test. " Whatever he may be," said one cheery speculator, who had laid his whole book for the great Epsom event against him, " they are going to show him at last, and I am bound to say that when James Praze does show them, they are apt to look deuced well *at both ends of the race.*"

Only a day or two after this remark, the sporting papers chronicled as the feature of the day the rapid advance of " King of the Huns " in the betting, both for the Two Thousand and the Derby. Dark, yes he was dark, as far as the public were concerned, but James Praze made few mistakes, and he knew all about it. And, in the first ferment that the news of a commission to back him occasioned, the whispers regarding his capabilities were wondrous. The trials that he was reported to have won were simply preposterous. According to some of his credulous supporters, he could give any amount of weight to anything at Newmarket, and the arbitrary assertion that he could give two stone to old "Logarithm," provoked the laughing rejoinder that the speaker was sorry to hear the old horse was dead. The next day it was stated positively that people would not be compelled to wait so long as they had expected for the "King's" appearance, that he would make his début in the Craven Meeting; in short, that "King of the Huns" was "going like great guns," and a certain starter for the Biennial. Some of the best colts for the year were entered for that, and as the race was run over the same course as the Two Thousand, should they compete, the pretensions of "King of the Huns" would be speedily settled. He would either be shown to be the great horse his friends declared he was, or the impostor his detractors pronounced him.

That there should be great difference between the love of a lover and that of a brother is natural; the jealousy which more or less tinges the first is absent from the second, and while that very colouring impelled Tom Bramber to place the worst construction on the missing girl's conduct, her brother's faith never wavered. He was grieved, he was worried, he was afraid Kate was in trouble of some kind, but his anxiety was not so great as to destroy his intense interest in the first appearance of his horse, the colt that he had looked after for the last two years, and on the back of which he secretly hoped to make his first appearance " in silk." Often Jim Darley pictured to himself the roar of thousands of throats shouting " ' King of the Huns' wins!" and seeing the "King's" number on the board, and Mr. Praze leading him back to the weighing room, and giving him, Jim, a word of encouragement as he did so. Talk about the pictures Kate used to paint for him, in which he figured sometimes as the master of foxhounds, and better still, sometimes as the huntsman of a crack pack! What were they to the glories of a jockey weighing-in for his first success? And then Jim would look forward to a triumphant career, in which he gradually arrived at the very top of his profession, and participated in the big retainers and general largesse, which reward the skill of the victorious horsemen of modern days.

The quaint little town in Cambridgeshire is filling up, and keen though the wind sweeps across the Heath, the London trains bring crowds to join in the fun. Lords by right, and lords by courtesy, genuine members of the Upper House, and the spurious nobility of the betting ring, jostle each other in the streets. There were chiefs before Agamemnon, and did not the betting ring of days not long gone boast its D'Orsay, its Lord Chester-field, and Lord Frederick? Members of Parliament

and members of Tattersall's rub shoulders in the
High, or on the steps of the Rutland. The old
stagers, who look upon the Houghton as the last
meeting of the legitimate season, and eschew
November racing, were all to the fore to see the
ball open once more. Hearty greetings are exchanged on all sides amongst men, many of whom
have not met for the last three or four months.
There is much racing gossip, and much interchange
of opinions over the big events of the coming season,
and above all there is much curiosity concerning
" King of the Huns." Is he the good-looking
colt his supporters declare him to be? Would he
win to-morrow? But on these points it is not so
easy to obtain judgment. Few of the visitors have
as yet been on the Heath, and those that have seen
the " King," are confined principally to those who
live at Newmarket, and professional horse watchers,
and among these latter, Mr. Bramber's colt has
apparently not found favour.

TIe betting at the Subscription Rooms that evening was brisk, and it was soon evident that those
connected with Mr. Praze's stable were very sanguine
about the success of their colt, notwithstanding that
in " Chorister " and " Ganymede " he would have to
encounter two of the best performers of the previous
year, both of which he would also run the chance of
meeting in most of the great three-year-old contests
of the present season. The Biennial Stakes in
consequence assumed an importance to which otherwise they had no pretension. Whatever colt might

win to-morrow he would undoubtedly, should his
victory be obtained easily, be looked upon as quite
at the top of the tree among those of his own age,
and the favourites for future events would most
certainly find themselves deposed from their pride
of place, should the dark outsider fulfil the hopes of
his trainer.   No secret was made that John Wrench
had been retained to ride the " King," that no
finer horseman ever finished over the Rowley Mile
was admitted on all sides, and that Mr. Praze's colt
would have every justice done him that jockeyship
could give.   As might have been expected, the next
day there was a large muster in the Bird Cage to
inspect the competitors for the Biennial, and many
good judges scanned " King of the Huns " narrowly,
and though, as was natural, differing more or less in
their estimate, picking holes in him here and over-
praising him there, upon one point they were all
agreed, that the great slashing brown colt was fit to
run for his life, and that if defeated it would be from
no lack of condition.

There is not much to choose in the betting
between " Chorister " and " Ganymede."   The
friends of both seem equally confident, and there is
plenty of money behind both horses.   With " King
of the Huns " it is different, although there are a
certain number of racing men who never allow a
colt of clever James Praze's to run without backing
it, still the people immediately connected with the
stable are neither numerous nor heavy betters, and
the investments consequently are much more

limited on the unknown " King of the Huns " than
those made by the more aristocratic stables to which
his well-proved rivals belong, and even as the horses
go down to the post, ten to one is offered against
the " King." The books are closed at last, glasses
are raised, the war of the Ring is still, a low hum of
muttered ejaculations fills the ear, broken only by the
shrill cry of some hungry fielder, who still defiantly
offers to lay against one of the favourites. There is
scarce any delay at the post, and the flag soon falls
for a capital start. " King of the Huns " is soon
seen well in front, and it is evident has all but over-
powered his jockey. But John Wrench is too fine a
horseman not to be equal to that emergency. He
makes no attempt to waste either his own or the
" King's " strength by fighting with him, but allows
him to stride along with a commanding lead. His
opponents, quite aware of the case, look upon it
that the horse must run himself out, and must then,
in racing parlance, come back to them, but as they
come down the hill to the bushes, the rider of
" Chorister " awakes to the fact that there is as yet
no sign of that happening, but it is in vain that he
and his brethren try to lessen the gap. Wrench, who
has now got his horse in hand, simply steadies the
" King " as they breast the ascent, and sails in the
easiest of winners by four lengths. A great shout
goes up from the fielders, as the number of the
winner is hoisted, for it is at once realised that the
betting on the Derby is completely revolutionised,
and offers to take two to one about " King of the

Huns" for that race are pretty frequent. The way
Mr. Bramber's horse had spread-eagled his field
showed him to be a colt of uncommon excellence,
and numerous are the enquiries now, as to Who is
Mr. Bramber? Is he here? When did he take to
racing?

Now this was just the question Mr. Praze was
asking himself as he led "King of the Huns" back
to the weighing-room. Where was Tom Bramber?
He had been so impatient to see this colt out, he
had so chafed because, in his wisdom, Mr. Praze had
declined to prematurely test the horse's powers, and
yet, although he had had due notice and the trainer
had expressed his belief that he would take a deal
of beating, Tom had never turned up. It had been
a great triumph, and amply repaid the trainer for
the dogged way in which he had waited for the
colt's powers to mature. Not only in a modest way
had they won a nice stake, but they also stood upon
velvet as regarded the Derby, and further, had
every reason to congratulate themselves on the
possession of, if not the best of his year, at all
events a very valuable colt. Jim Darley, too, whose
heart was swelling with pride at *his* horse having
in his own language polished off the swells, and
just shown them what he could do, was also much
disappointed at Tom's absence.

"He ought to have been here, he did, for he owns
him if I look after him, and the 'King,' he and I all
come from the same parish. It's too bad of him not
to have been here to see the horse win. Yes, my

boy," continued Jim as, having received the colt
over from Mr. Praze, he patted the "King's" neck
and led him away, "and they've got to see yet what
we can do, yes, you and I together," and Jim looked
forward to the day, not far distant he hoped, when
he in his turn should steer the "King" to victory.

But Tom Bramber was not to be seen at Newmarket that day, and all Mr. Praze could do was to
send off a telegram to him at his Wiltshire home to
inform him that "King of the Huns" had won the
Biennial in a canter.

CHAPTER VII.

"THE ROYAL HIPPODROME."

KATE might not know London very well, but she
was a young lady perfectly able to take care of
herself, and was very soon installed in modest
lodgings not very far from the Misses Rushey
Platt's establishment. She had severed that connection, and escaped a scolding, or "being preached
at," as she herself phrased it, by her furtive
departure, and the question now was, What was
she to do next? She was a practical young person,
and decided that as the earning her own living was
of paramount importance, the first thing was to get
hold of a morning paper, and see whether its
advertising columns contained anything that might
suit her. That vast epitome of the wants of our
fellow creatures always gives the idea that they
must speedily satisfy one another, but, practically

speaking, I am afraid things do not dove-tail quite
so cleverly. There are numerous cooks who want
places, and mistresses who require cooks, but when
it comes to the exchange of their respective needs,
these two sections are apt to differ considerably
about what constitutes a cook, similarly those
wanting desirable dwellings and those having them
to dispose of, differ considerably about the definition
of a desirable dwelling. Kate has not got very far
in her researches, when she gives a sudden start,
as her eye falls upon the following advertisement :

"MISSING SINCE JANUARY, 1867,
"Reginald Chacewater—left his chambers in the
Temple for the purpose of skating, feared to have
been involved in the lamentable accident in the
Regent's Park that afternoon. Anybody who can
forward any information about the missing gentleman to Herbert Chacewater, Chacewater Grange,
Bottlesby,* Wilts, will be earnestly thanked and
substantially rewarded."

What could be the meaning of this ? thought Miss
Darley. She knew perfectly well that, whatever
might have befallen Reginald since, he had
certainly come to no harm in the accident, and yet
it was quite clear from this that his own family
feared that he was amongst the victims of that
catastrophe. And then it suddenly occurred to her,
What ought she to do under the circumstances?
Ought she to tell them that Reginald had undoubtedly escaped with herself out of the Park that

evening; was it her bounden duty to write to Mrs. Chacewater and say so? But then the explanation as to how she and Reginald had come to be skating together on that afternoon was not so easy. At a glance she saw that it would be difficult to persuade people that their meeting had been accidental, and she smiled at the thought of what Miss Rushey Platt would say, should this version of that eventful day's skating come to her ears. Then again she no more wanted to disclose her present whereabouts than did Reginald Chacewater his, apparently. If she did she would be sure to be ordered to return home, and she was resolved not to go home, and finally Miss Darley made up her mind to keep her knowledge to herself on this occasion. What an unpleasant complication these two foolish young people were arranging for themselves, we shall see further on in this history.

The advertisement had upset the current of Kate's thoughts. Forgetful of her own needs, she could not help wondering what could have happened to Reginald Chacewater. That he should have any wish or cause to disappear of his own free will never occurred to her. She knew there was much robbery and violence continuously going on in London, as indeed may be said of all great cities; that people disappeared, or were found in the Thames, with much reason to believe that they had come to their end unfairly. She had heard that the missing man lived in the Temple, she did not know where the Temple was, and had a somewhat hazy knowledge of its locality, derived principally from "The Fortunes of Nigel," and she recollected that in Scott's famous novel the Temple was described as next door to Alsatia, and in that latter district according to the romancer law was lax, and drink was plentiful, a combination which usually results in crime. Could it be possible that in making his way back to his rooms, Reginald Chacewater had come to an untimely end? And then again her conscience pricked her, and she wondered whether she would be doing harm by her reticence. In the meantime, she would get her hat and go for a walk. She could think better in the open air than in that stuffy little sitting-room.

Miss Darley was not an experienced Londoner, and in attempting a short cut she, as one is very apt to do, missed her way, and found herself in a very respectable street with which she was unacquainted. She glanced right and left, seeking for some landmark that might give a clue to the repairing of her mistake, when almost unconsciously her eye fell upon a brass plate upon which was engraved the name Dr. Cotton. A few steps further, and a series of gaily-coloured posters proclaimed that she was in front of a building dedicated to the drama in some form. Kate paused to read the bills, and discovered that the form the drama took in this particular instance, was "horses," in fact, she was outside the circus in Argyle Street. At this moment a small door suddenly opened, and two or three men rushed out.

"Here, William!" exclaimed the foremost, "run for a doctor, quick. Fetch the nearest, there's one lives just up the street. I told you the horse hadn't got that last trick properly yet, but she would stop and try it. Deuced unlucky, all the other women gone home too."

But William was a man of slow perceptions, and before he started on his errand, required more definite instructions as to the whereabouts of the doctor he was desired to fetch. This was sufficient for Kate, who was one of those self-reliant young persons who would sooner do a thing for herself than feebly invoke assistance. She glanced for one moment at William's bewildered face, and then, swiftly retracing her steps, rang Dr. Cotton's doorbell. She found him at home, and upon hearing that it was an accident at the Hippodrome, he at once accompanied her back to the theatre. Now whether it was that singular curiosity which makes most of us wish in our younger days to go behind the scenes or whether Kate honestly thought she might render other help, I don't know, but she pushed forward with the doctor. She had hurriedly told him that the accident had happened to one of the ladies of the company, and Dr. Cotton not unnaturally regarded Miss Darley as also an actress belonging to the troupe, and said as he pushed his way in, " I shall want you, mind you keep cool and don't get flurried." And so Miss Darley passed the jealously-guarded portals of the stage-door without challenge. As for Mr. Slater, the proprietor, he knew from

experience, that when one of his young ladies came
to grief as he expressed it, to call another young
lady and a doctor to her assistance was the first
thing to be done, and as all the females of the
company had left the theatre after rehearsal,
with the exception of the unfortunate victim, he
was only too glad now to welcome a woman, let her
come from where she would.   After traversing
sundry dark passages, impregnated with a strong
smell of the stable, Kate found herself not only in
a theatre for the first time in her life, but actually
on the stage, so to speak.   The doctor made his
way at once to a little group in the centre of the
ring.   It was not the first time that he had been
called in there under similar circumstances.   The
sufferer was lying propped up with horse-rugs,
pretty nearly where she had fallen.   She was a
rather pretty-looking young woman, although her
face was now contracted from pain.   She shrank a
little as the doctor enquired into her hurts, and,
with Kate's assistance, made his brief examination.
   " I am afraid I have not been able to help paining
you," he said gently when he had finished, " and I
am afraid you are doomed to suffer a good bit yet
for the next two or three days, but you may comfort
yourself that it's nothing very serious—you have
sprained your leg very badly, but when we've once
got the inflammation down, you will be quite comfortable, though I am afraid there are some few weeks
on a sofa before you ; you can't hurry a bad sprain,
and it's always a tedious business.   And now, Mr.

5

Slater," he continued, turning to the proprietor,
" we must get this young lady home as quickly as
we can. I will send you an ambulance over from
the station, for she can't bear the jolting of a cab.
Just let her lie where she is till it comes," and then
the doctor was bustling away to fetch the required
help, when Mr. Slater stopped him.

"You are quite sure, poor thing, it is nothing
serious ? " he said.

The doctor nodded in the affirmative.

" I suppose," continued the manager, " it will be
some weeks before she can ride again ? "

"At least six," replied the doctor. " But, Lord,
it might be twelve, there's no accounting for
sprains."

" It's a great pity, poor girl, both for her and for
me. She is a great attraction, but if that's the
case, I suppose she had better get out of Town as
soon as she is well enough. It is no use her sticking
to the show if she can't take part in it. She is a
good girl and a plucky one, but I've always told her
she is a bit too venturesome. Horses, Doc'. you
see, are just like children, if you keep them too long
at their lessons they tire. She will bring them on
too fast, and that's what's the matter to-day."

The ambulance came in due course, and Minnie
Price (she was Josephine Vavasour in the bills) was
moved to her own home under the superintendance
of Dr. Cotton and Miss Darley. For the time being
the incident had driven all recollection of Reginald
Chacewater and the strange advertisement out of

Kate's head, and the adventure was destined to have
a singular effect upon the girl's future career.
Minnie Price fully deserved Mr. Slater's encomium.
She was a good, hard-working girl, and had, like all
her people, been brought up among "the horses."
They had all in some capacity or another been
engaged in the circus business as soon as able to do.
anything for themselves, but none of them had
perhaps, as yet, made such a mark as the unfortunate sufferer. She had combined good looks,
wonderful nerve, with an exceptional aptitude for
her profession. Miss Vavasour had honestly obtained her position as a star rider. She lived with
her mother, who was slightly crippled, the result of
a bad accident some few years ago in the Ring, since
which Minnie's earnings had sufficed for their needs.
Miss Darley had nothing to do just now, and was
naturally energetic, and so it came to pass that she
was a constant visitor to the sick girl, and indeed
took a considerable share in the nursing of her.
The pair rapidly became great friends, and this led
to Kate becoming an intermediary between Minnie
and the theatre. Minnie naturally desired to hear
news of her old companions there, while Mr.
Slater was genuinely anxious to hear how his
leading lady was progressing. Although undoubtedly desirous of having her once more in the
saddle, Mr. Slater was honestly interested in the
girl's recovery on her own account. He was a kind-
hearted man, and, if a little sharp-tempered with
his troupe at times when things were not going

5*

satisfactorily, was a good friend to them in the main.

Now all this had a peculiar fascination for Kate. She had always been fond of horses, and now she was being thoroughly initiated into all the minutiæ of circus life. She was present at their rehearsals, and in a very short time knew her way about the stables as well as any of them. She certainly couldn't stand on a horse's back, or skip through a paper hoop, but before three weeks were over there wasn't a nag in the Hippodrome that she hadn't sent over the bar, and as Mr. Slater enthusiastically said, " In six months Miss Darley, if she gave her mind to it, would play Turpin and his ride to York with the best of them." Miss Darley herself in the meantime had rather forgotten that necessity she was under, of doing something for her own living. She was living frugally and economically it was true, but all this time her little capital was wasting, and she was neither earning a shilling, nor had she arrived at the slightest idea how to set about it. To the circus people she was a mystery. How came this pretty, lady-like girl to have her life so completely at her own disposal? No friend ever accompanied her to the theatre, and though she was courteous and on good terms with all of them, yet there was a something about her which seemed to mark her out as of a class superior to their own. We know that she was not so in reality, but the last two years or so of her life had wrought a wondrous change in Kate Darley. Now that chance

remark of Mr. Slater's about her being able to do
Turpin's ride to York in six months, although she
had only laughed at it at the time, recurred to
Kate's mind, when she next took the question of
ways and means into consideration.   She must do
something for a living, why should she not try if Mr.
Slater would give her an engagement ?   It was work
that interested her, she knew all the people, and
though of course she had everything to learn, she
felt sure that it was a skill that she would both
willingly and speedily acquire.   She was already
great friends with Minnie Price, and she determined to make a *confidante* of her, and take her
opinion upon the matter.   Minnie, who had conceived an enthusiastic affection for Miss Darley was
delighted at the idea.   No fear that the day might
come when she would find Kate a dangerous rival in
her own theatre, occurred to the girl for a moment.
It had taken her years to acquire her own knowledge
of her art, and she knew that let Kate be as clever
as she might, it must be some time before she
could even master the ordinary mechanism of the
profession.   To merely sit on a bare-backed horse
cantering round the Ring, is not so easy a thing as it
looks.

Miss Darley had always been an object of great
curiosity to Mr. Slater, but when the day following
her discussion with Minnie she made this proposal
to him, he was, in nautical language, taken fairly
aback.   He had honestly thought what he had said
only in jest, that the girl really had all the makings

of an artist in the profession, but as for taking her as a pupil, that was a thing it behoved him to turn well over in his mind. "Who is she and what is she?" he muttered to himself. "She's a cut above us anyhow, and I'm blest if I shan't get into a scrape if I don't look out. Be shopped for abducting a ward in Chancery, or something of that sort. Then again, she is a very nice young woman no doubt, but who does she think is going to pay for her lessons, because, though no doubt she will pay for training, she won't bring a cent to the treasury for a good while; no, she must be bound in the regular way, and if she's not such a fool as to let out she ain't twenty one, well I'll chance it." And the result of all this diplomacy on both sides was that in two or three days Miss Darley had bound herself apprentice to Mr. Slater for three years at a very moderate salary, he, on his side covenanting to initiate her into the art and mysteries of "horse riding." Mr. Slater on his part carefully abstained from asking all unnecessary questions, while Kate on her side had no desire to make indiscreet or uncalled-for confidences.

CHAPTER VIII.

"CHILDREN OF THE SAWDUST."

The advertisement that had attracted Kate's attention was, as she saw, continued in all the London papers every day for a week. They were rife, too, in conjectures as to what had become of the missing

man, and those speculations varied according to the
ingenuity of the writer, but on one point they were
unanimous, that no trace whatever had been found
as yet of Reginald Chacewater, nor could any
reason be assigned for his mysterious disappearance,
That he had met his death by the terrible casualty in
the Regent's Park was now pretty generally scouted,
but a strong impression had grown up that he had met
a violent death in some of the lower dens of London.
Even the Squire, who had so sturdily refused to
believe that his son was no more, was becoming
shaken in his unbelief. But there was one man
firmly convinced that Reginald was alive and who
had solemnly vowed to discover him. Tom Bramber
had never wavered for a moment in his view of the
case. He was sure that Reginald had run away
with Kate Darley, and untiring in his efforts to find
them, but further than his steadfast belief, he was
no more advanced than other people. Still this
prevented him from relaxing in his endeavours; he
would find them, and then—well, what then? He
did not know, it would depend very much upon
circumstances, but if Reginald had wronged the
girl, he was determined to avenge her. How—well,
he did not exactly know how, but Tom had a fixed
idea, and let a resolute man only determine to be
what he called "upsides" with another, and the
means will be sure to come to his hand.

Reginald indeed, although he had acted on a
sudden impulse, had been far more successful in
effacing himself than an astute criminal, acting

with the most elaborate preparations, would probably
have been.   The only thing was that now he had
achieved his aim, he was beginning to think it
somewhat of a mistake.   To prevent all risk of
recognition, he had been compelled to select for his
retreat a place where he was thoroughly unknown.
He had taken refuge in the first instance in quiet
country quarters, but he was speedily convinced
that, if he wished to escape notice, a quiet country
village was the last place to reside in.   The simple
fact that you are a stranger at once provokes violent
curiosity to know who you are and what you are
doing there, so he rapidly fled from that to Chillingham, where he believed himself perfectly unknown,
but even in the biggest of towns it behoves you to
take some precautions if you wish to live from your
fellows a life apart.   For instance, it is prudent to
avoid all places of amusement, and this in itself
makes existence somewhat monotonous to a young
man of five-and-twenty, accustomed to indulge
freely in such amusements as came to him ; in short,
Reginald soon found the isolation to which keeping
up the part of being deceased condemned him,
was getting dull, intolerably dull.   He had awoke
to the fact that absconding from one's creditors has
its inconveniences, and began to speculate whether
the seclusion of gaol was not preferable to the
isolation necessary to keep out of it.   Now when a
man arrives at the conclusion that he has made a
fool of himself, the best thing generally is if possible
to retrace his steps.   There was no difficulty about

that in his case, he had merely to go back and face the danger from which he had run away, but one thing deterred him, and that was ridicule, the fear of which compels many of us to persevere in our wrong courses. His was a very indulgent father in the main, but there are limits, and though there is of course the record of the Prodigal Son, still he did not reappear for some years, and then did not bring a hungry pack of creditors at his heels. The killing of the fatted calf was a mild disbursement comparatively, to the satisfying of these latter. Then again, before resuming his place in this world, Reginald had vowed to distinguish himself, and to do that must of necessity be a matter of some time. No, if he had made a mistake, he would abide by it; the best thing to break the monotony of life is hard work, now was the time to write that play or romance which was to astonish the world. And so, having taken unto himself modest lodgings in that inland watering-place, wherein he had established himself, Reginald Chacewater sat doggedly down to his self-imposed task.

Mr. Slater was a circus manager on a colossal scale. He had not only the " Show in London," as he termed it, but one or two others travelling in the provinces as well, and the attractions of all these were exchanged as often as it was deemed the public required fresh stimulants. In the summer and autumn, these varied companies moved about pretty continually, but during the winter and early spring, Mr. Slater selected some large town

where he thought the public not only wanted amusement, but were ready to pay for it; and just now,
one of his companies was stationed at Chillingham.
Mr. Slater was a good-natured man, and not only
kindly, but often liberal to his numberless dependents,
many of whom, as he well knew, worked hard at a not
very remunerative profession, and no sooner did he
gather from Dr. Cotton that Minnie Price was not
only well enough to be moved, but would be all the
better for being taken away from the rigours of a
London spring, than he proposed that she should
go down to Chillingham, where one division of his
army was at present quartered, and he called upon
the sick girl, and made his proposition to her:

"You see, my dear, you are doing no good in the
fog and east wind here, the doctor says. Now,
Chillingham is a nice mild place compared to this,
you get the best of fresh air, hear the birds sing
and all that sort of thing. If you and Miss
Darell like to go down there together" (Darell was
Kate's assumed name), "she can be getting on
with her riding there, and the change will do
you good. They will be able to give more time
to Miss Darell than we can here, and then when you
are well enough, you can give the Chillingham
people a turn before you come back. They want a
novelty, the blessed public is death on novelties, and
as there is no getting their dollars without, well
novelties they must have."

So a few days later, Katie and her friend moved
down to Chillingham. If Kate had found there

was even more to learn in this new profession she
had adopted than she had expected, she was not in
the least discouraged at the result of the few lessons
she had had. She was used to horses, fond of them,
and she had plenty of nerve. She could see no
reason why she should not succeed, she had determined not to return home, and though she had
been very happy at Chacewater Grange, she had
great doubts about her getting on as an instructress
in another situation. That had been a rather
exceptional place. She was attached to the people
and they to her, and she knew that it would be absurd
to expect the same liberty would be conceded to her
elsewhere as she had enjoyed at the Grange. She was
a strong-willed girl, and on the whole quite satisfied
with the determination she had come to, a great
deal better indeed than Reginald Chacewater, working away in his solitary lodgings, and little thinking
that one to whom he was perfectly well known, was
living within a few hundred yards of him, and that
he ran the chance of recognition every time he
crossed the step of his own door. That they should
eventually meet was almost inevitable, but it was
precipitated by Reginald's impatience of his own
isolation. He could stand it no longer ; to exchange
ideas with somebody had become a necessity, and
one morning while gazing idly at the posters in front
of the gates of the public gardens that contained
the circus, he drifted imperceptibly into conversation with two or three of the employés who were
lounging there. That he should ask questions

concerning their occupation was natural, which ended by one chatty young fellow asking if he should like to see the horses. Reginald, only too glad to snatch at any distraction, jumped at the offer, and in a few minutes he found himself inside. After walking through the stables, his companion led him in to the body of the house. In the ring were some half-dozen performers rehearsing, and in his eagerness to watch them at their practice, Reginald pushed close to the ring side. One girl, who was evidently learning to stand upon a bare-backed steed as he cantered round the circle, especially attracted his attention. Not for one instant did he recognise her, for the place was too dimly lighted almost for that, but he was interested in her proceedings; he had hitherto only seen the members of the profession in all their glories, glittering in spangles, beneath the glare of gas, he had never seen them at their studies, and the girl at whom he was looking was evidently a neophyte. Every second or third round of the ring, she came off, not an awkward tumble, but lightly on her feet and laughing, though, at the same time, making an impatient remark to one of her companions. At last to save a fall she had to jump off close to where Reginald was standing, and as her eye caught his, she could not refrain from a slight start, for though Reginald Chacewater had failed to recognise her, Kate Darley had recognised him.

Turning away, Kate hurried after her horse, brought her lesson to an abrupt termination and quickly left the ring. She felt pretty sure that Reginald had not recollected her, but thought that in a stronger light and with more time in which to study her features the chances were that her face would recall itself to his memory. Now she was not at all sure that she wished this. Once more, to commence with, would arise the question whether she was not in duty bound to let his family know that he was alive, and that would probably involve the discovery of her own whereabouts. Then again, it was evident to her that Reginald had reasons of his own for acquiescing in the rumour of his death, and so disappearing from his home, as she herself had ; he had saved her life and it savoured of great ingratitude to betray him to all those whom he was apparently anxious to avoid. What his motives might be she could not conjecture, but it was clear that his incognito was of deliberate intention. She would keep his secret, and even should he at last discover she was the companion of his escape that afternoon in the Regent's Park—well, after all he had not known who she was, and was no more likely to recognise her now than then. But from that out, Mr. Chacewater took to frequenting the circus and dropped in constantly at " morning lessons."

For a few days Kate kept pretty well out of his way, but recognition came at last, and Reginald discovered that the girl he had saved from drowning at the sudden break-up of the ice was Miss Darell of Slater's Circus, but further than that, his knowledge of her did not extend.

"You may paint with a very big brush," quoth
Carlyle, "and yet not be a very big painter," and in
like manner you may write a very big romance and
starve while you are doing it.   Oliver Goldsmith
was a notable instance, by-the-way, of this latter.
Reginald Chacewater, although sanguine about the
ultimate success of the literary work he was now
engaged in, as it is good that all 'prentices of the
Guild should be, was not so foolish as not to know
that a man's work is not always estimated at his
own valuation; and even supposing that success
should crown his efforts, he was quite aware that
success in the career of literature by no means meant
money in the first instance.   He had to live, and
though he had brought away a considerable sum of
ready money at first, yet it was slowly melting
away.   And to procure more would necessitate
his avowing that he was still in the land of the
living.   As we know, his pride as yet forbade him
to do that, but a question that began to obtrude
itself, although as yet not pressingly, was what
employment he could procure that would bring
him in sufficient money for his wants, and that was
a recurring reflection which grew continally vaguer
and less satisfactory.   He saw Miss Darell and her
companions pretty well every day, but neither Kate
nor he ever made the slightest reference to their
past.   There might have been no such places as
Chacewater Grange or Bottlesby Parish for all
illusion they ever made to them, and yet they were
on very good terms, and saw a good deal of each other.

Though friendly with many of the ladies of the troupe, it was only natural that Reginald should talk more to Kate than the others. She was far more refined than her companions, who, good-hearted and good-looking girls though some of them were, were not exactly lady-like in their ways or speech. But it must not be thought that there was, at all events at present, any tender feeling between them. Kate looked at him with admiration as it was only natural she should at the heir to Chacewater Grange, the future lord of the soil of which her father was a cultivator. Then that he was good-looking and, as she firmly believed, the saviour of her life was not likely to lessen her feeling for him in that way, but they were not at all in love with each other, as anybody who noticed the frank intercourse between them would have at once determined. Reginald thought her a very pretty girl, and often wondered how one of her superior education and training had come to adopt such a profession, but he made no attempt to pry into Miss Darell's past, while Kate had no curiosity to gratify concerning his, as she already knew it. Reginald could not help contrasting Kate's quiet abstinence on this point compared with some of her sister artistes, who were not a little inquisitive to know how one whom they saw at once was a gentleman, came to be mixed up with them.

CHAPTER IX.

"SAM WARGRAVE."

NOT very far from Chacewater Grange lived Samuel Wargrave, Esq., a man who had recently bought a house and estate in the county, which, to use the old term, marched with that of the Chacewaters. Sam Wargrave, as the friends of his youth still called him, although amongst his acquaintance of the present day he would highly have resented such familiarity, was an extremely pompous, pushing, arrogant gentleman, who, beginning from nothing, had in divers ways contrived to amass a large sum of money. If people asked what Mr. Wargrave had been, his intimates would probably retort that "they would like to know what he hadn't been." He was a man who had dabbled in everything by which he thought money could be made, and, let it be what it might, his dabbling had usually turned out successful. He had done a little on the Stock Exchange, he had done a little on the Turf. He had speculated in a wholesale way in goods of all descriptions, from silks and satins to jams and calicoes, nothing came amiss to him. He was always going for "a corner in something," and, whatever the "corner" might be to other people, it generally proved profitable to him. Like many self-made men wealth had produced a craving for improved social position, and land and a country house he conceived gave stability quicker than anything.

" Your real swells," said Mr. Wargrave, " always have their box in the country, as well as their town house, though may be they can't afford to live in it.' It may have been terrible times he argued for landed proprietors of late years, " but at its present price, land is a very tidy investment." And so it came about that Mr. Wargrave finding Carlingham Park in the market had purchased it some three or four years before. Mr. Wargrave's family consisted of his wife, a son, and a daughter, all strongly imbued with his own views. The bluest-blooded lady in the land could not have stood upon her dignity more determinedly than Mrs. Wargrave. She had society gossip at her fingers' ends and talked of Duchesses and fashionable people as familiarly as if they were her intimate acquaintance. As for Mr. Horace Wargrave, the heir apparent of Carlingham, when he attained a commission in a Dragoon regiment he gave himself such intolerable airs, that it was speedily resolved that the " side must be taken out of him," and when a regiment has come to that conclusion they generally contrive to inflict a very salutary lesson upon the offender. Military discipline in short had licked Lieutenant Wargrave into a bearable shape.

As for Miss Wargrave, she was her father's own daughter. A tall, fair-haired, good-looking girl, who carried her head high and with exalted views

6

of her own pretensions and future. She was far too shrewd to overlook her father's and mother's vulgarity, and not to see that the position she wished to attain must come to her by marriage. A young lady best described by the line in the comic opera, " Of the highly-exclusive, top-towery sort." The man she married must be either county or titled, and having no false delicacy on this subject, she had already selected Reginald Chacewater as an eligible candidate for her fair hand. Although there never was a girl less likely to let her heart dictate to her head, still Clara Wargrave had a strong prepossession in Reginald's favour. And though his intentions had, so far, never been of such sort as she could construe into those of a lover, yet he had been fairly attentive, and had usually accepted all invitations to Carlingham Park.

She was not the least bit in love with him, but she liked him, and had thought it would be a good and advantageous thing for both that they should be married.

The Chacewaters were a good old county family, and had been settled in Wiltshire for centuries, while the eighty thousand pounds she would bring her husband would enable them once more to resume their proper place in the county.

Mrs. Chacewater had entertained similar views, and was always particularly civil and courteous to Clara Wargrave. She was not blind to the purse-proud vulgarity of the parents, but always contended that there was nothing wrong with the girl.

" She is a good-looking, lady-like young woman," she would say to her husband, "and if it so happens she and Reginald could fancy each other, it would do very nicely. Reggie ought to marry money, but he is just at that age when young men do what they ought not to do in these matters. I should be very glad if it was settled." To which the Squire made answer :

"That old Wargrave was a confounded cad, and he verily believed didn't know one end of a gun from another, but that money was certainly scarce, and the girl herself was well enough."

But whatever Mrs. Chacewater might wish, she felt there was an end to all this now. She did not, as we know, believe that her son was dead, but she did believe that he had levanted, and that Kate Darley was the companion of his flight. She had kept her own counsel, and confided her suspicions to no one, but this would destroy all prospect of her hopes being realised as effectually as if Reginald had perished beneath the ice. But though she had come to this conclusion, though she might be doomed to disappointment with regard to this marriage, she yearned to know that her only son was not dead, that in course of time she should see him once more. And the way to ascertain this she had made up her mind was to discover Kate Darley. It was easy for her to set enquiries afloat in that direction ; the girl had lived in her household, been the favourite companion of her daughter, and it was but natural that she should take much

6*

interest in her welfare, and feel both grieved and alarmed at her sudden disappearance in the great London whirlpool. But no results came of her researches, any more than they did of the fierce and untiring pursuit of Reginald by Tom Bramber.

Nothing is more sure nor singular than after the loss of dear friends or relations, the first great gust of grief over, the way we inevitably drop back into our old habits and customs. The first sorrow for our dead past, our duties in this world fortunately compel us to once more exert ourselves and leave us no time to sit eating our hearts out. It is not that those that are gone don't linger sadly in our memories, but we who are left have our lives yet to live. Despite that lingering belief that Reginald was still alive, he was none the less sincerely mourned for at the Grange, and more than once the Squire and his wife felt that the uncertainty concerning him was even more painful than the positive knowledge that he was no more. At the end of two or three weeks Mr. Chacewater had resumed his usual avocations, was pottering about his fields on his favourite cob, and gossiping with his neighbours and tenants. An especial favourite at the Grange was the Rev. James Marton, the Rector of Bottlesby, a hale, active, country clergyman of the old-fashioned sort, who, though doing his duty, and thoroughly liked and respected in his parish, was a sportsman to boot. Mr. Marton did not hunt himself, but he saw no harm in sometimes going to see the hounds throw off, and all through

the season seemed very accurately informed as to
their doings. A good, steady shot, and throwing a
very decent fly, Mr. Marton passed a healthy and
cheerful life with much satisfaction to himself and
his flock. If the service at Bottlesby was devoid
of choristers, and was what in these days would be
denominated of primitive fashion, yet the Rector
could preach a stirring sermon, and few men in a
pulpit could more thoroughly hold the attention of
his auditors than the Rev. James Marton. Besides,
all Bottlesby knew that in time of real sickness or
distress, they could always count upon genuine and
substantial assistance from the Rectory, as well as
advice.

Now, though no frequenter of race-courses, it
may be easily supposed that a man like the Rector
took an interest in the prominent events of the
Turf, as did the Squire, and when the two met, such
matters as the Derby were wont to be touched upon
in the course of their conversation. The supposed
loss of his son had caused Mr. Chacewater of late
to hold aloof from society, and so, when he encountered the Rector, one bright May morning, he
hailed him with avidity as one laden with all the
freshest gossip of the neighbourhood, a matter in
which he felt himself woefully behindhand. Very
pleasant indeed was the chat between the two old
friends ; how the price of stock had ruled in the
neighbouring markets, how the spring corn was
looking, how that recalcitrant old Darley was going
on, and whether any tidings had been heard of

pretty Kate, were all matters upon which the Rector had much to say, and the Squire to hear. Then came what was going on in the neighbourhood, and amongst other gatherings the Rector mentioned that he had dined two or three nights before at Carlingham Park.

"A pleasant party, no doubt," said Mr. Chacewater. "I can't say Wargrave is a man I can quite cotton to, but, to do him justice, he always gives you a good dinner, and his wine is of the best."

"No," replied Mr. Marton, "he is a little boisterous in his manner and rather vulgarly proud of his wealth, but he gives you of his best, and is a liberal enough man if you ask him for his assistance about anything."

"Yes, unlike so many men who have made money, he is free-handed, though what made him settle in the country I can't imagine; anyone less given to country pursuits couldn't be."

"I think we've done him some slight injustice," replied the Rector, "one can't call him a sportsman, because he don't shoot and he don't hunt, but he showed the other night much interest in and knowledge of the Turf."

"I should never have suspected him of that.' said the Squire sententiously.

"Nor I," replied Mr. Marton, "but after dinner the conversation got, as it always does at this time of the year, on the Derby, and there, to my amazement, Mr. Wargrave proved very much at home. There was nobody there who had the performances of the competitors so thoroughly at his fingers' ends, nor who made such shrewd comments upon them."

"Ah! that must have been interesting," rejoined the Squire. "And what does Wargrave think of our horse? I mean that horse that is entered in young Bramber's name, ' King of the Huns'?"

"Well, to my astonishment, Mr. Wargrave seemed to have a very poor opinion of it; he admitted he was a very fine-looking colt, and that he won the Biennial in a canter, but wound up with the remarkable dictum, ' "The King" is a nice colt, but he'll win no Derby.' Well, I ventured to observe, ' but, Mr. Wargrave, if " King of the Huns " will not win, perhaps you can tell us what will ?'

"' Yes, Mr. Marton,' he replied, ' " Chorister " will win the Derby this year.' "

"Why!" exclaimed the Squire, " ' King of the Huns' beat 'Chorister' far enough in the Biennial. What on earth is to prevent his beating him again at Epsom ? "

"Just what I said," rejoined the Rector, " but Mr. Wargrave looked at me with a smile, as if compassionating my innocence, and replied, ' " Chorister," sir, you will find will win the Derby. As for " King of the Huns," I don't expect to see him in the first three.'

"' But if he beat " Chorister " at Newmarket, why shouldn't he beat him at Epsom ?' I asked.

"' Because if I know anything about horse-racing,' was the reply, ' the money will stop him.' "

Now the Rector and Mr. Chacewater knew, like
all men of the world, that racing was not always
conducted honestly. There are unscrupulous
people on the Turf who do not play fair, as indeed
there are in every vocation by which money can be
made. There is cheating at cards as well as cheating in the selling of tea and sugar. Coals do not
always weigh what they are represented to. The
probity of the Stock Exchange is sometimes questioned, and it has been asserted that in the matter
of warranting a horse, a Bishop is no more to be
trusted than other people. But it was perhaps the
first time that either of them had been warned of
the unfair play beforehand. They also knew that
men who lose their money over racing from a horse
not running up to his usual standard are too prone
in their disappointment to proclaim the whole affair
a robbery upon no grounds whatever. It is not
regular racing men who express these feelings as a
rule. They know that you might as well accuse a
crack cricketer, who habitually made large scores,
of playing unfairly, because on some occasion he
did not trouble the scorer. But upon this occasion
they were warned by a man who seemed to know
what he was talking about; that this thing would
happen, and that a horse who, to their knowledge,
was thoroughly well, would not win a race which
those connected with him most certainly expected
that he would do. Now Mr. Wargrave, in their
eyes, was certainly no sportsman, but he might
know a good deal about racing for all that; he had

the character of being a shrewd, clear-headed man,
and though they had undoubtedly no knowledge of
his family tree, they had always understood that
his money was of his own making, and that he had
nobody but himself to thank for it. There was
considerable debate between them as to not only
what they ought to do, but what they could do
under these circumstances. They both agreed that
to ask Mr. Wargrave what he either knew or
suspected would be useless. He would probably
take refuge in generalities, and say, " Oh, nothing
more than that so much money had been laid
against 'King of the Huns,' that he thought it
improbable he would win." And it was quite
possible that he had been speaking thus vaguely
when he made the remark. He was a man given
to expressing his opinion in pompous and positive
fashion. Still, in such small business matters as
had fallen within their knowledge, Mr. Wargrave
had been generally clear-headed enough.

After considerable discussion they came to the
conclusion that all they could do was to warn Tom
Bramber that they had good reason to believe there
was a conspiracy to interfere with " King of the
Huns " for the Derby; that in what form this
villainy would be perpetrated they were unable to
say, and could only recommend him to take every
precaution against the horse meeting with foul
play either in the stable or on the race-course.

CHAPTER X.

"A FALL IN THE BAROMETER."

If the Rector of Bottlesby held Mr. Wargrave and
his family in no great esteem, his daughter Lucy
had a considerably more pronounced opinion regarding them.   The residents of a thinly scattered
country neighbourhood have to take Society as it
comes or there would be no Society.   New comers
may not always be to your liking, but they have
to be accepted.   The circle is too thin to be very
exclusive, and when the new settlers are backed by
a long purse, their reception naturally becomes
warmer in a ratio equal to their capabilities of
entertaining.   Owners of big domains and lordly
mansions can be content to pretty well limit their
entertaining to their own houses, but the minor
gentry of the country must mix with one another.
Lucy Marton was far too sensible a girl not to
understand this, and never suggested to her father
that they should not know the Carlingham family
because she herself could not bear them.   She was
not blind to their pompous arrogance, but she
would have declared that the thing that irritated
her most was the offensive air of patronage assumed by one and all of them.   Mr. Samuel Wargrave, in his new *rôle* of wealthy landowner, would

have said no doubt that it was the duty of men in his position to be upon friendly terms with the country clergy, to ask them to dinner, etc., but in reality he took credit to himself that he condescended to do so, and never allowed himself to reflect that these men were probably at the Universities when he was sweeping out the shop or office from which his prosperous career began. All honour to the wealth that comes from honest industry, but some of Sam Wargrave's early associates would have laughed and replied, "There is a good deal in what you call honesty, and you must give it a very wide acceptation if you are reckoning up Sam's little games." But though she scarcely knew it herself, perhaps the mainspring of Lucy's prejudice arose from perceiving that Clara Wargrave had made up her mind to become Mrs. Reginald Chacewater if she could. Although no words of love had actually passed between Reginald and herself, they had known each other from childhood, and Lucy had come to regard him rather as her peculiar property. She would have indignantly denied that there was any feeling between them ; but she could not endure the thought of poor Reggie throwing himself away upon a girl so utterly unworthy of him as Clara Wargrave. But it is possible, when it came to selecting, that Lucy would have been hard to please on that point.

However, all that was done with now. Lucy cherished no hope of his being still alive, and in mourning for him, as to a great extent she did in secret, she undoubtedly began to have some inkling of the truth and recognise that her feeling for Reginald had been considerably stronger than she had had any idea of. Very much against her wish, she had accompanied her father to this dinner at Carlingham. It had been an invitation of some standing, and sorry as they might feel about Reginald Chacewater's sad fate, he was no relation to them. The accident had occurred over two months ago, and Mr. Marton did not consider they were warranted in sending an excuse. She had felt very indignant at what she termed the heartlessness of the Wargraves, because they very naturally abstained from alluding to the man who was gone. "Clara Wargrave," she muttered to herself, "is exactly what I always thought her. A girl with no more feeling than an oyster for anyone but herself. Poor Reginald, a short time ago, when she thought he would suit her as a husband, she was purring in his ear, and stealing soft glances at him, and now she might have forgotten that he ever existed."

This was not quite the case. Clara Wargrave, no doubt, was of a phlegmatic disposition, but she was exactly in the same position as Lucy, and whatever her feelings might be, could make no outward demonstration of her grief.

Miss Marton chanced to be seated near the door, and rather apart from the other ladies, when the gentlemen came in from the dining-room, and the conversation concerning the big race at Epson had not as yet died away. She did not profess to be a student of the Calendar or know anything about racing, but she did know that what was estimated the great prize of the year was the Derby, and she did know that the favourite, "King of the Huns," was a horse sprung from her own part of the world, and was the property of Tom Bramber, one of her father's parishioners, and the consequence was, Mr. Walgrave's strongly expressed opinion that "King of the Huns" had no earthly chance for that race made considerable impression upon her, and when some three or four mornings afterwards she met the young farmer close to the Rectory, and he raised his hat in reply to her "Good morning, Mr. Bramber," she ventured to hope that his horse was going on well.

"That's just where it is, Miss," replied Tom, "to the best of my belief the 'King's' as well as ever he was, but the Squire sent for me only two days ago and tells me he hears that they won't let me win the Derby, and recommended me to take precautions against foul play."

"Well, Mr. Bramber, I don't know much about such things, but there can be no harm in your taking precautions, surely."

"Well," said Tom, smiling, "that's just what I thought, and so I wrote off to Mr. Praze, who has care of the horse, and told him."

"Just so, and what does he say?"

"That it's all nonsense, that that sort of idle

talk is always flying about before a big race, and winds up by saying, 'Tell me who *they* are that say such things,' and that's just what I don't know."

"It so happens that I can tell you where the Squire derived his information, because I happened to be dining at Carlingham that night, and it was from Mr. Wargrave we heard it."

"Mr. Wargrave," replied Bramber. "Why, what does he know about horse-racing? Why," continued Tom, laughing, "there's not a gentleman round knows less about sport than he does."

"He talks about racing, anyway, as if he understood that," replied Miss Marton, merrily. "At all events, for your sake, and the honour of the county, I hope the 'King' will prove victorious," and with a bright little nod she bade him good-bye.

"It's just what Praze says," thought Tom. "Mere idle gossip. Not likely a man down here, who has got nothing to do with it, can know what's going on at Newmarket, much less a chap like this Wargrave, who don't what I call know a horse when he sees it. He's a bragging lot, from all accounts, just the sort who'll lay down the law about everything. I'll just drop Praze a line to tell him it's all moonshine, and that if he's got a spare bed I should like to run up to Newmarket and take a look at the colt myself."

Considerably to his surprise, Tom Bramber received a telegraphic reply to his letter, "Want to see you, come at once," was the laconic message—

" PRAZE." And that same afternoon saw Bramber arrive at the trainer's house.

Dinner over, and enquiries about the " King's " health satisfactorily answered, "There's no such thing as a certainty in racing," remarked Mr. Praze, sententiously, " but our Epsom chance is an undeniably good one. Such tales as you wrote to me about are generally mere idle gossip, but there's gossip and gossip, and what's rubbish in most men's mouths becomes worth paying attention to in the mouth of another. Now this Wargrave, tell me, is he a big, blustering man, Christian name Samuel ? "

Bramber nodded assent.

" Ah ! " rejoined the trainer, " If Sam Wargrave said that, there's something in it."

" Why Mr. Wargrave is not a racing man ! " exclaimed Bramber in astonishment.

" No," replied Praze, " but he dabbles in it now and again ; he is great friends with two or three of the shrewdest men on the Stock Exchange, who, though not avowedly on the turf, are quite as deeply involved in it as anybody. Tattersall's can't teach the Stock Exchange much. From all which you understand that what Sam Wargrave says is not to be put down as mere 'talk.' It's quite possible some of his old friends may have given him a hint that the ' King ' won't win, without in the least telling him what's going to happen to him."

" And what do you think is ? " replied Bramber, eagerly.

" Nothing here," rejoined James Praze. " I

think I can be sure that he will leave Newmarket all right."

" And afterwards ? " said Tom, anxiously.

" We shall have to keep our eyes remarkably wide open," returned the trainer.

The result of Tom Bramber's visit was, that when he left Newmarket he was by no means so confident of winning the Derby as on his arrival. Another thing, too, which attracted his attention, as it did that of many others conversant with the Turf, was, that though all training reports from Newmarket representing " King of the Huns " as galloping in grand form, though on public running he stood out as decidedly superior to all his antagonists, yet he never advanced a point in the quotations at Tattersall's. He did not go back in the betting, but instead of advancing as the race drew near, and creeping up point by point, as the news of his being in great health came to London morning after morning, he remained steady ; he did not recede in the market, but at a price there seemed always plenty of money to lay against him. It too often happens in Turf matters that the predictions of the prophets of evil prove true, and those well versed in the mysteries of the betting market noticed that some of the most noted of these were very persistent in prophesying the downfall of the " King," both by deed and word. If there is much excitement in the winning of a great race, there is much nervous irritation, when you deem the coveted prize within your grasp,

to be persistently told that it will escape you. No
reason is assigned, nothing but a shadowy menace
of danger.   Such menace calculated to induce
belief that the prophets intend to take steps to
ensure the fulfilment of their denunciations.
Although Tom Bramber's time and thoughts were
all concentrated on the discovery of Kate Darley,
yet this mysterious something that threatened the
success of "King of the Huns" temporarily
changed their current.   It was not only the pecuniary difference it would make to him, and that
in his eyes was a very considerable one, but like
others of his type, he couldn't bear to be beaten.
To be beaten honestly and squarely, well, though
he didn't like it, he could bear that, but to be
tricked out of the race, to know that his horse
had not fair play.   He wouldn't stand that if he
knew it.   Who were these scoundrels from whom
Wargrave got his information, and what was it they
intended doing?

There were so many ways in which a horse could
be prevented from winning.   Praze, too, seemed
strangely lukewarm about it.   It was quite as
much his interest, in fact, as far as sheer money
went, more so, that the horse should win, as
his—Bramber's—and yet he said he could only
guarantee the colt's safety while he was at Newmarket.   Why not?   Why couldn't he keep watch
and ward over him at Epsom, just as well as in his
own stables?   And then Tom wondered how the
villainy contemplated against him was to be met.

7

Small comfort to be got out of Mr. Praze's sage remark that they must keep their eyes remarkably wide open. What rubbish! Of course they must, and see that a good many other people kept theirs open too. Then Tom reverted to the great search which was the main object of his life. Not a trace had he discovered of the missing couple, and he was puzzled now in what direction to make a fresh cast. No matter, let him only get this Epsom business off his mind, and he would start anew. It was a curious thing that, although Mrs. Chacewater and Tom Bramber believed Reginald and Kate Darley had gone off together, and were anxious in the extreme to ascertain their whereabouts they had taken different roads to the same end. Whereas, Mrs. Chacewater directed all her enquiries to the discovery of Kate, Bramber was unceasing in his endeavours to find Reginald, but hampered his agents by the statement that the man he sought was accompanied by a young woman.

CHAPTER XI.

"THE DERBY FEVER."

SOME few years ago, what may be termed the Derby fever, was wont to run very much higher than it does now-a-days. It, so to speak, smouldered all the winter, gathered strength during the early spring, and reached its height in the month of May. Country gentlemen, especially at that time, felt they must run up to London, and see the great annual problem solved, and from the Derby week till after Ascot many were the cheery dinners eaten and hearty handgrips exchanged between old University friends, old brother officers, etc., men who had been sworn friends in bygone times, but whose paths had now diverged, and who seldom met, except on the occasion of this yearly holiday. There are just as many dinners eaten, and much the same sort of thing goes on still, no doubt, but the interest in the great Epsom race has undoubtedly waned. Horses never fetched such prices, and never were such big stakes run for, and yet somehow, to old hands, it seemed that there was more genuine love of the sport formerly than there is now. I suppose it's the old story, we are cloyed. Even the school-boy has to cry, " Hold, enough ! " at last, to jam tarts. We have too much racing at present.

It does not necessarily follow that because men are connected with horses, they either know or care anything about racing, and the circus people were probably as indifferent to it as any folks in England ; but still there were one or two there who had so far yielded to the furore of the hour as to take a few tickets in sweeps, and that these men should occasionally talk about their modest speculations was natural, and this at last attracted Kate Darell's— as we must now call her—attention. Not six months ago, when she often got a letter from her brother Jim, which was sure to contain gossip of a turfy nature, she recollected that he had been very full of a horse called " King of the Huns," that he had

7*

dwelt a good deal upon the great things expected
from him. That he would carry off the Derby he
looked upon as an assured thing. Kate was a good-
natured girl, and had perhaps at the same time
a desire of gaining credit for some horsey knowledge with her present companions. She wished to
do them a good turn and gratify her innocent
vanity at the same time. As one who lived at
Newmarket, and was getting his living in a racing
stable, Miss Darell believed that her brother knew
all about such matters. He had not written of late,
for the best of all possible reasons, he did not know
where she was, but there was no reason he should
not. She would write to him, and tell him to hold his
tongue about it. She could trust Jim. If she told
him he was to keep her secret he would do so. And
she would keep Mr. Chacewater's, there was no
reason that she should say anything about him,
and then once more did Kate wonder what object
he could have in still allowing his friends to believe
him dead. The more she thought of this the more
Kate was puzzled. She herself had run away from
her friends for reasons quite satisfactory to herself.
That her mother would be very unhappy about it
was likely, but she knew her father too well to
think that he would trouble himself very much
about what became of her or Jim; besides, nobody
for one moment supposed she was dead. The Misses
Rushey Platt had seen her since the accident and
could vouch for her having escaped unhurt, besides
young men of Reginald's age have no reason to run

away from home ; they can go if they wish to, and
none can hinder them. And the running away
from one's creditors was a thing outside her experience. Another thing she thought singular
about Reginald Chacewater, and that was that he
had not been discovered. She knew that he had
been advertised for, and it seemed to her, in full
possession of his identity, extraordinary that they
did not recognise him as the missing man. She
forgot what a very short time our minds retain such
notices as these. By the next day we have usually
forgot what the description of the missing man was
like, and by the day after, that there is a man
missing at all.

In pursuance of that decision, Kate wrote at once
to Jim Darley, and then, affecting great interest in
the forthcoming race, invested a half sovereign on
" King of the Huns " in a sweep, and hinted darkly
that she had relatives at Newmarket, who often
told her about all these sort of things in their
letters, but she should no doubt hear from them in
the course of a few days, and if she heard satisfactory news of " The King," she should back him for
another half-sovereign herself, and would recommend them all to follow her example. Her sisters
of the sawdust were aghast at the recklessness of
the neophyte. In due time came a letter from Jim.
He was delighted to hear from his sister, and scolded
her well for keeping him in ignorance of her whereabouts, but he was so engrossed by the approaching
triumph of " his horse " at Epsom that he forgot to

mention what it strongly had behoved him to
mention—to wit, that by her mysterious flight she
had given rise to much scandal.   He was too young
to point out that a stain on her scutcheon, though
easy of acquirement by a woman, is apt to be difficult of effacement as the " damned spot " that so
troubled Lady Macbeth.   Kate, pleased with her
work and the progress she was making in it, gaily
proclaimed the triumph of " The King," and The
Royal Hippodrome were not only "on" to a man,
but also, in their little way, to a woman.

Although Reginald had never meddled much
with racing, it was not likely that a man of his age,
and who had gone through Cambridge, had not
seen plenty of it.   The Heath, Ascot, etc., were all
familiar to young Chacewater.   It is true that when
he went to Ascot he took it more in the light of a
large garden party, where one flirted and lunched
and had a good time generally, but still, taken even
in that way, people always combine a little betting
with it, and he was much amused when he found
the circus all suffering from a severe attack of
Derby fever.   Faith in " The King " was preached
by the whole troupe, and the anxiety to proselytise
is never stronger than it is amongst women, when
they dabble in horse-racing.   Miss Darell, indeed, .
was immense upon the occasion, and painted a
small wager placed upon " The King " as an investment in the mines of Golconda !   Reginald
laughed.   Money was getting scarce with him, but
he too promised to stake his sovereign on what he

jestingly described as "The Greatest Certainty of Any Age."

" Think, Miss Darell, what a line for the bills."

" Miserable unbeliever, how dare you mock me, but you must do as you have promised, Mr. Waters " —his assumed name. " It will be such fun, we've all agreed to have a great supper together to celebrate the victory."

" Hurrah ! " replied Reginald. "Great Derby dinner. Unparalleled attraction. No money taken at the doors."

" Do be quiet, Mr. Waters. I am sure I've heard or read something about winning your money like a real swell. The great thing, as far as I remember, is to look as if you had lost it."

Reginald bowed to the rebuke, but felt that there was small danger of these children of the arena welcoming success with any such stoicism.

Mr. Samuel Wargrave usually took himself to the Metropolis betimes. It was not that the season made so very much difference to him. He could not be described as elect of Society, but he most sincerely wished to push his way into it, and to be what he called in his own vernacular "in with the tip-toppers." With this view, he had bought an estate and was attempting the rôle of a country gentleman, but ever if a man was thoroughly bored by country life, it was himself. He had not a single pursuit that accorded with woods and green fields. He preferred the flowers in Covent Garden immeasurably to those in his own. He was essen-

tially a man of cities, and his whole and somewhat
varied life had been passed among them, chiefly in
London, but he had followed unknown industries
both in Liverpool and Bristol.   To escape as early
as possible from what to him seemed the solitude of
rural life was the natural instinct of all of us when
wearied past endurance.   He liked the hum of the
town, his spirits rose at the sight of the crowded
streets, and really regarded his residence at Carlingham Park as a penance necessary to the ad-
vancement of his aspirations.   So early April had
seen Wargrave duly settled once more in the
Metropolis.   Reginald Chacewater would have been
much surprised to know that Clara was sincerely
grieved at his supposed death.   Miss Wargrave was
a vain, ambitious young woman, and fully aware
that their circle of acquaintance in town was by no
means of a refined order; indeed, she did not
scruple to confide to her mother that she looked
upon them for the most part as vulgar wretches.
Sparse though it might be, she knew that the society
they mixed with at Carlingham was composed of
much better bred people.   She was eager to push
her way up the social ladder, and looked disdain-
fully down from a higher plain upon old friends
and acquaintances.   Married to a young man of good
family like Reginald Chacewater, and backed by
her father's money, she had thought attaining such
a position as she desired a mere matter of time.
She had plenty of tact, taste, and strong common
sense.   She was a showy, and by no means a bad-

looking girl, and took very good care that both her maid and her milliner should do her ample justice, whatever else they might say. No one had ever been able to assert that Clara Wargrave was not well dressed.

Now without affirming that young men are scarce from Clara's point of view, they were. Amongst all her acquaintance in London she could not point out one that she wished to marry. No doubt there were many of impecunious young men who would have answered her purpose, but then what is the use of that when you never come across them. At Carlingham eligible bachelors were scarce. Reginald had seemed to fulfil every condition, and, therefore, Miss Wargrave most sincerely bewailed his luckless disappearance. She had to begin all over again, and the fair Clara was impatient. A well-born husband was an essential in her scheme, and she was now at a loss for one even in prospective. She had plenty of confidence in herself, and though her common sense told her that she might not quite succeed in subjugating Reginald Chacewater, she had little doubt that he would speedily perceive all the advantages of a marriage with herself. As for love, that was an old world-worn tale of our grandmothers, and even if it wasn't, this very advanced young lady would have asked what *had* it to do with marriage? It is only quite the common people make such ridiculous marriages now-a-days. So that altogether Miss Wargrave grieved much more sincerely for the lost Reginald than Lucy Marton gave her credit for.

At Bottlesby the interest about the Epsom race has rapidly reached the boil, and the talk at the Farmers' Ordinary on market days becomes extremely turfy. Was not " King of the Huns," the favourite, the property of Tom Bramber, one of themselves, and had not most of them " a poond or two on Tom's horse "? Every year had the Squire and the Reverend James Marton discussed whether they should go up and see the great equine battle of the year fought, much to the amusement of their feminine belongings. It was a time - honoured joke this sham discussion, for the Squire had been present on every anniversary of the big race for more years than he cared to recollect, while as for the parson, Lucy was wont to say that the only piece of turf slang she had ever understood was when Reginald, then a freshman at Cambridge, had said to her, on the conclusion of a debate on the subject, " Lucy, my dear, it's odds on your papa being a starter." But though greatly interested in the result, more so indeed than usual, Mr. Chacewater was very decided this year, and James Marton hadn't the heart even to raise the question. He had been as fond of poor Reggie as if the boy had been his nephew. And believe though the Squire might that his son was not dead, yet, in the face of that unsolved mystery, neither man felt willing to encounter the turmoil of London in the Derby week.

CHAPTER XII.

"KATE DARLEY'S DÉBUT."

IT was at length decreed by the ruler of that branch of Slater's Circus to which Kate was attached that she should make her first appearance in public. She had now served an apprenticeship of a good four months, and had proved a wonderfully apt pupil. She could even jump through easy hoops from the broad padded saddle, if the pace was but moderate. But she was not thought good enough in that line yet by the ring-master to make her *début*, and indeed they had plenty of young ladies to fill those parts, but it so happened they had no one to do the *haute école*. Poor Minnie Price had been their star artiste in this particular line, and the poor girl had not sufficiently recovered from her sprain as yet to be able to ride. The manager considered it to be a considerable attraction, and thought Kate would do it quite sufficiently well to make an appearance. " Her youth and good looks," he urged, " will make up for her lack of experience. She was a good horsewoman when she came to us, and her previous knowledge will stand to her better in that *rôle* than in any other, and then——"

" You know, Mr. Waters," he exclaimed in a sudden burst of enthusiasm, " by Jove! she is in

looks a thorough lady, and in the high school
business that always fetches the pit and gallery."

Kate's heart beat quick upon learning that the
hour was at hand when she was to make her first
obeisance to the public. She felt nervous. What
artiste really good for anything is not at that first
plunge? Most of our leading actors would tell you
that a first night is always an anxious time. I can
imagine a young author feeling dreadfully ashamed
on the appearance of his first book; I can picture
him skulking about, and looking askance at those
he meets, and wondering whether they know that
he is the composer of those three volumes of
dreadful rubbish. I know there is the complacent
neophyte as well, who feels no anxiety on the
subject. A writer whose first book sometimes
proves his last. Nervousness has caused failure in
many a first essay from the stage to the cricket-
field. Kate, too, had a sharpish struggle with the
ring-master. While quite agreeing with Miss Darell
that she couldn't dress "too much the lady" for
high art equitation, their ideas a little differed as
to what that exactly meant. The ring-master's
views unmistakably savoured of the sawdust; in
his heart he had a leaning for a Di Vernon hat and
feathers; and as for habit, Kate declared that he
wanted her to wear one the date of which might be
described as "when all the world was young." Miss
Darell at last appealed to the manager, who at once
pronounced in her favour.

"Dress the character in your own way, my dear.

I'm not afraid of your failing in any way, least of all in that."

Flushed with her triumph, Kate was leaving the theatre when she encountered Reginald. She stopped and suddenly exclaimed:

" Mr. Waters, don't you ever come here at night ? I don't remember ever seeing you at a performance."

" No," he returned, " that is my working time, for I am a busy man, although, I daresay, you do not think so."

" Ah! I am afraid," rejoined Kate, " I never thought about it, but I hope you will come on Thursday. I am to make my first appearance in Chillingham that evening."

Miss Darell did not think it necessary to confide to Reginald that it was her first appearance altogether, any more than she thought fit to tell him that she was aware of his identity.

" I shall be only too glad," he replied. " Let's hope your success on Thursday will be only the forerunner of that of ' King of the Huns,' next week."

" Don't laugh," was the rejoinder. " I only wish I was as sure about the first as I am about the second."

" Ah! with me it's just the other way," rejoined Reginald. " I wish I was quite as sure about the second as I am about the first."

" Mind you come," said the girl with a laugh and nod, and then she flitted off to her lodgings.

Should dire necessity compel one to efface one-self, after the manner of Reginald Chacewater, a source from which discovery is more liable to come perhaps than anywhere is either from our own servants or those of our friends and acquaintance. They know so much more about us than we do of them, and recognize us when we have no recollection of them. They are very ubiquitous in these days. That dreary old servant we read about who keeps his place for twenty years, during the last fifteen of which he had been an abominable nuisance to the whole family, is a thing of the past. You were staying in Scotland, perhaps, last year, there was a housemaid there you occasionally passed on the stairs, and to whom you gave a slight *douceur* on leaving. You don't recollect her when you meet her in the service of some other friends in Devonshire, but the chances are the girl has neither forgotten you nor your name. In oblite-rating oneself in these days there is always danger of recognition to be apprehended from the domestics who come across us, and it so happened that Mary Forster, a Bottlesby girl, who some two years before had been a housemaid at Chacewater Grange, was now in service at Chillingham ; a girl with all the thirst of amusement natural to her age, and, not uncommon with her class, a great weakness for a circus. Upon the rare occasions on which this young woman could get away from her employment her greatest delight was to attend an afternoon performance of Mr. Slater's troupe. The entertainment was always varying, and consequently offered fresh attractions, though, for the matter of that, this enthusiast would have been content to look on at exactly the same performance for a month. That this young woman should contrive to snatch a glance at the local paper, which always contained the programme of the Royal Hippodrome, was a matter of course, and the discovery that the new star, Miss Darell, would make her first appearance before a Chillingham audience on Thursday night inflamed her with curiosity. Miss Darell was announced with a great blare of trumpets as the great favourite of half the hippodromes in Europe, and Mary Forster felt that if she could possibly manage the evening out on Thursday next, it was imperative that she should assist at Miss Darell's *début*.

As a man well-known to them all, Reginald Chacewater found himself put into an excellent seat on the eventful night; although it had amused him to watch their practice and rehearsals, and to study the inner life of the profession, Reginald had never yet witnessed a performance. He had of late, from prudence, abstained from going to any places of amusement, and the lights, the crowd, and the spectacle all combined to raise his spirits, and make him feel like thoroughly enjoying himself.

A circus is usually a popular entertainment, and there are few people who cannot pass two or three hours most agreeably in watching the horses, acrobats, and spangled-attired performers in the different phases of their varied show. A storm of

applause welcomed Miss Darell as, on a foam-flecked
black steed, she cantered lightly into the arena,
reined her horse up short, and bowed gracefully to
her audience. With her dark hair knotted closely
round her head and surmounted by the most
orthodox of hats, and with a workman-like habit
which fitted her graceful figure to perfection, Kate
Darell was looking her best and brightest as she
faced an audience for the first time; excitement
had brought a slight flush to her cheeks, and the
house at once recognised that whatever else she
might be, it was an uncommonly pretty girl that
was acknowledging her reception. Even Reginald
was surprised. He had thought Miss Darell a very
pretty girl on the day they escaped from the
Regent's Park, but, often as they had met since, he
had only seen her in the half-light of the circus at
rehearsals, and then attired in a pot hat and ordinary
skirt, and looking rather hot and dishevelled from
her exertions. Pretty, no doubt, but he had never
quite recognised how pretty till this evening. Her
horse was a perfectly well - trained one and
thoroughly *en rapport* with herself. Well versed in
the tricks of the *manège,* he obeyed implicitly
every motion of her heel and hand, as she put him
through nearly the entire *rôle* of his accomplishments. Two or three of these Kate's good taste
led her to reject, as, although clever, she was
conscious that they were not graceful, and that
neither she nor her steed would appear at their best,
and Kate's idea of the *haute école* was that every-

thing should be done with consummate ease, and
above all gracefully.

Another storm of applause followed the conclusion
of her performance, and having acknowledged the
ovation of her admirers, Kate cantered off to
receive the congratulations on her successful first
appearance.

If Mary Forster had sat entranced all through the
performance, she had been thunder-struck when
Kate first rode into the Ring. She had seen Miss
Darley, while at Chacewater Grange, too often in
hat and habit not to recognise her at once. She
had always heard that she rode remarkably well.
" But, lor," she murmured to herself, " to think
that she can ride like that ! " And then Mary
began to wonder when she took to it, how long
she had been at it, etc. Then the vagaries of the
two clowns with some hats, which they seemed to
delight in wearing anywhere but on their heads,
distracted her attention, and for the time put all
thoughts of Miss Darley out of her head. Although
she had left the Grange about two years ago, and
barely six months after Miss Darley had come there,
still Mary never doubted that she and Miss Darell
were one and the same person.

The show was all over, and Reginald, well-used to
the ins and outs of the place, made his way behind
the scenes to shake hands with Kate, and say a few
words of gratulation on her success ; and fortunate
for him was it that he did so, had he not, the probability is that he would have stumbled across

8

Mary Forster, and that she would have recognised him just as surely as she had done Kate. That Mary would talk her evening's amusement over with her fellow-servants was a matter of course, and that she should dilate on how she had once lived in the same household with the new star, this Miss Darell, was sure to come to pass. Indeed, Mary would have much to say on the subject, and already considered that her previous acquaintance, although in a humble capacity, with such a public character as Kate, gave her a factitious importance. All this would matter very little in Chillingham, but it was not likely that she did not keep up some correspondence with the Grange. Nor, when next the spirit moved her to write there, was it probable that such a tit-bit of gossip as this would be kept out of her letter. The news that Mrs. Chacewater is vainly seeking seems likely to reach her before long without any effort on her part. And that will prove the truth of her theory, and, in finding Kate Darley, recover her son.

Having thoroughly enjoyed his evening, and at the same time feeling that he had never done justice to Miss Darell's personal attractions, Reginald was in high spirits, and tendered his congratulations with more warmth and geniality than he had ever infused into his intercourse with Kate. The girl was struck with the change, and flushed and pleased with her own success, responded in like manner, and from that night their acquaintance became on a more intimate footing. The ladies of the troupe smiled, looked knowing, and speedily settled that the pair were fast ripening into lovers, of which, whatever the future might have in store, the pair at present were most certainly unconscious. Very good friends, no doubt, enjoying each other's society, and seeing a good deal of each other. Kate's professional duties compelled her attendance at the Circus nearly every morning, and, as we know, Reginald had constituted it his favourite lounge. But it is difficult for people to remain on terms of close friendship without any reference to their antecedents, more especially when each has one point on which their curiosity is excited with regard to the past. Miss Darell was thirsting to know, not only upon what work Reginald was engaged, but also why he persistently kept his existence concealed from his family, while he, on his side, had a great desire to learn what Miss Darell's life had been before her connection with the Royal Hippodrome. Her superiority of manner to themselves had been matter of remark when she first came amongst them, from Mr. Slater downwards, but who she was, or what she had been, as they told Reginald, they knew no more than he did.

" Might be a live countess for all we know to the contrary ; carries her head high enough at times, but she's not a bad sort all the same."

It was quite clear to Reginald that any information he might want about Miss Darell must come from her own lips, and that she was far too clever a girl to be entrapped into confession by

8*

insidious cross-examination. Her eyes sparkled sometimes at some "fishing" question which he conceived most craftily put; he knew he was detected, and could almost have laughed at the dextrous ease with which it was parried. It amused the girl to think that while she knew perfectly well who " Mr. Waters " was, he was completely in the dark as to who Miss Darell might be, and she could sometimes hardly suppress a mad desire to turn the conversation upon Chacewater Grange and Bottlesby parish, and cover the impostor with confusion. But no, she must find out Reginald's reason for silence before she allowed him to know who she was.

Rather an important day that Thursday had been in the annals of the Darleys, had Kate but known it, for in the morning Jim also had made his début, and had for the first time been allowed to take a prominent part in the trial, which was to satisfy the stable that their faith in " King of the Huns " for the Derby was justified.

CHAPTER XIII

" THE TRIAL."

THE sun shines brightly down upon Newmarket Heath, although what wind there is blows rather keenly, as it is wont to do there at the end of May, let the day be ever so fine. A small group of men and horses have gathered together on the far side, and it is evident that a discussion of considerable interest has just commenced. The heaving flanks and dilated nostrils of the four horses pacing round and round the group before-mentioned indicate clearly that they have just been galloped, and it is the results of that gallop that Mr. Praze, Tom Bramber, and Wrench are now talking over.

" Well," said Bramber, " I think we may say now that the Derby's all over."

Mr. Praze smiled as he replied, " Yes, if the ' King ' will only do as well on the Downs as he has done on the Heath, I think we may say it is. About good enough, John, isn't it ? " he added, turning to the jockey, " though you hadn't much in hand at the finish."

" No," replied Wrench, " it was about all out of my horse. You haven't told me what the weights were, but I suppose you asked him a pretty stiff question ? "

" Yes," said the trainer quietly. " I set him to give old ' Logarithm ' a stone, and I don't think there's a colt that he'll have to meet next Wednesday could do that, nor even the half of it."

" No," replied Wrench, " he ought to win."

" He ought to win," broke in Tom Bramber impetuously. " Hang it all, you mean he will win, man ! "

Mr. Praze shot a keen and anxious glance at the jockey, and then said quietly, " What is it, John ? "

" Temper," replied Wrench laconically. " I've got an idea that he may take it into his head to show it when he gets into a crowd."

" I've never seen a sign of it, yet," said the

trainer, and beckoning to the lad upon " King of
the Huns " to stop, he walked quickly across to the
horse, and as he caressed his neck glanced attentively at him.   It was only the glance of a moment,
but James Praze was favoured with what he had
never noticed before in the " King," namely a good
look at the whites of his eyes.   Stepping back
quickly to the side of the other two, he said, " What
makes you think so, John ? "

   " Well, this," returned the jockey, " the trial was
run exactly as you proposed, the two young ones
racing with one another, brought us along a cracker
as far as they could.   At the end of the mile they
were about done with, and the one Darley was riding
swerved nearly over me from sheer distress, in fact
he would have done so outright if it hadn't been for
great efforts on the part of Jim—that boy will ride
some of these days—then, as we had arranged, old
' Logarithm ' came to the front, and I called upon
the ' King ' to go up to him.   Well, there's no
nonsense about it, but for a few strides I thought
· he was going to shut up.   It seemed quite as if he
was going to sulk, and refuse to try any more.   I
sat quite still upon him, afraid even to touch him,
and then he went on again and, as you saw, won
clever at last."

   " He's bred to stay," remarked the trainer medita-
tively.   " We have tried him to stay, and he can
stay."

   " Quite so," replied Wrench, " but he's a nervous
colt, and a queer-tempered colt besides, take my

word for it. I came through with him in the
Biennial, was right in front all the way, and there
was consequently nothing to interfere with us. I
can't do that at Epsom, there's plenty of room and
it's all straight on the Rowley Mile, at Epsom there's
Tattenham Corner to get round, and then there's
likely to be a large field."

Mr. Praze made no further comment on the
jockey's observations, but turning to Bramber, said,
" 'King of the Huns' is as fit as I can make him. If
John there don't win on him next Wednesday, it
will be either from bad luck, or confounded obstinacy.
I've never known him to show temper yet, but men
are like that, smooth enough as long as things go
right and they can get their own way."

Mr. Praze made no further allusion to there being
any unfair play threatening the horse, and when
Bramber asked him what precautions he proposed
taking at Epsom, he merely said, " He'll leave Newmarket all right on Monday, and I'll take very good
care that he's well looked after at Epsom. I'm
not very much afraid of any harm happening to him,
but Sam Wargrave, years ago, was in with a lot who
didn't talk lightly. I won't say they did anything
wrong, more especially Wargrave himself, but it was
very odd that when they didn't think much of a
horse, and bet against him, he didn't as a rule win."

Mr. Praze was a cautious man, he understood the
ins and outs of his profession thoroughly, and quite
recognised that, with no unfair play in the case, bad
luck often dogs the steps of those who go racing.

in the betting. The consequence of these tactics was, no favourite was ever more unsteady for the great race than " King of the Huns." The public was fairly puzzled ; no sooner had the opposition driven him back to seven or eight to one than those who believed in him came to his support and placed him once more fairly at the head of the poll. The sporting papers hardly knew what price to quote him at ; and if this caused considerable excitement in the racing world during those last three or four days, you may judge there was much talk on the subject in the Royal Hippodrome at Chillingham.

Kate had had a line from her brother just after the trial, in which that young enthusiast assured her that there never was such a horse as the " King "; that he would win the Derby by the length of a street ; and that if she wanted new bonnets, now was her time to get them, free gratis and for nothing. And when Kate gleefully communicated the news to her friends, Slater's troupe were flushed with elation, and regarded Miss Darell as an inspired prophetess. Although only some three or four days had elapsed between Kate's début and the eve of the Derby, yet Miss Darell and Reginald had grown more intimate in that short space of time than they had done in the whole of their previous acquaintance. Some of the pleasantest friendships of our lives are formed in this wise. Thrown together by stress of weather in a dreary hotel when travelling, or three or four days passed in a country house, sometimes make us discover attractions in people, who, long though we may have known them, never particularly interested us before.

There could not well be a man more unsuited for the enterprise he had embarked upon than Reginald. He was of a gregarious temperament, utterly unfitted to lead a solitary life. He had no wish to proclaim his doings on the house-tops ; but, on the other hand, he was not a man to keep his hopes and fears to himself. He had a craving to share his aspirations with somebody ; and now that he really was working hard, and sanguine about that work, he felt dreadfully in want of somebody to confide in. He had plenty of friends, some literary strugglers like himself, others, men still on the bottom of the ladder of their various professions, but all high of heart, and given to drawing glowing pictures of the time to come, but he was all alone, he was dead, slain by his own hand. In his utter dearth of acquaintances, he had taken to passing his mornings pretty regularly in the Royal Hippo-drome ; and though upon excellent terms with the whole troupe, Miss Darell was the only one who had even a pretence of culture and refinement ; and the impulse to speak to her of what he was doing, and his hopes concerning it, was at times almost uncon-trollable. Nonsense, what folly ! Why confess his secret to this circus-rider ? Why ? Simply because, circus-rider or not, he felt that she was different from any woman he had ever met. She seemed so to sympathize with him in his loneliness. Kate

was a warm-hearted girl, and that he was depressed and unhappy about something or other, was scarce likely to escape her notice. Her knowing all about him, and the affection she entertained for his family, naturally induced her to be kind to him, and that a young man in Reginald's place should mistake this for sympathy, is easy to understand. It never occurred to him that Miss Darell could see nothing to be sympathetic to him about, and in brooding over the unpleasantness of his present position, quite forgot, as we are all apt to do, that it was entirely of his own making. And so it came to pass that some three or four days after their friend-ship had glided on to this more intimate footing, he confided to Kate the work he was engaged upon, and all his hopes and fears regarding it. Kate, as we know, was a girl fond of reading, and of a vivid imagination. She had discussed books many times in the last two or three years, but she never en-countered anyone who made the slightest attempt at writing them, or even ventured to believe in their capability of doing so. She thought an author must be, *de facto*, a clever man, and some little awe was now mingled with the interest with which she regarded the embryo writer before her. She did not reflect that the authors who can claim that epithet, are a very small percentage—" Of making many books there is no end, and much scribbling is a weariness of the flesh "—quoth the Preacher, or something like it.

Was ever there a young author who could with-

stand the temptation of talking over his first book?
Why should he not? It is human nature. Did he
not hope it would be a success, he would never have
gone through the trouble of penning it, and success
in the springtime of life is, or ought to be, what we
all aim at, and if fame but come with it, the wine
of the gods, for once at all events, has touched our
lips. That this mighty secret should draw the two
young people closer together than ever was only
natural. Reginald was ever willing to discuss the
difficulties of his story with her, for, instead of an
elaborate treatise on the law of copyright, calculated
to advance him in his profession, Mr. Chacewater
was engaged in the composition of a romance in
three volumes. "What solicitor, do you suppose,
would send a brief to a man who has written a
burlesque?" said a well-known dramatist of the
present day, on being asked if he ever went on
circuit; and the writing of a novel would, I should
fear, lead likewise to extinction as a barrister. That
all this looked remarkably like the prelude to their
falling in love with each other there can be no
denying. Kate, too, really did take considerable
interest in the story he was telling, and on more
than one occasion her quick imagination suggested
a way out of difficulties that troubled him. That
the girl had something of the romancer in her
nature was evident. We must remember the stories
with which, when they were children, she used to
amuse her brother Jim. Authors are sensitive
beings, and this might have marred the harmony

now existing between them; but Kate was practical
as well as imaginative, and it never entered into
her head that the writing of tales was a vocation
for which she had any gift. She was getting on fast
in her new profession, and was so naturally graceful
with it all, that her companions all prophesied a great
future for her. She was very independent too, and
had once or twice declined to essay some new trick
of equitation, on the grounds, not that she could not
succeed in doing it with practice, but "there's not
a lady in the troupe can do it except by severe
effort, nor do I believe there ever will be. All
riding in the Ring to be good for anything must be
done easily." They could not taunt her with being
afraid, for she was only apt to be too venturesome.
Just as she had decided that a sedentary life would
not suit her, so now did Kate's common-sense warn
her where she and Reginald Chacewater were
drifting to. She liked him; yes, owned to herself
that she liked him very much, and she felt pretty
sure that he liked her. "But," she asked herself,
"how long can this go on? And if we get to care
about each other, what's to become of us then? He
can't remain dead all his life; he can't marry me,
his family would never allow it; for both our sakes
I shall have to put an end to this; at all events for
my own. I cannot leave the circus; I have bound
myself to Mr. Slater for so many years. If I only
knew why—what Reggie's motive can be in thus
concealing himself from all his family and friends?
I dare not ask him; but surely it would be best for

him, best for me, that he should acknowledge at
once that he is alive and well."

From these reflections, and the glib way that Mr.
Chacewater's Christian name had passed through
Miss Darell's brain, it was evident that her conjecture was correct, and that the pair were lovers now
really, although, perhaps, some little distance yet off
being avowed ones.

CHAPTER XIV.

" THE FIRST GAME OF THE RUBBER."

A BEAUTIFUL Derby morning, and London is in
all that simmer of excitement which only the
University Boat-race and the old Epsom contest
seem able to evoke.   Of late years we have seen the
erection of other shrines in the great City's vicinity,
to which the votaries of racing within her gates
flock forth to worship; but to the real, un-
adulterated Cockney there is only one race in the
world, and nothing but dire necessity prevents his
attending the Derby.   That he does not know the
names of the horses engaged, that he will probably
be taking his pleasure in his own way while the
race is being won, and that on his return to Town
he is positively in happy ignorance of the name of
the winner, matters nothing.   It represents the one
annual outing, and it grieves him sorely not to
assist in the celebration of the great festival.
Despite all the chops and changes of the market
during the last few days, " King of the Huns " has

settled down a strong favourite at last.   His arrival
at Epsom has been duly chronicled, and the news
that he has done a rare good gallop over the entire
course has also reached Town, and his detractors are
for the time silenced, or at all events abstain from
betting against him, which, in the parlance of the
Ring, comes to pretty much the same thing. A few
hours more, and the wires will be flashing the
name of the Champion Three-year-old of the season,
veritably from pole to pole. Curious that such a
message should be wider spread, and perhaps more
anxiously looked for, than intelligence of revolutions
or the fate of kings.

Mr. Sam Wargrave is there, in one of the biggest
boxes on the grand tier, resplendent in white hat,
white waistcoat, straw-coloured kid gloves and a
dust coat, beaming upon everybody, patronising
everybody, hospitably asking men of all sorts to
come up and have just a snack and a glass of wine
at his box after the race—if the snack does not
include pâté de foie gras, perigord pies, etc., etc.,
there will be stormy times awaiting Mr. Wargrave's
retainers on his return to Town—and to one and all,
if asked, does Mr. Wargrave confide that he has got
" his little bit on ' Chorister,' " and that he thinks
he will win cleverly.   Further, asked by some of his
shrewder acquaintance what makes him ignore
" King of the Huns," Mr. Wargrave somewhat contemptuously expresses his opinion that the
favourite is a mere " miler," and will never get
the course

"Really, Sam?" said one of these gentlemen, with marked emphasis, and looking Mr. Wargrave keenly in the face.

"Very much really, my dear boy," was the reply, and once more begging him not to forget to turn up for lunch, Mr. Wargrave winked genially at his questioner.

The gentleman laughed as he turned away, and, as he made his way back to the Lawn, muttered, "He knows his way about, does Sam, and a hint from him at the last moment on the race-course is usually worth attending to. 'His little bit,' indeed! It would make me very uncomfortable, I know, to have such a little bit on a race. However, I'll follow his hint, and just have a pony on 'Chorister.'"

The usual scrutiny is going on in the Paddock, with the usual diversity of opinion. There is a tendency in human nature to believe to the last in the ship that carries your fortunes, and those whose money is invested on horses are given to be blind to their defects, be they of form or condition, till the fiat of the judge has dispelled the illusion. As unkind things are said of the competitors as may be heard anent the fashionable beauties by the loungers on the rails in Hyde Park during a summer afternoon. Eyes keen to detect the flaws, and, in their anxiety to detect them, overlooking such good points as a colt can boast of. However, if they have their traducers, these high-bred animals rejoice also for the most part in blind and foolish

9

worshippers. At the further side of the Paddock, the trainer of "Chorister" is talking earnestly with William Stainer, the jockey who is about to ride the horse in the forthcoming race. Mr. Brett is a little, cat-like man, with small, keen eyes, enough to go through you when they fairly catch yours, but he has a somewhat shifty glance, and it is not often that he looks the person he is conversing with honestly in the face. Still if the trainer's countenance is not prepossessing, he is a man of good repute, and numbers amongst his patrons men whose probity is utterly above suspicion.

"Now, William," he said, "you thoroughly understand your orders. You are to wait upon the favourite till you are round Tattenham Corner, and then come right through — your horse can't stay, but he can go quick. The slower the race is run, the better for you, but mind, don't lie too close to him, but wait upon the favourite."

"All right, I understand, but it's not much use. 'King of the Huns' slipped us in the Guineas, you know, but he had the foot of me all the same."

"Quite so, William, quite so," rejoined Mr. Brett blandly; "but there's always the luck of Tattenham Corner, you know. Get safely round that, who knows, perhaps the 'King' won't; then, do as I tell you. Strangle in."

William Stainer nodded, and then walked quietly off to look after his mount. A fine horseman, with a first-class standing in his profession, he was also of unblemished character; but it is not to be supposed that he had not a tolerable inkling of what Mr. Brett and the "Chorister" party were counting upon. It was all nothing to him, no wrong proposal had been made to him, his business was to do the best he could for his employers, and if any mischance should befall "King of the Huns" in coming round Tattenham Corner, to take advantage of it. He knew his horse was tremendously fast for about six furlongs, and, should they not begin racing in earnest till that distance from home, felt that, except the favourite, he held his field pretty safe.

Almost simultaneously with the above, only in a different part of the Paddock, a like conversation was taking place between Mr. Praze and Wrench, and at which Tom Bramber was assisting.

"Now, John," said the trainer, "I've nothing much to tell you about the colt. He can race and stay, and is as fit as hands can make him. Ride him as you like, only one thing, keep as clear of the crowd as you can, and keep on the outside round the Corner."

"That's giving away pretty well two lengths, you know, Mr. Praze."

"And the 'King' can give it, or six either," broke in Bramber, with his accustomed impetuosity.

Wrench looked at Tom in a pitying way. He did not believe in giving a point away anywhere in race riding.

"You've got your orders, John," replied the trainer curtly. "Once more I repeat, 'lie out-

side.'"   And as he walked away with Bramber, he
said, "He's the best horseman in England, and
there's none straighter; but he's as obstinate as a
mule, and thinks there's no one can ride like him."

A few minutes more, and the two paused to have
a look at the "King," as with Wrench on his back
he paced proudly by on his way out of the Paddock.

"I suppose I am to stop here, sir?" exclaimed a
voice in rather piteous tones, which proceeded from
a small knot of stable lads, apparently left in charge
of some horse-clothing."

"Ah, Jim," said Tom Bramber, "you want to see
your horse run, I suppose?"

The boy made no reply, but the way his face lit
up at the suggestion, made words quite unnecessary.

"Stop, come here," suddenly exclaimed the
trainer, and thrusting his hand into his pocket he
produced a handful of loose silver.   "Now," he
continued, "you know all about the course, you
led the 'King's' gallop over it only yesterday.
Mind you attend strictly to my orders.   Take the
first fly you can pick up, and drive as quick as you
can to Tattenham Corner.   Make your way in to
the railings on the outside.   You'll have trouble,
the crowd's gathered pretty thick there already, no
doubt, but mind, you've got to do it.   Stick there
till the horses come round, then keep your eye on
the 'King,' and take particular notice of what
happens.   Off with you, you've no time to spare."
And so saying, Mr. Praze waved his hand, and in

obedience to the signal Jim Darley vanished as fast
as his legs could carry him. " Now, Tom, we'll go
up and see it. Our horse is all right. If any foul
play is intended, it will take place in the race, and
Tattenham Corner is the most dangerous point."

The story of the Derby is an oft-told tale, and
yet to the man who loves racing no two Derbys are
alike. From the year when the "West" won by
a neck—a neck I was too young to understand—to
the day when favourite after favourite compounded
in the mud, and Fordham drove home a powerful
coach-horse, " Sir Bevis," on the upper ground to
victory, I can call to mind no two struggles for the
championship of the year, which were not marked
by many differences. It is its continued variety
that gives to racing its greatest charm.

Mad with excitement at the idea of somehow
being concerned in the great race about to be run,
and anxious to see his horse, as he proudly calls it,
make hacks of his opponents, Jim Darley speeds
gaily upon his errand. By dint of free expenditure
of the change Mr. Praze has given him he is
quickly at Tattenham Corner, and there, as the
trainer has anticipated, he finds the crowd already
clustered thick round the rails. However, with a
little pushing and a little cajolery, in a very few
minutes he has got an excellent place and, with
nerves strung to the highest tension, awaits the
coming of the horsemen. The preliminary canters
are all over when Jim gains his coign of vantage,
the competitors are all gone down to the post, and

there is that anxious delay that always more or less
heralds the start for the Derby. All the few
shillings he is able to muster are staked upon the
success of the "King," and he has wound himself
up to such a pitch of nervous anxiety as far exceeds
that of most of those who have got thousands on
the result. To do him justice, the money has little
to say to it, though shillings and thousands are
mere relative terms in proportion to the means of
those betting them. It's the success of the colt
that he has tended and watched over for the last
two years, and of whom perhaps, except his sister,
he is fonder than anything in the world. And now
the hoarse roar of the crowd proclaims that the
competitors are on their way. Anxiously he strains
his eyes towards the nearest point at which they
are visible. He just catches a glimpse of their
caps as they gallop through the furzes, and then
they are once more lost entirely to view. He can
see but a little distance from where he is, and before
the horses meet his eye, comes the thunder of their
hoofs. Then comes a perfect babble of tongues, as
of a score or more all speaking at once, in language
more forcible than polite, and then like a whirlwind
a confused mass of horses and silken jackets swing
round the corner. In a second, Jim's quick eye
has picked out the black and scarlet hoops of
" King of the Huns." He is on the inner side the
turn, and next the rails. Another instant and a
big colt ridden by somebody in a black jacket closes
in upon him; there is a slight collision, and Jim

can see that Wrench is very nearly driven over the
rails, and then they sweep on, and Jim Darley can
see nothing but a confused troop of horsemen fast
vanishing in the distance, and is oppressed with a
hideous misgiving that the black and scarlet hoops,
on the success of which all his very soul is centred,
is considerably in the rear. Jim has not been at
Newmarket for two years without knowing that a
collision may mean the upsetting of a horse in
either his stride or his temper, and he feels sick at
heart, and wroth with the world generally, as he
struggles to disentangle himself from the crowd in
which he is wedged.

It may be that Jim was in a great hurry in discharge of his mission, to get back to the Paddock,
and recount what he had seen to Mr. Praze. In
conjuncture with that it must be borne in mind that,
although the discipline of a racing stable had
schooled him in great measure to retain it, he had
naturally a hasty temper, and, moreover, was now
suffering the bitterness of defeat. It is possible
that Jim was pushing his way somewhat rudely
through the crowd. At all events he came into
collision with a bullet-headed young man, who
returning the shove that Jim had given him with
interest, remarked sarcastically:

"If you have lost your two-and-six, you little
varmint, you needn't be in such an everlasting
hurry to wash it down. Backed a fiddle-headed
wrong 'un, I suppose."

The young man spoke entirely at random, but in

his present state of mind, Jim immediately took it as an aspersion upon the "King." There was a sharp exchange of the amenities usual on such occasions, which speedily resulted in more extreme measures. Jim's opponent was not only older and bigger than himself, but had apparently a decent knowledge of using his fists, and though Jim showed plenty of dash and courage, when at the end of a couple of rounds the crowd separated them he had had most perceptibly the worst of it, and was fairly on the road to a pretty severe thrashing. Sad at heart, he made his way slowly back towards the Paddock. If ever anyone was conscious that his first Derby day had proved a failure, it was Jim Darley. His horse had been beaten, he had been a good deal knocked about, he had lost his money, and, worse than all, he was not only very late in getting back from the errand on which he had been sent, but he was in a sorry plight in which to meet his master. Mr. Praze was a strict disciplinarian, and likely to be sharp on any one of his servants who should misconduct himself on the race-course.

Mr. Praze had excellent eyes, and practised ones to boot in the matter of racing. He saw there was a scrimmage at the Corner, and when a few seconds later there smote upon his ear the cry of "The favourite's out of it," and he could see nothing of the black and scarlet hoops, he dropped his glasses, turned to Bramber, and said quietly: "We're done, Tom."

"What on earth's happened to the 'King'?" exclaimed Bramber.

"Temper," replied Mr. Praze. "Yes," he continued, as the number went up, "'Chorister' it is, and Sam Wargrave is right once more. Now come along to the Paddock, and let's hear what Wrench has to say for himself."

The jockey's explanation was terse and to the point. He was knocked into at the Corner, his horse sulked, and he had never been able to induce him to really gallop afterwards. The trainer said nothing, but he made a pretty shrewd guess at the real state of the case. He was still standing looking at the "King," the spur-marks on whose flanks showed that John Wrench had tried other means than coaxing to persuade his horse to do its best, when Jim Darley, vainly trying to staunch his still bleeding nose, made his appearance. Mr. Praze looked at him with intense disgust.

"You're a nice object," he said at last, "to belong to a respectable racing stable. I sent you away on business of some importance, and not to amuse yourself by fighting the first quarrelsome blackguard you found on the Downs. Looks as if he had his fill of amusement, don't he?" he continued, turning with a grin to Tom Bramber.

"I couldn't help it," replied young Darley. "It ain't quite my fault, I was bound to fight. I didn't take on a chap a good deal bigger than myself for fun; but I did what you sent me to do, Mr. Praze, first."

"Ah, then you can tell us exactly what took place at Tattenham Corner?"

"Yes," replied Jim, and then proceeded to give a very graphic account of what he had there witnessed.

"Temper, temper," moralized Mr. Praze, "there's no calculating on man or horse when their temper gets the better of them. There's John Wrench, in his obstinacy, will go inside, exactly where he was told not to go. Then there's the 'King,' the moment he is interfered with, sulks, and won't try another yard. Here's Jim Darley, who was sent to look after the pair of them, must indulge in a quiet little fight before he comes back. Well," he continued, glancing first at the boy's blood-stained countenance and then at the " King's " spur-gored flanks, "these two have been paid in full for making exhibitions of themselves, and if somebody would only horsewhip John Wrench within an inch or two of his life, I should go to bed comparatively happy. Temper, nothing but it, has lost you your first Derby, Tom Bramber."

CHAPTER XV.

" DOMESTIC DIFFERENCES."

WHAT on earth " Cockchafer " was started for had been a question much mooted at Epsom just before the Derby. His owner was a gentleman utterly unknown to the public, racing, indeed, under one of those fictitious names, which the law permits to be registered. He was a sporting publican who only kept two or three very moderate horses, which he usually ran on country race-courses; that a horse of his should be even entered for the Derby was a pure chance. Mr. Praze, like other people, had marvelled somewhat why this outsider had gone to the post. His previous essays in moderate company had shown that he had no pretensions to appear in high-class contests. Mr. Praze marvelled no longer, he understood it all now. " Cockchafer " had been started for the express purpose of interfering with " King of the Huns," and had fulfilled his mission only too successfully. The imperturbable trainer had been too long on the Turf to be surprised at anything. He had seen many a good race lost by a similar mischance, and many a good horse design-edly defeated by the same means. That the owner of " Cockchafer " had been a mere instrument in the hands of others, had probably been paid to start his horse, and was not even cognisant of the orders given to his jockey, Mr. Praze had little doubt. He regarded the whole business as the work of what he inconsistently termed the " War-grave lot." He admitted that he could not actually connect Sam Wargrave with the two or three men whose persistent opposition to a horse in the betting was always the precursor of defeat. He confessed that no case of malpractices had ever been brought home to this little clique of speculators, but he regarded them with profound distrust, and believed them to be utterly unscrupulous. So far the

"Wargrave lot" had hitherto never crossed his path, and Mr. Praze was not given to trouble his head about other people's doings, as long as they did not interfere with himself. He was a dangerous man to meddle with, giving much time and displaying much ingenuity as a rule to the repayment of those who ventured to turn the tables upon him. On his return to Newmarket, Mr. Praze resolved to devote himself to the return match with all the energy he possessed, and to be "upsides" with his enemies in some shape before the year should be out.

That there should be a long talk between the trainer and Tom Bramber over their mutual disappointment may be easily imagined, that Mr. Praze should give vent to the above sentiments with somewhat vicious expression, and that Tom Bramber should suggest the advisability of breaking somebody's bones forthwith, but whether the owner, rider, trainer, Sam Wargrave, or the Stock Exchange generally, was not quite so clear, was quite in accordance with his character, but the trainer quietly rebuked him:

"Leave it to me, Tom, leave it to me. Temper lost you the Derby; if the 'King' hadn't sulked, he was so much the best of them that he could have won in spite of the scrimmage. I intend to be quits with those thieves, never fear, but it's no use gassing and blowing all over the place. What a deal of good it would have done you if you had only been apprenticed to me for five years when you were a lad. There's nothing like a well-managed racing stable to cure an infirmity of temper."

"You don't seem to have been very successful with the 'King' at your academy, anyway," retorted Tom grimly.

It was a cruel stab, and for a moment the trainer winced.

"Ah," he said, with rather a forced grin, "Epsom seems rather unlucky ground for us, or else I was just going to quote the 'King's' schoolfellow, Jim Darley, as much improved in that respect."

The mention of Jim Darley recalled his sister vividly to Tom's recollection, and his resolve to prosecute his search high and low to discover Kate's whereabonts, as soon as the great race at Epsom should be over. It was over now, and a pretty *fiasco* it had been as far as he was concerned, and he supposed that would be the result of this next undertaking. If he found her, it would only be to discover that she was living with Reginald Chace-water, and he feared with no wedding-ring on her finger. He had vowed to revenge her wrongs, should that be the case, and it had begun to dawn upon him how that was to be done was not so easy to determine. He was interrupted by his companion:

"Tom, you are wool-gathering," remarked Mr. Praze. "It's no use your puzzling your brains about how we're to be quits on these thieves—you had best leave all that to me."

" I should think it was very simple," rejoined Bramber. " Our horse was so far beaten in the Derby that he is sure to stand at longish odds for the Leger. We know he wasn't beaten on his merits at Epsom, and therefore as soon as betting begins in earnest, we must back him to win us a good stake."

" Oh, no," said Mr. Praze, " that wouldn't quite do. Plenty of people know that our horse was interfered with as well as we do, and besides, Tom, I must—I must indeed, give that Wargrave lot a thorough lesson. Now I want you to promise me one thing. You will say nothing, and you won't make a single bet on the Leger. Leave all that to me; in fact, don't go near Tattersall's. I have got it all in my head, and I think by the time the game is played out, they'll be rather sorry that they took it into their heads to meddle with James Praze."

Tom readily gave the required promise. At the present moment he felt utterly sick of race-horses and race-courses, and quite indifferent as to the future of " King of the Huns." His mind was absorbed with Kate Darley, and a great passion, even when apparently hopeless, will often temporarily extinguish a man's other faculties. Until he knew what had befallen Kate Darley, Bramber felt that he was incapable of attending to anything else. He had gone back with the trainer to Newmarket, after the Epsom carnival was over, and was to depart that morning for Bottlesby, whence, after a couple of days devoted to putting the affairs of his farm in order, he intended to start upon his quest, though in what direction that search should be prosecuted he was still in hopeless uncertainty. That the losing of money bringeth sadness and depression, and its converse hilarity and high spirits, is the usually accepted result of all speculation. "Next to the excitement of winning, give me losing," cried Fox, and there spoke the spirit of the true gambler, to whom the money was but as mere counters, it was the game that interested him. How men take their reverses is an interesting study to the observer of human nature. Mr. Praze, for instance, has accepted his in a decidedly revengeful spirit, no uncommon phase.

"Wealth is not everything," quoth the philosopher. "No," retorts the cynic, "but it means so much, that, give it me, and I'll make you a present of what's left." If there was a party present at the Derby that year, that ought to have been thoroughly pleased with themselves, it was the Wargraves. Mr. Wargrave had not only won a very nice stake over "Chorister," but had placed several of his friends on good terms with themselves, by advising them to follow his example. That "little snack" after the big race had turned out the sort of luncheon that a man who knew what good living was would expect to find at the great Epsom carnival. The champagne had been iced to a turn, and few of his many friends forgot to look in upon his box. Clara, too, arrayed in what her *modiste* vowed was a poem in millinery, conscious of looking her best, a winner of dozens of gloves and other fripperies, and surrounded by a troop of admirers, should have been in a state of beatitude, and yet she was not.

"Man never is but always to be blest," applies equally to women. To say that Clara Wargrave was constant in her affections would be hardly descriptive of that young lady's feelings, but she was pertinacious in her desires, which perhaps answered the same purpose. She had plenty of worshippers at her shrine that afternoon, but they were all of the wrong kind. She had set her heart, as we know, upon rising in the social scale, and the devotion of these young men from the City, and of such did those who whispered soft nonsense into her ears mostly consist, had no charm for her. She was not in love with Reginald Chacewater, but she had meant to marry him, and Clara Wargrave was unwearying in the pursuit of anything she set her mind upon.

And more men are married in this way, than suspected, or, at all events, if they have a vague perception of the truth, could be brought to admit it. Nobody better aware of this than Clara, no one could have summed up more accurately the advantages that could be arrayed on her side by such an arrangement, and she was serenely confident in eventual success, but Reginald's death had put an end to all this. Clara had been most honestly grieved at his melancholy end. She really did like him in her way, but it was not precisely that, there was no one to take his place, there was no one of her acquaintance who combined all that Reginald represented. A husband, no, she need be under no anxiety about that, there were plenty of these young men from that City which she so despised, and from which she sprang, who would gladly come forward as suitors for the hand of Sam Wargrave's daughter. But none of these at all promised to realise Clara's ambitious dreams. Miss Wargrave chafed because amongst her father's many guests that afternoon there was not one of the class she had set her heart upon. Now when Miss Wargrave chafed, she was at no pains to disguise it from her domestic circle. Her mother, partly from being of a similar temperament, and partly from finding it more comfortable to range herself on her daughter's side than to place herself in opposition, generally chafed with her, with the inevitable result that even on an afternoon of such sybarite enjoyment as this, one became conscious of a decided crumpling of the rose-leaves.

Sam Wargrave's home life had grown unpleasant to say the least of it, during the last few months. It was rather hard upon him, but he was quite as desirous for the success of Clara's schemes as that young lady herself. It was in furtherance of that end that he had purchased Carlingham Park, and it was really not his fault that Reginald Chacewater should have proved the only suitable young man in that neighbourhood. In London his acquaintances and intimates were of the kind that had flocked to

10

his luncheon at Epsom, and as he replied testily to the petulant upbraidings of his daughter upon his never bringing anybody home to dinner who was either worth talking to or desirable to know:

"I can't help it. It isn't my fault, I don't know any nobs. I am quite willing to be chummy as far as I am concerned, but I don't manage to get the chance somehow here. We know everyone round about Carlingham, and I've fed 'em, and, as you know, done the thing properly; as for there being so few young people about, it's unlucky, but it can't be helped. It's a thousand pities that young Chacewater was drowned last winter, you and he were just made for each other, my girl."

"I liked Reginald Chacewater, very much, papa, it's very likely it would have ended in my marrying him, if, poor fellow, he had only lived, but it's not to be supposed that I can waste my life fretting about a man who is no more. You know between ourselves our position is by no means what it should be. Now," continued this matter-of-fact young lady, "the question is, how is this to be mended? As for Horace, he is a fool—you put him into a good and expensive regiment, and make him a handsome allowance, and nothing comes of it. He never brings any good men home with him, and mark my words, whenever he does marry, he'll do something awfully foolish."

"I am afraid you are right, Clara," said Mr. Wargrave. "I've given him a fair start; I can't give him brains, but I'll tell you what I can do: if he goes marrying without my consent, I can leave him to keep his family on his own hook."

"Don't talk nonsense, papa," replied Miss Wargrave. "Horace will never be self-supporting, and you know it. Now if we are to get on in life, it must be through ME, and if I am to get on in life it must be through my marriage"—there was no diffidence in this young lady—"and to get married, a girl must meet suitable young men. Now, papa, that's your business, you must find them."

"Don't I keep telling you I can't," replied Mr. Wargrave, now fairly at bay. "You wouldn't have me advertise for them, would you? Do you want me to write begging letters all round the Peerage, asking if they've a younger son, willing to wed a girl whose father can give her fifty thousand pounds —made in business?"

"If you can't discuss the matter without being coarsely abusive, papa, it is high time our conversation terminated," and as she spoke she rose from her chair, and swept angrily out of the room.

Sam Wargrave looked grimly into the fire. Similar scenes to this were now of constant occurrence between him and his daughter. The fair Clara was generally given credit for much serenity of temper, but it is compatible with one of those serene tempers to become more exasperating than one of the most hot-headed and passionate description.

"Ah," muttered Sam Wargrave, "I never thought I'd be so sorry for poor young Chacewater as I am

10*

at this minute. That girl drives me just wild. How the —— can I introduce her to fellows I don't know? She makes me just mad. Marry a swell, I wish she could, nothing would please me better, but to expect me to work the oracle is downright foolishness. That poor Chacewater chap was just the thing. What a thundering pity he ever learned to skate!"

CHAPTER XVI.

"BOTTLESBY GOSSIP."

THERE was a cry of woe amidst the members of the Royal Hippodrome when the telegram announcing the winner of the Derby reached Chillingham. Like other false prophets, Miss Darell was, to speak figuratively, deposed from her ped, and the subject of much good-humoured banter. As for that supper, there were grim jests as to of what that now Barmecide feast should consist. Some of the humorists of the company drew pictures of the cakes and ale and dainty dishes that should have decked the board, and of the Lenten fare that, now their golden dreams were dissipated, must be their substitute. Kate's friends at Newmarket were pronounced lying prophets, and everybody recalled the wise old adage, " Don't never prophesy unless you know."

Amongst this light-hearted company there was infinitely more jest than lamentation over their disappointment. If nobody counted more mad very much, in like manner the reverse was of no very serious consequence to any of them. Kate herself was perhaps more disappointed than the rest, and she mainly on her brother's account. Jim, in his last letter, had been so confident about his horse winning, and she felt sure that he would take the failure of " King of the Huns " very much to heart.

In the meantime Miss Darell was increasing rapidly in favour with the Chillingham public, and Reginald Chacewater, since the night of her début had gradually dropped those precautions against recognition that he had previously taken. He frequently appeared in the evening now in the front of the house, and he was very often Kate's escort in the Public Gardens and on the Promenade. In spite of her prudent resolutions, Kate seemed inclined to let things take their course, at all events for the present. Something like a fortnight had elapsed since the black and crimson had come to such infinite grief upon Epsom Downs. No great lapse of time perhaps, but when young men and maidens have arrived at that very confidential state into which Reginald and Miss Darell had imperceptibly glided, it becomes very like living in a house in which the fire is smouldering, and may leap into life and burn fiercely at any moment. If those good resolutions of hers ever do recur to Kate, she shuts her ears close to them now. She argues that it is very pleasant, it must come to an end before long, why should she not enjoy it while she may ?

And when the separation does come, well, it is she who will suffer most, and if she elects to bear the pain, in return for a few days of happiness and dreamy lotus-eating, it matters to no one but herself.   Kate Darell rarely bestows a thought upon that other admirer of hers ; that she knows of his devotion it is needless to say.   Whenever did a girl overlook that, let the tribute be of ever so small a value in her eyes.   True, Tom Bramber as yet has never declared himself; Kate knows, nevertheless, that she had but to hold up her finger to bring the stalwart young farmer to her feet.   She has thought of his disappointment, as well as her brother's, in connection with the Epsom failure.   The winning of the Derby she knows is a thing of which most men feel proud, but still she has not felt anything so much grieved for him as she has for Jim.   In fact Tom Bramber has as yet made no impression upon her heart, and ruefully he acknowledges to himself that she has given him no sign of encouragement.   Things are not what he conjectures between her and Reginald, but let that matter end as it may Tom is so far right, his love suit is going very much awry.   It is little use laying siege to a heart already garrisoned, and Kate is in little mood just now to listen to words of love from other lips than those of the man who saved her from a watery grave in the Regent's Park.

At length it became rumoured about Bottlesby that Kate Darley had been seen.   The report in the first instance was vague and shadowy as such rumours usually are. She had taken up with some strolling players.

"Pretty come down this for one who held her head so high."

"It's only what might have been expected from one of old Darley's children. It was all very well for Madam to take her up to the Grange, and think she was going to make a silk purse out of a sow's ear, but Kate Darley always was a wild one, and it wasn't likely she would ever settle down and get her living as a decent girl should." Then it was whispered about that Kate was riding in a circus. Well, they did think she would never have come to that, and after a little all this gossip came to Mrs. Chacewater's ears. By dint of cross-questioning here and there pretty sharply, she found, considerably to her astonishment, that the source of all this talk sprang from the Grange, and that it was from among her own household this report had arisen. Mrs. Chacewater at once made enquiries, and speedily found that her cook had received a letter from a girl now in service at Chillingham, who had formerly been housemaid at the Grange, and that this girl, who knew Kate Darley perfectly well by sight, had seen her riding in the circus there. Mrs. Chacewater was strangely moved at the intelligence. She had cherished a hope, as we know, that her son was still alive, and that could she but find Kate she should also find Reginald. Now this conviction was shaken. Surely if Reginald had eloped with this girl he would never allow her get her living in a show, for, although liberal enough in her ideas, Mrs. Chacewater had but hazy views concerning the equestrian profession, and an undefined notion that it was by no means respectable. She never could have believed that Kate Darley could have embarked on such a career. Nevertheless, now Kate was discovered, she must ascertain if Reginald was with her. She could not well go herself, to do that would be to arouse hopes on the part of her husband which she knew might never be realised, and she could devise no plausible excuse for going to Chillingham. It was a delicate commission, and she could think of no one to whom to entrust it. While puzzling her brains as to who on earth she could employ in this emergency, chance put an instrument into her hands at which she grasped with more avidity than prudence.

That luckless race over and Tom Bramber, once more resolute to prosecute his search for Kate Darley, returned to his task with more energy than ever. That the gossip of Bottlesby should reach an active man who was out and about all the parish and its neighbourhood in a very short time was a matter of course, and Tom's first thought was that it was a thundering lie, and that could he but bring it home to a man he would cram it down his vile throat. Tom, whose theatrical experiences were gathered from country fairs, held the " play actors " in small esteem, but as it was only the tale of an idle woman's tongue, he determined to proceed at once to Chillingham and see for himself. This happened to reach the ears of Mrs. Chacewater, through Miss Marton; and being in complete ignorance of Tom's passionate admiration for Kate, she thought it possible to ask him to enquire into the truth of the current report. It was odd, she thought, that he should be going to Chillingham, but Mr. Bramber was a busy man, and combined a good bit of horse-dealing with his other avocations. Chillingham was a popular hunting centre, and like all such, as Mrs. Chacewater knew, a place in which there was always a likelihood of either picking up or disposing of a good horse. It was moreover very accessible, being only about three hours journey from Bottlesby Station. She accordingly sent down word to Tom Bramber that she desired to see him before he went away, and the young farmer duly presented himself at the Grange in reply to her summons.

"Good morning, Mr. Bramber," said the lady, "only you must be sick of condolences or I would say how sorry we all were for your disappointment."

"Yes, ma'am," rejoined Tom, "It was hard luck to know you ought to have won, to know you had the best horse in the race, and then to be beaten is rather rough on one. We must only hope for better luck another time."

"And may that time come soon," said Mrs. Chacewater.

"Thank you," replied Tom, "but the picking up a colt good enough is not so easy," and then he pondered what it was that Mrs. Chacewater wanted with him, for that he had not been sent for to discuss the past Derby he felt sure.

"I heard casually from Miss Marton last night that you are going up to Chillingham, Mr. Bramber."

"Yes, ma'am," replied Tom. "I am starting by the twelve train."

"You have of course heard the talk in the village."

"Yes," he returned sternly. "A lie set afloat by some evil-tongued old woman. I only wish it had been a man who had said it."

"Dear me," replied Mrs. Chacewater. "I had no idea that you took such a warm interest in Kate Darley."

"You see," stammered Tom, rather abashed, "I have known 'em since they were quite little ones. I have known them all their lives, and so take a sort of interest in them."

He was not thirty, and though she still did not grasp the truth, yet it did strike Mrs. Chacewater that there was something incongruous in his fatherly interest in such a pretty girl of eighteen as Kate Darley.

"They are a bit wild both of them, but Kate is far above mixing herself up in any such brazened foolery as that."

"I quite agree with you, Mr. Bramber. Kate Darley is far too good for such a life, nor do I believe she would give pain to those who are attached to her by taking up such a mode of earning her living. I am as anxious as I am sure you are to

contradict this report which is circulating in the
village, and I wish to be able to contradict it with
authority—you understand."

" I think so," replied Bramber quietly.

" It will be no trouble to you to give up one
evening and spend it at the Royal Hippodrome at
Chillingham, and convince yourself that Kate
Darley takes no part in the performance. On your
return I trust we shall be able to give it a positive
denial."

" All right. I quite understand what you want,
ma'am. Have no fear but what I will do your
errand, for it happens also to be what takes me to
Chillingham." And then Tom bade Mrs. Chacewater
good morning, and left that lady no little disturbed,
for it had dawned upon her at last that Mr.
Bramber was in love with Kate, and that if her old
theory should prove correct, and Reginald have
been the companion of her flight, there was likelihood of hot words between the two men, if
they met, as meet they were almost bound to do,
should gossip prove true. Was Reginald with this
girl, and if so, what were the relations between
them ? Know whether she was right or wrong in
that fixed idea of hers she must, but she shuddered
at the idea of a fracas between the two men. She
had no fear for her son physically—what Chacewater had ever felt that, or blenched for the scions
of the house on that account ? but she shrank from
the disgrace of an open scandal such as this would
be should Reginald and young Bramber come to

blows over this girl. A pretty story that would be to have flying about the county, and then she wondered what else she could do. Tom had said he meant finding out the truth concerning Kate, and if, as she now believed, he was thoroughly in love with her, it was not likely he would falter in his determination. It was done now, and she must abide the result. From the word spoken and the arrow sped, there is no retraction.

CHAPTER XVII.

"A PARTING KISS."

Tom Bramber on his way to Chillingham presents a very different front from that he has shown about Bottlesby. There he has boldly denounced the whole scandal as an infamous lie, he has told Mrs. Chacewater that he felt sure there was not a word of truth in it, that Kate Darley was far too proud a girl, to go before the public in that fashion or to associate herself with a lot of mere strollers ; still adhering closely to that belief of his in which all shows, circuses, and theatres are a mere ornamental fringe to fairs generally, where the shows are conducted under canvas, and the performers dwell in huts, Tom regards these latter as very little superior to the gipsies. It has been all very well to bluster it out at Bottlesby, but in his heart of hearts is a horrible conviction that it is true. What could have possessed Kate to take up with such a life he cannot even guess. Still stranger, what could have induced Reginald Chacewater to mix himself up with such a lot of vagabonds? It must be borne in mind that Tom has never seen the inside of either a regular theatre or a circus. He moves about the country a good deal, and has much experience of country towns, but then small country towns in an agricultural neighbourhood rarely boast of a theatre, a corn exchange or a big room at the principal hotel sufficing for such entertainers as are speculative enough to venture amongst them. Although he has been to Chillingham before, yet it is rather out of his beat, and though it certainly does boast a theatre, the building stands in an inferior part of the town, is poorly attended, and keeps its proprietor in a state of chronic insolvency.

On his arrival he puts up at a quiet commercial hotel in one of the leading thoroughfares, and then strolls off to discover the whereabouts and take stock of the Royal Hippodrome. He finds it in the Public Gardens, a large building, dedicated in the summer chiefly to flower shows, concerts, etc. On to this the enterprising Mr. Slater has built canvas stables, made a Ring in its centre, and transformed the whole place into a bright and handsome Hippodrome. The doors are at present closed to the public, for it is the intermediate time between the afternoon and evening performances. Outside them, however, are gaily printed bills of the entertainment, with a list of the artistes appended thereto. Tom eagerly scans this latter, and his heart gives an exultant throb as he finds there is no mention of

Miss Darley on the list.   Still he has come to Chillingham to clear up this story, he will witness the
performance this evening, and ascertain with his
own eyes that Kate Darley takes no part in it.   It
will be time enough on the morrow to make
enquiries as to whether she ever was connected with
it.   When Tom takes his seat that night he is
amazed at the splendours of the building.   Still
more is he thunderstruck at the large audience
that are gathered together, and though still scanning
each fair equestrienne narrowly, he has well nigh
put away from his mind the idea of Kate having
anything to do with the company, and is carried
away with enthusiasm at the varied and clever
performance.   At length there is a slight pause,
broken only by the badinage which passes between
the Clown and the Ring-master.   He can see that
the audience is eager and excited, and hurriedly
asks his neighbour what is coming.

   " Ah, it's the first time you have been here," was
the reply.   " Coming ?   Why, Miss Darell !   Who's
she ?   Well, I reckon she's about the prettiest girl
you ever saw or ever will see outside of an 'oss," and
in another moment, Kate, looking most bewitching
in the nattiest of hats and the daintiest of habits,
cantered into the Ring on her famous black trick
horse " Beppo," and commenced to go through her
act of high-art horsemanship.   Three or four times,
in obedience to imperceptible signals from his mistress, did " Beppo " go kicking and backing round
the Ring, in a manner sufficient to even discompose

a western " Cowboy," during all of which Kate sat
fixed and immovable, as if she were a very part of
her horse. Then at a touch of her hand, after two
or three saucy bounds, he quieted down and went
through all the tricks of the *manège*, and then,
amidst thunders of applause, Kate bowed gracefully
to her audience and quitted the ring.

As for Tom Bramber, he sat like one transfixed.
Never, he thought, had he seen Kate Darley look so
lovely. Her horsemanship had always bewitched
him, but he had never seen her ride like that. If
the Bottlesby scandal were true, he had pictured
her in short spangled skirts jumping clumsily
through paper hoops, after the manner of the fair
equestriennes he had witnessed at the two or three
fourth-rate circuses which it had so far been his lot
to see. Jumping through a hoop can, even in the
hands of a most accomplished artiste, never be a
graceful performance. It is not like skating, where
grace is usually the result of practice. Tom had
naturally a keen eye for both grace and beauty, and
the perfect ease with which Kate sat her horse, and
the way her light figure swayed with his every
movement, was to him what the picked picture of
the Royal Academy is to the connoisseur, a thing to
feast your eyes upon as long as you may. Like the
prophet who blessed what he came to denounce, so
Tom, who had come sternly determined to condemn,
was simply lost in admiration. He felt he could see
no more, no sooner was it evident that Miss Darell
did not intend to reappear than he rose and made

his way out of the theatre. He must get into the
fresh air; he wanted to think. What did it all mean ?
Yes, Kate Darley was a circus-rider, but a circus-rider
of a very different pattern from that which he had
imagined. Reginald Chacewater too, where was he ?
He certainly had not figured in the Ring; but if
Kate was with him, how was it he allowed her
to night after night appear in public ? Could it be
that he was all wrong in this supposition of his, and
that the disappearance of the two was merely a
coincidence that had taken place in utter inde-
pendence of each other ? One thing was certain,
to Chillingham he had come, and at Chillingham
he would remain, until he had ascertained whether
Reginald Chacewater was in the place, and, if so, what
was the connection between him and Kate Darley.

For the next two or three days Tom Bramber
pertinaciously attended every performance in the
Royal Hippodrome, and filled up his spare time by
making enquiries in every direction for a Mr.
Chacewater. Six months had elapsed since the
accident in the Regent's Park, and the names of
the sufferers were well-nigh forgotten ; but the fate
of Mr. Chacewater had been so much canvassed at
the time that here and there a recollection of the
name still remained in men's memories. The public
had long ago made up its mind that he was drowned
then and there, and that the theory put forward at
the time of his being still alive, was merely one of
those hallucinations which occasionally possess the
near relatives of the dead, loth to believe that one

loved so dearly had been snatched from them, and it regarded Tom as a man slightly touched in the head. But it was not long before it occurred to Tom that such enquiries were useless. If Kate now went under the name of Miss Darell, the chances were that Reginald had also a *nom de guerre*, and that the most likely way to come across him was to keep as strict a watch as he was able on Kate herself. He had attended half-a-dozen performances at the Hippodrome, and his assiduous attendance soon attracted the notice of the officials at the doors. It was soon further remarked that if he sometimes came late, and at others left early, he never missed one minute of Miss Darell's turn. This soon became talked of among the company, and Kate was rallied not a little about her unknown admirer. As yet she had not seen him, and was not best pleased to hear that she had one. She did not know why, but she had an undefined sense of danger in the air. She felt uneasy about this man, who, she was told, never took his eyes off her while she was in the Ring. It could matter nothing to her, but it might mean harm to Reginald. What if it should be somebody in search of him, and what if Reginald should fly and once more endeavour to evade his pursuers? He was evidently in hiding from some one. Ah, she did not want that just yet. Not three weeks ago, and she had thought it best that she and Reginald should part, but there was no need for that just now, she argued. It would be quite time for him to go when he said anything

11

foolish. His friendship was very dear to her, and then—— Well, Kate Darley flushed and found she could humbug herself no longer. Friendship forsooth! She was falling over head and ears in love with the man.

The gossip of the *coulisses* quickly reached Reginald's ears, and was spoken of between Kate and himself, but the former had made up her mind that before she avowed her knowledge of who Reginald was, she would, at all events, endeavour to have a look at her mysterious admirer. Chacewater had succeeded in concealing his identity for so long that he had pretty well lost all apprehension of being discovered, and, though curious to see him, had no suspicion of who Kate's admirer was, nor that he in any way concerned himself. He determined that night that he would attend the Hippodrome and have a look at this unknown admirer of Miss Darell. He was always there, and any one of the officials could point him out. But it so happened that he was so absorbed in his work that night that he took little count of time, and when, starting from his writing-table, he rushed round to the Hippodrome, he found that the hour appointed for Katie's turn was long since past, and they told him at the door that she had already left the Ring. For a moment he stood undecided, then, having determined not to go in front of the house, he made his way round behind the scenes, with a view of seeing Kate before she left the circus. Miss Darell, attired in her walking dress, met him in the passage outside the dressing-rooms, and enquired anxiously if he had been in front that evening.

He replied in the negative.

"Because, Reginald," she replied, "my mysterious admirer is no other than Tom Bramber, who knows you as well as I do. What your object is in letting all the world believe you dead is no business of mine, and I will keep your secret; but rest assured that if Tom Bramber catches sight of you he will recognise you at once."

"Why, who on earth are you?" he exclaimed, not a little surprised to find that he was known.

"Kate Darley," she replied, "the daughter of one of your father's tenants, and formerly governess to your nieces at the Grange. My lips are closed; but if you want to remain unknown, take my advice and leave Chillingham at once."

"And what do you intend to do?" he asked gravely.

"Stay here," she replied impatiently. "Bid me good-bye, and go," and as she spoke she extended her hand.

"I don't want to be discovered just yet most certainly," he replied, as he pressed her hand. "Good-bye, Kate my dearest," and drawing her suddenly to him, he pressed a warm kiss upon her lips. "Once more good-bye, dear. Keep my secret." Another warm squeeze of the hand, and he was gone.

"Yes, Reginald, I will keep your secret," said the girl, "till it pleases you to discover it. Ah," she murmured to herself, "Heaven grant I may only keep my own."

11*

CHAPTER XVIII.

" TOM GETS HIS ANSWER."

THAT Tom Bramber was no adept at the detective business was obvious. His being so slow to recognise that the fugitives would most likely have to be sought under assumed names was proof of this ; but the most important mistake he made in the new line he had taken up was in forgetting that he was perfectly well-known to those he was in search of, and in taking no precautions to prevent their becoming aware that he was on their track. The natural consequence of this had come about. Reginald knew of his presence at Chillingham before Bramber had discovered him, and at once took steps for the prevention of that by leaving the town. All unconscious, Tom steadily pursued his quest. He hovered about the Hippodrome, firmly persuaded that where Kate was, there also he should find young Chacewater. He had scraped acquaintance with some of the men connected with the troupe, and haunted the place at all hours, both during the performances and at odd times, much as Reginald had been in the habit of doing, but with this marked difference, that whereas Reginald was privileged to enter the building and gossip with the performers during the morning rehearsal, Tom never passed the doors except as one of the paying public. In his somewhat clumsy way, he began to push enquiries with regard to the man he sought. He knew by this it was useless to ask after him under his own name, and as he was afraid to be too direct in his questioning, he was at first unsuccessful; but the abrupt disappearance of Waters was naturally spoken about in the Hippodrome, and at once attracted Tom's attention. Having once obtained his clue, it was easy to put questions as to what manner of man this Waters was, and from the description given of him, Bramber had little doubt that Waters was the assumed name of the missing man. He learnt, moreover, that Waters, though not belonging to the troupe, was quite one of themselves, that he disappeared without saying good-bye to anyone, nor did anyone know what had become of him. "Unless," added the clown reflectively, "it's Miss Darell. He was uncommonly sweet upon her. She may know."

"Do you suppose he has left the place?" enquired Tom. "I have a strong idea that I used to know this Waters at one time."

"Safe to have done, I should think," replied the clown. "Why he was never out of the place. We used to see him regularly every day."

"Ah," said Tom, "if it was the man I mean I should have known him again, but I have never set eyes on him, and I have been here pretty often too, the last week."

"Ah, yes," said the other; "but he hardly ever came in to see the performances; he used to come in in the morning at rehearsals to chat with us all, and Miss Darell in particular. He had known her before she joined us, though she only began here, and we can't make out anything about her, she must have quarrelled with her friends we think. She seems to have been brought up a cut above us; not that there's any confounded nonsense about her, she is good friends with us all, and we all like her."

All this was confirmation strong of what Tom suspected. There could be no doubt about it. Reginald had run away with Kate Darley, and they were living here together as Mr. and Mrs. Waters. Were they man and wife? That was the question. If so, his mission was ended. And, hard though it might be, that he should have loved, and loved in vain, still he could bear it, and wish her happiness with all his heart. It was not likely a girl would hesitate between the heir of Chacewater Grange and his tenant. He only wanted to assure himself of that, and then—well, he would go back to Bottlesby, sell off everything, give up the farm, go away, and try to forget. His views about the circus-riders had changed considerably during the past week, and as he feasted his eyes daily on Kate's pretty face and graceful figure, he came to the conclusion that his love was hopeless, and became as despondent as men in their youth are wont to be when their love is rejected. But how was he to ascertain this? He had thought it all so easy when he started from home, and now he did not know exactly what to do.

His intention had been to confront the young
Squire and drag the truth out of him, and whether
Reginald willed it or no, he had felt pretty sure he
should be able to convince himself on the point he
wanted to know. But now, just as he had discovered him, Reginald had again vanished; and to
get the truth from a man you must, at all events,
be able to get at him. The one way left him was
to question Kate Darley; and Bramber was much
too earnest in his love not to think of that with
some apprehension. Kate was a high-spirited young
woman, and, as he knew, of a fearlessly independent
character. It was quite likely that she would
fiercely resent any meddling in her affairs on his
part. If he wanted to know whether his love was
hopeless, he most certainly did not wish to destroy
such small chance as might remain to him by
involving himself in a bitter quarrel with Kate. In
fact, never was man more perplexed than Tom
Bramber, as to what his next move should be. That
his own chance was an utterly forlorn one, he could
not but admit. What object could Reginald Chacewater have for pretending to be dead, and taking
an assumed name, but that he had run away with
Kate? And then as he mused on that vow of
vengeance that he had breathed, should Kate's
finger wear no wedding-ring, it for the first time
dawned upon him that where a woman loves, she
has scant thanks for those who seek to avenge her
wrongs for her. And so, sore perplexed, Tom
Bramber gazed daily with increasing admiration at

Miss Darell's spirited performance, but still hesitated
to seek an interview with her.

The pertinacious watch that Tom was keeping
upon Miss Darell quickly attracted the attention of
the employés of the Hippodrome. They saw that
he hovered about the stage door even to see her
come out, and, at a respectful distance, sometimes
followed her home. All this was told to Kate, and
was the subject of some jesting on the part of her
companions. It irritated the girl; it was exasperating to have her footsteps dogged in this
manner. She never saw him herself, except when
she was in the Ring, and then she would at times
catch sight of him in the front seats. She grew
more angry with him every day. What business
had Mr. Bramber to come down to Chillingham and
pry into her life? She was nothing to him; he had
never even told her that he loved her, but she knew
it very well for all that. If it hadn't been for his
coming here, where he was not wanted, Reginald
might have been still in Chillingham, and there
was no blinking the fact that she missed him dreadfully. It had been very pleasant, that last week or
two of lotus-eating. There was nobody now to stroll
about the Promenade with, to take her to the band,
or even for an occasional drive on Sundays, that is
to say no one she cared about, for there were
plenty of young men in the Company of the Royal
Hippodrome quite willing, at the slightest encouragement, to become Miss Darell's cavalier on
such ocasions. But though upon good terms with

her companions, and well liked, she was intimate
with none of them, with the exception of Minnie
Price, the girl she had supplanted, who was still
not sufficiently recovered from her tedious illness to
take her place again in the bill ; so while Tom
Bramber still hesitated, and was casting about how
best he might question her, and so ascertain from
her own lips the truth of that matter which had
brought him to Chillingham, Kate's wrath waxed
hotter and hotter. His conduct, she said spitefully,
was aggravating in the extreme—how dare he play
the spy upon her like that ? Let her only meet
him face to face, and she would tell him frankly
what she thought of his behaviour; and then
Kate thought ruefully of that other, for whom
the appearance of Tom had been the signal to
vanish.

At length Tom determined to write and ask
Kate at what time it would suit her to see him. It
was a good, manly letter. He told her that if she
wished to know by what right he had traced and
followed her to Chillingham, for he made no disguise of his having done so, it was by the right of
an honest man to ask the woman he loved, and
would fain marry, if that were possible, and hear
her answer from her own lips. He thought that her
reply might give him some clue to her feelings, if
not a hint of how matters stood between her and
Reginald. His heart beat quick, as love's messenger, in the prosaic form of the Boots of the
hotel, placed a note from Kate in his hand. His

anticipations were disappointed. Miss Darell's rejoinder was laconic in the extreme :

"I will see you to-morrow at twelve.

"Sincerely yours,

"KATE."

Tom smiled grimly as he read it. "There's no
chance for me," he muttered. "I was a fool ever
to think there was. As Praze would say, there's
temper in every one of those half-a-dozen words.
There will be a regular storm to-morrow, I suppose,
and much good I shall have done by trying to put
things straight. I wasn't very hopeful of my own
chance, but I did think I might either be a help to
Kate in her need, or able to offer her my honest
congratulations with a sore heart though it might
be. Now I suppose it will all end in a quarrel,
everything has gone wrong and going wrong—d—
it all, Praze is right. Temper's at the bottom of
all the mischief in this world. There's the 'King'
lost his temper and got beat, Jim Darley lost his
and got thrashed, Kate and I are going to lose
ours to-morrow and quarrel. If I had only come
across the young squire here there would have been
a deuce of a row between us and then the thing
would have been complete. What a fool I was to
come here, what a downright idiot a chap makes
of himself when he gets to feel real bad about a
girl."

Very pretty looked Kate the next morning, as
Bramber was shown into her little drawing-room.

She rose to receive him as he entered and, after a haughty inclination of her head, stood erect, a slight flush upon her cheeks, and the light of battle in her flashing grey eyes. The summer sun glistened on her close-coiled silken tresses, reflecting in the golden light the varied shadows of the raven's wing.

" You wished to see me, Mr. Bramber," she said, " and I most certainly wished to see you. I wished to know what is the meaning of this unmanly pursuit, under what pretext you seek to pry into my affairs, by what authority you mix yourself up in my comings or goings ? "

" By the authority of love, the great love I bear you must be my warrant for having followed you here."

" And do you suppose, sir, that because you happen to admire a girl, it gives you a right to track her as if she were a hunted criminal ? Has it never occurred to you," she continued almost contemptuously, " that a girl may reckon other admirers beside yourself ? "

" Kate, Kate, only hear me ! " he exclaimed.

" And that if they all," she continued mockingly, " watched over me with the untiring vigilance of yourself, life would become unbearable, intolerable ? "

He writhed beneath her merciless tongue, for he was well aware that he had no plea to justify the strict supervision he had exercised over her during the past week.

" One question only, Kate," he replied in a low

voice. "Answer me that and I will trouble you no more."

"With a view to that latter relief, say at once what is it you wish to know."

"Are you Reginald Chacewater's wife?" he rejoined doggedly.

"And pray how does that concern you, I should like to know?" And then as the whole significance of the question crossed her mind, the blood rushed to her temples, and she half bowed her head. Then quickly raising it again: "No, I am not, and after the insult implied by your question, I trust we shall meet no more," and, with the slightest obeisance to him, Kate rang the bell in token of his dismissal.

That scandal was busy with her name had never as yet crossed Kate's mind. That when she had disappeared it should be at once concluded that she had a companion in her flight, and that in her own neighbourhood she should be held to have shared the usual fate of girls who love not wisely but too well, had never entered her head, but that Tom Bramber should not only suspect Reginald of being that companion, but further conjecture that she was not his wife but his victim, filled her with confusion. She had maintained a proud front in Tom's presence, but she was bowed to the dust with shame to think that she could be believed to hold such a position; she ground her teeth, and the passionate tears welled up into her eyes as she thought of it. And if this had occurred to Tom

Bramber, why not to everyone else at Bottlesby? Bramber was doubtless only repeating what all Bottlesby was saying. Reginald was like the ostrich, he thought he had hidden himself, and that all the world believed he was dead. The world was only laughing at him, and, worse still, jeering at her. Dead! No, young Chacewater had run off with the daughter of one of his father's tenants, and had pretended to be drowned. Funny idea, but Reggie was always a little eccentric. And then she thought of how tongues were wagging round her old home. How should she ever dare to look her stern old father in the face again? Tom Bramber, yes, he was loyal still, though she had flouted him, had asked, despairingly though it might be, whether she was Reginald Chacewater's wife. Was it likely that question would occur to anyone about Bottlesby? They would scoff at the idea of her being anything but his mistress. What did they think of her at the Grange? It was not true. She was innocent, but how was she to prove it? Kate not only realised, but even exaggerated the difficulty of her position. She and Reginald had disappeared simultaneously, and were both discovered at last living at Chillingham. Who would believe her assertion that all this was pure accident, that they were acquaintances, and that till the very last Reginald had only known her as Miss Darell of the Royal Hippodrome. The sole person who could corroborate her story was Reginald himself, and at the present moment she had no idea of where he was. Still, surely she should hear from him before long; now he was known to be alive, to attempt further concealment would be useless. It was not likely that Bramber would make any secret of his being still alive, and that clearly ascertained, she thought his discovery would speedily follow. It was all very well for her to disappear, it was not likely that anyone would take much trouble to find her, and yet Tom Bramber had done so. With Reginald Chacewater it was different. The son of a rich country gentleman, vigorous search was sure to be made for him. In the eyes of Kate Darley, the lords of Chacewater Grange were of much greater importance than the world generally gave them credit for, and so the girl comforted herself that Reginald would speedily be compelled to emerge from his obscurity, and would then in all honesty bear witness that accidental and innocent had been their brief acquaintance.

CHAPTER XIX.

"MY SON IS YET ALIVE."

TOM BRAMBER returned to Bottlesby with a heavy heart. He had learnt all that he wanted to know, and at present there was no more to be done. That first dream of vengeance that had filled his mind, that determination to right Kate's wrongs at any cost, had as we have seen evaporated. He had found that it was easier to imagine than to put in practice, and that it was very questionable whether Kate would be even grateful to him should he attempt it. He had made up his mind to leave his old farm. Whether he should take another in some other part of the country or whether he should emigrate to Canada or Australia, he did not know, but he would leave Bottlesby. As for what course he should take with regard to Reginald, well, he had plenty of time to think that over while arranging his affairs. One thing was certain, that Reginald had left Chillingham, and that, even if he would, at present he did not know where to find him. That Mrs. Chacewater would send for him to know how he had prospered on her errand, on hearing of his return, he felt quite certain. He resolved to spare her all needless trouble on that point, and betook himself to the Grange the next morning.

" Well, Mr. Bramber," said the lady, their greetings once exchanged, " have you found Kate Darley ? "

" Yes," he replied, " and what the village says about her is true in the main. She is a rider in a circus, but there are circuses and circuses, as I dare-say you know, ma'am, and this is no such miserable show as I have been accustomed to see at the fairs round about."

" I understand," said Mrs. Chacewater. " Yes, 1 have seen circuses in London and other big towns and know, of course, they are very different from those you see at country fairs. Is she well, and did she ask after us ? It is certainly not the life I should have either suggested or approved of for her.

had I been consulted. I can only hope she may do well in it. Thank you for making enquiries for me. I hope you *prospered* on your *own* errand ? " And the lady somewhat emphasised her last words.

"The less said about it, ma'am, the better," returned Tom, "I wanted to know something, and I know it now. But there are some things there is not much comfort in knowing," and Tom stopped abruptly.

Mrs. Chacewater waited for him to say more, but Tom remained mute. He had got to tell her that her son lived, and he was turning over in his own mind how best to do so, for he had not an idea that she suspected the fact, and had a hazy recollection of grievous results produced by the announcement of such tidings too bluntly.

" Excuse me, Mr. Bramber," said the lady at last, " did you ask Kate Darley to marry you ? "

" No, ma'am," replied Tom almost roughly, "nor am I at all likely to do so," and once more he relapsed into silence.

" I have no wish to intrude further into your confidence, but is that *all* that you have got to tell me ? " And she looked almost hungrily into his face.

" No," said Tom. " I have something very important to tell you. I have a great bit of news for you, if you think you can bear it, if you can promise not to go fainting or anything of that sort."

She nodded assent.

" Mr. Reginald is alive. He escaped all right that day last January in the Regent's Park."

Mrs. Chacewater turned very pale. She had hoped this thing, but the confirmation of that dim and distant hope made her heart stand still. Her first-born was restored to her. What mattered all else?

"Is he well?" she asked, in an almost awe-struck whisper.

" I've not seen him," replied Bramber, " but there is no possible doubt of his being alive and perfectly well. He was in Chillingham till a few days ago, and I spoke with those who knew him, and had seen him frequently. Where he may be now, I can't say, but he is most certainly alive."

" Thank you very much, Mr. Bramber. I will ask you to leave me now, for I want to think. One question more. Has Kate seen him?"

" Yes," rejoined Tom. " I will say ' good-bye' now, Mrs. Chacewater; you had best get over the news a bit before we have any more talk. Shall I send anyone to you?"

" Thanks, no, I only want to be alone," and, much relieved by the way Mrs. Chacewater had borne his intelligence, Tom took his departure.

She sat quite still for some little time after Bramber had left her, and at first could only murmur prayers of thankfulness that her son was yet alive, but soon the more worldly part of her mind re-asserted itself, and her thoughts reverted to this complication with Kate Darley. In the first tumult of her joy she would have recked little what sort of a bride Reginald brought her, and would have

12

welcomed Kate, of whom she was really very fond, warmly, as her daughter-in-law, but as she became calmer, she remembered that previous matrimonial scheme, upon which she had been wont to speculate. Kate might be all very nice, but one of the tenants' daughters was no fit mate for the heir of Chacewater Grange. The Chacewater estates required propping up, it was necessary that Reginald should marry money—money and position if possible—but essentially money. Miss Wargrave was perhaps not all that could be desired, but her father made no secret of it that she would bring fifty thousand pounds to her husband, and then Mrs. Chacewater reflected that even if Reginald and Kate were not wedded, the complication still existed, and that an entanglement of that nature was perhaps more to be dreaded than an imprudent marriage; and then having collected her ideas, she hurried off to tell her husband that their son lived.

The Squire's sensations in the first instance were those of unmixed delight, but he speedily experienced a revulsion of feeling. Why Reginald had disappeared was a thing his wife and Tom Bramber had held a theory of their own about, and had kept it rigidly to themselves. Though sceptical for a long time, the Squire had come eventually to thoroughly believe in his son's death, but, upon hearing he was still alive, the reason of his disappearance became to him clear as daylight. It was a beautiful idea, no doubt, of Reginald's, and doubtless often occurred to impecunious youth. To vanish from the wrath of their creditors for a space, and then to reappear from out of the darkness, famous and wealthy; the dream of a young man, and seldom realised. The theory at all events had not occurred to Reginald Chacewater's creditors, they accepted the tidings of his death without hesitation. The Squire settled their bills without demur. Poor Reginald was gone, and there must be no blot on his memory, but those fully accounted for the missing man's acquiescence in the rumour of his own death. The story of the Prodigal Son does not bear too literal an interpretation, and when the news of his probable return is heralded by the consciousness that not only much money has been paid for him, but that much awkward explanation has yet to be given of his unaccountable absence, it is not to be wondered at that a strong feeling of anger took possession of Mr. Chacewater towards the culprit. Reginald might not reappear at the Grange for some time, but the news that he was alive, there could be little doubt, would not be long before it was all over Bottlesby, and the county generally. Countless would be the enquiries as to what induced him to cause such pain to his parents and all friends by this extraordinary conduct. Mr. Ch - water experienced the irritating sensation of having been made a fool of, and he certainly had a warrant for thus thinking. Reginald had not only without compunction played with his father's and mother's affections, tricked the former into paying his debts, but actually made him the subject of ridicule in his

12*

own neighbourhood, as the victim of a practical joke.

With the exception of the mistress of the Grange, Tom Bramber had been very reticent with regard to his visit to Chillingham. He made no secret that he had been there, but then all Bottlesby knew that in pursuit of business he occasionally did go there, but though he was asked more than once whether he had seen anything of Kate Darley, he either evaded the question or bluntly answered in the negative. But he saw no reason for concealing the fact of Reginald being alive, and said that though he had not seen him himself, he was quite convinced that it was the case, although why he did not come home, he couldn't imagine. Which afforded much food for conjecture in the neighbourhood. The Squire too made no secret of the discovery of his son to his old friend the Rector. Where he was he didn't exactly know, but he certainly did not perish beneath the ice last January. And so the news speedily came to the ears of Lucy Marton and, on their return to Carlingham Park at the end of the London season, to the Wargraves. It took a great deal to move Clara, but her eye glistened and her heart swelled with elation at the idea, that the prize she had striven so hard to grasp was still within her reach, and instead of the web which she had been so carefully weaving having been ruthlessly swept away by the great Destroyer, there was but a temporary rent in it, and that Reginald Chacewater was still alive to fall a prey to her fasciuations. Sam

Wargrave was perhaps as pleased as his daughter.
His search for that eligible young man, despite his
best endeavours, had so far proved unavailing.
Nobody as yet had commended himself to Clara's
taste and requirements like Reginald Chacewater,
and now that it had been ascertained that he was
alive, his reappearance at the Grange would surely
be only a matter of a few weeks. In furtherance of
this end, Mr. Wargrave was more profuse than ever
in his entertainments. Garden and dinner parties
followed each other in rapid succession that August
in Carlingham Park. Mr. Wargrave drove over to
the Grange himself to hope that, after the happy
intelligence, the Squire and his lady would at once
mix again with their neighbours as before. Should
Mr. Reginald turn up, they should only be too
pleased to see him, of course he was always included
in their invitations. " Don't be afraid, Mr. Chacewater, I'm not inquisitive. I'm not given to poking
my nose into my neighbours' affairs. Young men
will be young men; perhaps he had outrun the
constable; perhaps he had backed that horse of
Bramber's rather too stiffly, though I told you all
down here again and again that 'Chorister' would
win. That's all nothing to me, there's a hundred
reasons a young fellow might have for keeping out
of the way for a bit. However, I do hope you will
excuse a short invitation, and that we shall see you
all at dinner on Thursday week. Good-bye," and
with this Mr. Wargrave stepped into his dog-cart
and drove off.

He had not got very far on his way home before
he encountered Tom Bramber, and, being a man
who under all circumstances had ever an eye to
business, he pulled up, and with that somewhat
boisterous affectation of geniality under which he
habitually veiled his innate cunning and vulgarity,
said, "Morning, Bramber, promises to be a grand
harvest; I hope for once you are satisfied with your
prospects."

"I have seen better and I have seen worse,"
replied Tom surlily. He did not like Mr. Wargrave,
and had good reason to suppose that he, or at all
events his friends, had something to say to the
ignominious display of "King of the Huns" at
Epsom. "But I don't complain."

"Don't complain," replied Sam Wargrave with a
loud laugh, "I should think not, with such a yard
of ricks as you are bound to have."

Now it really was very creditable to Mr. Wargrave that he should have picked up the jargon of
farming with such fluency, for his life had been
passed in cities, and he knew nothing of agricultural pursuits.

"You will find your tenants will tell you a
different tale," rejoined Bramber. "It will be only
a moderate wheat crop, even if we have the luck to
get it in good order."

"Ah, well, you are taking a gloomy view of
things," replied the master of Carlingham Park,
"but what's the odds to you? You have a harvest
to gather, on Doncaster Moor next month, that will

make up for half-a-dozen bad years. We know the
Derby running was all wrong, and 'King of the
Huns' will show us it was, in the Leger. I hope
the horse is going on well?"

" I believe so," rejoined Tom, "but I haven't
heard from Newmarket for the last week or two,"
and slightly raising his hat he rode on.

Tom indeed had troubled his head very little
about the "King's" welfare of late. His whole
mind had been engrossed with Kate Darley. Now
that was all over, and he was concentrating all his
energies in making arrangements for the getting out
of his farm as soon as possible. He had received a
few lines from Praze now and again, assuring him
that the horse was going on well, and always
reminding him of his promise not to interfere in
any way with the betting market. " You shall
stand whatever you like in my book," wrote the
trainer. " When we meet at Doncaster I will show
you exactly what I have done. Till then you must
trust me implicitly." In his present mood this just
suited Tom Bramber. He cared nothing about the
horse, he didn't care very much even whether he
won the Leger or lost it. There was the never-
failing instinct that it was better to win money
than to lose it, but just then Tom was too taken up
with his love troubles to care about anything else.
If he had any other feeling concerning success at
Doncaster, it was that those whose machinations
had caused the defeat of his horse at Epsom might
burn their fingers over the race on the Town Moor.

That Praze was earnestly desirous of the same end he knew, and felt that if anybody could bring that satisfactory result about, it would be the astute trainer. One thing which struck him, when later in the day he thought over his interview with Sam Wargrave, was that while that gentleman had spoken so positively in May of "Chorister's" approaching victory at Epsom, he seemed completely to ignore the probability of his beating the "King" at Doncaster. It struck him as so singular that he thought it worth while to write a line to Mr. Praze, and tell him of Sam Wargrave's change of opinion.

CHAPTER XX.

"THE WARGRAVES' GARDEN PARTY."

Harvest is in full tide and Carlingham Park is all *en fête.* It is a fine old house, and the gardens with their well-kept terraces, and beds glowing with brilliant colouring, lend themselves admirably to such a gathering as this. Sam Wargrave has collected all the country side to celebrate, as he says, the success of "Chorister." In the pretty though not extensive park are erected marquees for not only all the Wargrave tenants, but half Bottlesby to boot. Wickets have been pitched, and the retainers of Carlingham are doing battle with the men of Bottlesby, whose wives and sweethearts are there to enconrage their exertions. In the gardens are collected all the families of the neighbourhood ; daintily dressed damsels, and men clad in gorgeous flannels, flit about the croquet ground. Ices, cups of tea, and refreshments of all descriptions are proffered in a profusion that makes the servitors of the Park envy the cool dress of their brethren in the cricket field. If Sam Wargrave is keen about the making of money, no one can gainsay but what he spends it with a lavish hand. To make himself popular and to extend his connection with the county is an object with him, and to entrap the leading magnates of the county within his gates, he is willing that his gold shall flow like water.

He had won a good bit of money over the Derby, and when his daughter suggested the giving of a garden party on a grand scale assented at once.

" We can't get hold of the people we want in Town," said Miss Wargrave, " but people are easier to catch I think in the country, more especially if you give an entertainment of this nature. People who might demur about dining with us, won't hesitate a moment about attending a garden party on a large scale, and only ask the tenantry and the Bottlesby villagers to play cricket and take a day's outing in the Park, and if it's only a fine day you will snare everybody within driving distance."

Sam Wargrave listened to the wisdom of his daughter, eager and pertinacious as ever in her efforts to ascend the social ladder, and the result fully justified her expectations. All the neighbourhood was there, and all the neighbourhood freely admitted that the new master of Carlingham

certainly understood how the thing should be done.
The Chacewaters were there, though, no little to
Miss Wargrave's disappointment, the truant Reginald was not with them, and Miss Chacewater
confided to her bosom friend Lucy Marton that
they had no tidings of him and no idea of where he
was.   Lucy thought sadly of the last time she had
been at Carlingham ; it was at that dinner-party in
the spring, just before the Wargraves moved up to
London, when the supposed death of Reginald was
in everybody's minds, and the Grange was a house
of mourning.   She remembered how angry she had
felt then at what she regarded as Clara's heartless
indifference.   And now, something like Mr. Chacewater, she thought what a deal of real sorrow had
been wasted on that graceless offender.   In her
heart, too, she was conscious of having been
betrayed into the discovery of a feeling for the
culprit which she had not suspected.   She could
keep her own secret, but the old, frank confidence
that had existed between her and Reginald was
gone for ever, and on his return they must either
be a good deal more to each other or a good deal
less.   He had surprised her love by a sorry trick,
and she felt a little sore with him in consequence.
But for the belief that he was lost to her for ever,
she had not awakened to what her real feelings were
towards him.   That freak of Reginald's had brought
trouble on a good many people ; but for that Kate
Darley would probably hardly have known him, and
listened with a very different ear to Tom Bramber's

wooing. His mother, too, would have been spared
much anxious pondering as to his relations with
Kate. In short, so far, the results of Reginald's
brilliant idea had been the exact opposite of that
which he had intended—the temporary postpone-
ment of a settlement with his creditors, until such
time as he should be able to discharge his liabilities
without calling upon his father to assist him, had
eventuated in their being at once paid in full by the
Squire. It was altogether an unpleasant afternoon
for the Chacewaters. That all their friends should
be full of anxious enquiries about Reginald, as to
where he had been, how the mistake had arisen,
and when they expected him home again, was only
what might be looked for, but they were none the
less irritating for that. The Squire indeed, speedily
became extremely testy over such questioning, and
retorted sharply: "How should he know? It
was easier to predict whence the wind would
blow than what would be the movements of a young
man of Reginald's age. That from his own careless-
ness and stupidity, he had left them for months
under a terrible misapprehension, and that he would
probably favour them with his company again when
he got tired of his present life." Of what his
present life consisted, and where his present life was
led, Mr. Chacewater said nothing, for the best of all
possible reasons, that he did not know, and this
alone, now that he had recovered from his first
delight on finding that Reginald was alive, was day
by day making the Squire more angry.

Sam Wargrave moved about amongst his guests, pompous and somewhat patronising as usual. The former he could not divest himself of, but he had guests there to-day who he knew would submit to none of the latter, and though it was not natural to him, Mr. Wargrave managed to show sufficient deference to people of higher standing than himself, nor, to do him justice, did he fall into the opposite extreme so common to men like himself— Sam Wargrave never cringed. He was full of good-humour that day. Clara's idea had been a great success, and he knew that it had been so; his invitations had been accepted by two or three families whose acquaintance he much desired to make, but who had not so far troubled to call upon him. In the course of the afternoon he came across the Rector, and as he shook hands exclaimed:

"Delighted to see you, Marton. It's some time since we met."

" Yes, I haven't seen you since the day I dined with you last spring a few days before you went to London. We Wiltshire men rather scoffed at you for a prophet then, but we hailed you a true prophet later."

" Hey, what? What do you mean?" said Sam Wargrave.

" What, don't you remember your prediction?" said the Rector smiling. " Why, you told us all that 'Chorister' would win the Derby. What you did not tell us was what a jolly afternoon we were to have afterwards in celebrating his success."

"Ah, I recollect now," said Wargrave. "I
remember, somebody gave me a hint that there
was a screw loose with the favourite. However, I
fancy Bramber was a very unlucky man to lose the
race."

"I read something in the papers about a scrimmage at the Corner," rejoined Mr. Marton, "but
the 'King' made no show at all. It is rather apt
to be the case I think when a man only owns one or
two horses, he is given to over-estimate them. His
parents usually think an only child a prodigy."

"I don't know how that may be," replied Wargrave, "but I mean what I say. I look upon 'King
of the Huns' as the best of his year, and think he
will show you so next month."

"This is a complete retraction of all former
beliefs," said the Rector laughing. "We've made
a convert of you in Wiltshire. Unfortunately I
haven't the faith in our champion that I once had.
I am afraid there will be no celebration of his
victory——"

"More unlikely things have happened," rejoined
Mr. Wargrave chuckling. "I tell you what,
Marton, I'll do this all over again, blest if I don't,
if 'King of the Huns' wins the Leger, and I tell you
he will."

"I am sure I hope so," replied Mr. Marton.
"Beyond local patriotism, all Bottlesby now will
have an interest in his success," and then the Rector
moved on to speak to some other friends who caught
his eye

If reputations are easily lost, they are at times easily won, and in no case perhaps does success bear fruit so largely and so speedily as in the profession of prophecy.   There is an almanack still I believe enjoying a large circulation, which, in the days when the century was young, predicted a week of terrible storm and tempest, and the storm and tempest were so to speak, there to order.   The proprietor of that almanack was a made man, not only he, but his family for generations to come.   He was supposed to be an infallible judge of weather, and though his subsequent vaticinations proved quite as inaccurate as other people's, people, especially in the country, where they are more credulous than in towns, shook their heads, quoted him with reverence, and wound up with "Bless you, he knows"; moreover they are still shaking them. Now of all lines of prophecy, none perhaps is so popular as that of horse-racing.   I sometimes wonder, taking into consideration the grand army of amateurs, whether the professors of this art do not almost outnumber those they prophesy to. Now Sam Wargrave's prediction about "Chorister" had made a great impression on the minds of those who heard it, more especially after the event.   We all look ruefully back at that advice which if followed at the time would have led on to fortune, and only wish we had done what Jones told us to do with regard to Montezumas, utterly ignoring that had we embarked in all the speculations Jones has been for years whispering into our ears, we

should have been left poor indeed. That Mr. Wargrave had said all along that "Chorister" would
win the Derby was by this well known all round
Bottlesby, and much eagerness was evoked to know
what his oracular lips might have to say on the
subject of the Leger. He had been so short a time
back at the Park that there had not been much
opportunity to question him on that point, and now
there was no necessity for it for, delighted with the
success of his entertainment, Mr. Wargrave was
going about amongst his guests, positively beaming
in the gratification of his heart, trusting they were
all enjoying themselves as much as he was, and
assuring them he should have a gathering of the
same kind next month, if "King of the Huns"
won the Leger. Such a pleasant piece of news as
this, as might be expected, spread like wildfire, and
before the sun went down, all Bottlesby knew what
Mr. Wargrave deemed likely to happen at Doncaster.

"It is very strange, Papa," said Lucy, as she and
the Rector drove home in the delicious summer
evening in all the brilliant light of the Hunters'
moon, "that they should know nothing of Reginald
at the Grange. Jessie told me that though they
know he is alive, they don't know where he is, nor
what he has been doing since last January."

"Jessie told you that?" rejoined the Rector medi-
tatively. "I can only say that you know more
about it than I do. Herbert Chacewater is very
reticent upon the subject, and has evidently no

wish to discuss it. He had to receive this afternoon lots of congratulations upon his son being unexpectedly restored to him, but he got unmistakably very irritable on being questioned about the matter, and therefore I refrained from seeking to learn anything about him, but I'll own to being curious in the extreme about the whole thing. That he has purposely mystified everybody about his death is evident, and that he must have had strong reasons for doing so is equally clear. He has got, I am afraid, into a big scrape of some kind, and instead of going straight to his father, as he should have done, has foolishly distressed us all very much by thinking to obliterate himself."

" Do you think he has been in a very bad scrape, Papa?" said Lucy in a low voice.

" Nothing probably but what, if he would confide in those nearest and dearest to him, might be put right. I am very fond of Reggie, he is a straightforward young fellow, and if he only had application would play his part in this world."

"But you haven't answered my question, Papa."

" Well, Lucy, I am afraid it is. Reggie and his father have always been on excellent terms, and that he shouldn't come to him for help in his difficulties looks bad. You see, although Jessie may not know, it does not follow that the Squire is in any such ignorance. On the contrary, I suspect he knows all about it, and is very wroth in consequence."

" Could you not try and mediate between them ? " asked Miss Marton

"I would in one moment," rejoined the Rector, "if I only knew what was the matter. But you see I am in the confidence of neither father nor son."

Lucy said nothing for some time. Both she and her father were thinking of Reginald, and the Rector was turning over in his own mind whether it was possible for him to be of any use in the matter. On arriving at home they paused for a few moments in the hall to light their bedroom candles, and as they were doing so Lucy said :

" Papa, I think to-morrow morning you ought to manage to see Mr. Bramber."

" Why ? " exclaimed Mr. Marton, in visible bewilderment.

" Well," said Lucy, " you see, some weeks before the race, Mr. Wargrave knew 'King of the Huns' would not win at Epsom, and said so. Now he tells us ' King of the Huns ' will win at Doncaster. I don't know what it means, but the horse is Bramber's, and I think he ought to be told what Mr. Wargrave says."

" Yes, there's something in that," rejoined the Rector. " Tom might as well know ; it can't do any harm at all events, though I should think he is a better judge of the ' King's ' chance than Mr. Wargrave can be."

" I have an idea too, Papa," said Lucy, " that Mr. Bramber can tell you more about Reginald than anybody else round Bottlesby," and, taking up her candle, she nodded good-night to her father and tripped upstairs.

13

CHAPTER XXI.

"THE RECTOR'S DISCOVERY."

As soon as he had finished his breakfast the next morning and skimmed the newspaper, Mr. Marton started off to have a talk with Tom Bramber, and, after some little enquiry, found him where he least expected on a fine morning in harvest time, namely at home. Mr. Marton expressed his surprise that Tom was not afield, superintending his men.

"Well, the fact is, sir, you see," replied Tom, "I've a deal to do just now, and I am obliged to leave the overlooking to some of the men. I can trust mine pretty well. I've been a decentish master and they know I stand no nonsense."

"Well," said the Rector, with a glance at the pens, ink and ledgers littered about the table, " you know best, but I should have thought all those accounts could have waited till the corn was in. Besides, man, it's a sin to lose such a day as this if you can possibly help it."

"You see, sir," replied Tom, " the fact is I am going away, and I was just making a bit of a valuation as to what the plant, stock, etc., might be likely to fetch."

"You don't mean to say that you are going to leave us. you who've been brought up in the parish,

who know every man and woman in it as well as
I do myself, you can't mean that?"

"Yes, I do," replied the other. "Things have
gone all wrong with me of late, I must go away
from Bottlesby and begin again in a new place."

"I've known you since you were an urchin," replied
the Rector, "not much higher than my stick, and
should be very, very, sorry to part with you, and so
would the Squire, and, for the matter of that, all
Bottlesby. In short it can't be done, Tom. You
are one of the institutions of the place. Now then,
out with it. What's the matter?"

"A good deal's the matter," replied Bramber,
"that is to me, but you can't help me, nor, as far
as that goes, can anyone else. There are some
troubles you know we have got to bear alone."

"That's true. I'm not going to bother you, but
you'll tell me one thing. If it's anything to do
with money, you're bound to give the Squire and
myself the chance of helping you if we can."

"Thank you, sir; thank you," replied Bramber.
"All Bottlesby knows that the Squire and the
Parson will stand by them in difficulties, but it's
not that. There's troubles a deal bigger than money
ones you know."

"Yes, and as you say, that we must face by ourselves. You must forgive me, but I thought perhaps,
Tom, that you had been a little bit too fond of
'King of the Huns,' and tempted to venture more
money on him than you could afford. It's the
curse of racing, it tempts men to do that. Is he

13*

going to atone for the disappointment he caused
you at Epsom? Mr. Wargrave told us all so the
other day, and says the Epsom race was all a mistake."

"Mr. Wargrave is quite right, it was. He
mayn't be much good to hounds, and he owns up
to not being much of a shot, but he does understand racing. The 'King' is well, that's all I
know, leastways he was, the last I heard of him, but
Praze don't talk much about it this time; he was
for him so sanguine last that he's not likely to be
over confident this."

"We must hope for better luck on the Town
Moor," rejoined Mr. Marton. "There's one thing,
a man doesn't get out of a big farm like yours all
at once, Bramber, and I hope something will happen
yet to make you change your mind. Now I want to
talk to you about another thing. It was you who
found out Mr. Reginald was alive, but you didn't
see him, did you?"

Tom eyed his questioner suspiciously, and then
said, "No, but I know for certain that it is so."

"You heard that at Chillingham, didn't you?"
continued Mr. Marton. "That's where the circus
which Kate Darley has joined is performing, is it
not?"

"Yes; you mean kind, I daresay, sir. She's
there, but she's nothing to me, and I don't want
to be cross-questioned about her proceedings
simply to provide gossip for the old women of the
village."

Tom was getting visibly angry, but if ever there was a man who could awe the turbulent members of his flock by the ready assumption of his high calling, it was the Rector.

"Do you suppose, Bramber," he said sternly, "that I am asking these questions with a view to mere idle gossip? Do you think I should be fit to hold the post that has been entrusted to my care if I confined myself to talking to you twice a week from the pulpit? It is my duty to seek out those that are heavy laden, and to help them in their troubles. Was it Kate Darley who told you that Mr. Reginald was alive?"

"Yes, but I knew it all along."

"Then why didn't you speak," exclaimed the Rector, "and save all the misery his friends have undergone?"

"Because I wasn't quite certain," replied Tom.

"You knew, and you weren't quite certain? What do you mean by all this quibbling and equivocation? Tell me the truth at once. Shame on you, Bramber, that I should even have to ask you for the truth."

"I am no liar, Mr. Marton," replied Tom, now thoroughly at bay. "I only guessed what you might have all guessed, that when Mr. Reginald and Kate Darley disappeared, they had gone off together. We all knew for certain that Kate was not drowned. I didn't see why Mr. Reginald should be either. When I found Kate Darley was at Chillingham, I found, as I expected, that Mr. Reginald was there too, or rather he had been, for weeks."

"Stop, stop," cried the Rector, "I never dreamt of this."

There was silence for a minute or two between the two men, and then in a low voice Mr. Marton asked, " Is he married to her ? "

" No, curse him ! " said Tom, springing to his feet, " and that's what's the matter," and without waiting for another word from his companion, he fled from the room.

Seldom had the Rev. James Marton felt more troubled about the affairs of one of his parishioners than he did about Reginald Chacewater's, as he walked homewards. That he should have made such a *mésalliance* would, the Rector knew, be a bitter disappointment to his father and mother. That the pretty, graceful, lady-like little thing had been educated much above her station, and though a marriage not likely to meet the approval of his friends and relatives, yet it was capable of being glossed over with that negative phrase that it might have been worse. But if, as Bramber positively asserted, no marriage had taken place between them, then, from the point of view of a clergyman and a man of the world, Reginald had committed both a sin, and a well-nigh irretrievable blunder. That there was the slightest connection between Kate Darley's flight and Reginald's disappearance, had never crossed his mind. He could not even recollect ever having seen them together, the busiest tongues in

the parish had never hinted at such a possibility
in his hearing. And then he wondered whether
Herbert Chacewater was aware of his son's escapade.
He must be ; that would account for Reginald's non-
appearance at the Grange, for his seizing upon the
report of his death as a lucky accident in his favour
with the desire of being temporarily lost to view.
The whole thing seemed clear enough to the Rector
now. One thing only perplexed him sorely, and
that was what use to make of his discovery.
Whether he had not better keep his mouth closed
simply, or whether it was possible for him to interfere with advantage to anyone.

A jockey's life, especially in the early part of his
career, is by no means a bed of roses, and Jim
Darley always looked back upon the Spring when
" King of the Huns " was disgraced at Epsom as
about the darkest period of his younger days. Jim
believed in his sister as thoroughly as he did in his
horse ; a disquieting rumour had reached him from
Bottlesby, but of that he had taken little heed ; he
knew better. Kate was getting her living in a circus,
well, why shouldn't she ? That was all right
enough, there was no more harm in that than in
what he was doing himself. But one thing had
struck the boy very forcibly. On his visits to Newmarket, which in the early part of the year had been
pretty frequent, Tom Bramber had always noticed
him, spoken to him, and had something to say
about Kate. He had only been there once since the

"King's" defeat, and then, hard as Jim had tried to catch his eye, Tom had studiously ignored him, and far from speaking to him about Kate, had vouchsafed him nothing but a slight nod in reply to his salutation. Then, unbounded as was his faith in his horse, what were they going to do with him? They had prevented his winning at Epsom, were the same rascally tactics to be used against him at Doncaster? Who was to ride him? Was that obstinate idiot Wrench to have the mount again? If Wrench had only done as he was told, well then the "King" would have won easily enough, but he thinks he knows more than anyone else and pays no heed at all to what's said to him. Who would ride the "King" for the Leger per- plexed more people than Jim. It was a vexed question in the stable. That Wrench should do so was commonly supposed, he did a great part of the riding for Mr. Praze's stable, but still it was noticed amongst the boys that the crack jockey had never been down to give the colt a gallop at exercise since Epsom, though before that time he had often done so. As for Mr. Praze, he was as inscrutable as the Sphinx, and never to his most intimate friends dropped the slightest hint. Fidgetty about his sister and anxious about his horse, Jim Darley was going through a trying time, but receiving, though he did not know it, a grand lesson in his art, and one which moreover may be applied to life gener- ally. He was learning to "sit and suffer," which being interpreted means, in turf parlance, to have

patience in difficulties. Still Jim's anxiety grew
absolutely feverish, as Doncaster drew near. His
belief in Mr. Praze was unbounded, and the work
done by his charges was, of course, all directed by
the trainer. The " King " looked well, and it would
be a keenly critical eye that could have found much
fault with his appearance, but, for all that, Jim felt
quite certain that he was not doing such strong work
as he had in the early part of the year. That
no man could teach Mr. Praze his business was an
axiom at Newmarket. If Praze didn't understand
how to wind a horse up for a race then there was
no one there who did. Jim had not ventured to
suggest this idea of his to anyone, nor had he
even heard it mooted, and yet there were plenty of
lynx-eyed judges on the Heath not likely to fail in
detecting such a weak spot in a Leger candidate,
if it were there. The one thing reassuring to Jim
was that that turf barometer of a horse's forthcoming
prospects, the betting market, kept steadily rising.
There was no strong order out evidently to back
" King of the Huns," but, for all that, it was apparent that he was greatly and persistently backed,
whether by the public or his stable it was difficult
to say. No large bets were made about him, nor
could any one individual be precisely identified as
his supporter, but whenever there was betting on
the Leger going on, there always seemed to be
somebody who wanted the odds against " King of
the Huns," to a small sum, and whereas after his
defeat at Epsom.fifteen to one was easily obtainable,

speculators were glad to take about half the price now.

Jim Darley had served two years of his apprenticeship, and it was a sore disappointment to him that as yet no opportunity had been given him of " donning silk."   There were boys at Newmarket younger than himself who not only could boast of having had more than one chance in that way, but some few who were already held to have distinguished themselves, and bade fair ere long to be in considerable request.   Jim had at one time looked forward to Tom Bramber as likely to beg Praze to give him a chance.   He thought he might ask this favour at his hands, but it was close upon three months since Bramber had been seen at Newmarket, and Jim felt that that occasion had not been one to prefer his petition to either him or the trainer.

CHAPTER XXII.

"GAME THE SECOND."

AUGUST is gone, and amongst its stirring events, stirring, that is, to the racing world, brought with it the York meeting.   There was good sport witnessed over the Knavesmire, but the only matter notable as it concerns this history was the strong demonstration made in favour of " King of the Huns," who for the first time was supported in real earnest fashion to win many thousands.   Whom this outlay was for it was not easy to determine.   The money was booked to two or three well-known

members of Tattersall's, but nobody supposed that
they were more than bookers in the business.
They had never been identified in that way at all
with Praze's stable, but there was one professional
gentleman, whose engagements had necessitated his
presence in the great Cathedral city, who watched
the proceedings of the betting ring with considerable interest, and that was John Wrench.   That
something of this kind might happen, he had been
expecting for some time.   He knew, none better,
what had happened to the " King " at Epsom, and
though neither Praze nor Bramber had said much
at the time, he knew they were displeased with him
for not obeying orders, and lying well on the outside coming round Tattenham Corner.   If " King
of the Huns " started for the Leger, he supposed
that he would ride him, but he had heard nothing
about it, and had no great fancy for the mount.   In
Wrench's own opinion, the horse had completely
lost his temper, and was never to be relied on.   " A
right good horse when he likes," had been the
jockey's verdict, " but never to be depended upon.
If he takes it into his head there's not a colt of his
year has a chance with him, but he's much more
likely to sulk, and refuse even to try to gallop.
But if," thought Wrench, " it's the stable who are
backing him in this way, he must have satisfied
them at home that he has got over his tantrums,
and is quite a reformed character, and if that is the
case, I should like not only to ride him, but to be
allowed to stand in a small stake with them on my

own account." Still eagerly watching the pulsations of
the market, Wrench noticed that a prominent member
of the betting ring, who had more than once acted
as agent for Praze's stable, took occasion, twice or
thrice, to lay against "King of the Huns." John
Wrench was puzzled, he could not understand which
way the wind blew, and resolved that he would run
down to Newmarket, and have a talk with Praze,
as soon as he could spare the time. But, as a leading
jockey, Wrench was in great request, and it so
happened that it was not until just before the
Leger that he was able to pay the Newmarket
trainer the visit he intended.

James Praze's string were doing steady work on
the Bury side of the Heath, when the jockey
cantered up on his hack, and said carelessly, ' Fine
morning, Mr. Praze. Your lot all doing nicely I
hope ? "

" Yes," replied the trainer, " I have nothing to
complain of. Mine are all pretty fit."

" That's right." replied the jockey. " How's the
Derby impostor ? He was backed for a lot of money
at York, as if somebody had fancied his chance
again. You've never said anything, but I suppose
I'm to ride him ? "

" Not exactly," rejoined the trainer quietly. " You
don't suppose I shouldn't have booked you before
this, if we'd meant that. You don't fancy the
horse for one thing, and Mr. Bramber didn't fancy
your riding of him at Epsom for another."

This was so far true, that Tom had not thought

the horse was done justice to upon that occasion, but the taking away the mount from John Wrench for Doncaster was solely Mr. Praze's doing, and due to the jockey's having paid no heed to the trainer's instructions.

"Very well," replied Wrench, considerably nettled, " then the sooner I announce that I am to let, the better. I think you might have let me know before, but it's always the way with men who just own one or two horses. When their wretched old screws don't win, they say it's all the fault of the jockey. ' King of the Huns ' is a coward, as whoever takes my place at Doncaster will very speedily discover. All the same," said the jockey, casting a searching glance at the trainer, " there's somebody don't think so, judging from what I saw at York," and with this parting shot, to which all the same he attached no particular meaning, John Wrench cantered off.

And so it came to pass that, a little later on, Jim Darley was struck almost dumb with surprise. Work was over for the morning, and Jim had just finished doing down his horse, when the head lad looked into the loose box, where the " King " was just nibbling at a handful of hay, and told Jim he was to go up to the house, as Mr. Praze wanted to speak to him. Wondering what on earth his master could want with him, Jim lost no time in repairing to the parlour, where the trainer still lingered over his breakfast.

" Two years ago, Darley, when you came to me," said Praze, " I told you that if you paid attention to orders, and kept your temper, you had the makings of a horseman, and your chance would come. Well, it has come. You will be wanted to ride ' King of the Huns ' in the Leger."

Jim's eyes glistened, and it was all he could do to refrain from exclaiming, " Oh, Mr. Praze ! "

" You see," continued his employer, " the horse is no doubt a little queer in his temper, and it is quite likely he will do more in your hands than he would in Wrench's. Now, don't get conceited and run away with the idea that you can ride with John. If he gets alongside with you at the finish, it must be on one a good many pounds worse than yours, or he'll make mincemeat of you. Remember, I'll forgive you if you're beat, but if you forget what you're told, you needn't look forward to wearing silk again whilst you are in my stable. One thing more. You ought to have learnt by this time to hold your tongue. Now don't go blowing around that you are going to ride ' King of the Huns.' That'll do for the present. You'll hear what more there is to say at Doncaster."

There was a full muster at the pretty little Yorkshire town that September. Men, who had been up in Scotland for the first month of the grouse, pulled up in shoals on their way back to Town, to witness the great race of the North: whilst Manchester, Sheffield, and the other big towns within hail of the Yorkshire border poured in their contingents, all anxious to gaze on the fray.

Still, thronged though the place was, and vainly as
Praze searched at all the well-known trysts, he could
neither see nor hear anything of Tom Bramber. He
was anxious to see him, for had he not asked Tom
to leave all speculation on the race in his hands?
And it behoved him to render an account of his
stewardship. But no, he could see nothing of him,
nor could he hear from any of their mutual
acquaintance that any one had set eyes upon Tom.
Considerable surprise was expressed when it became
known that Wrench was not going to ride the
" King." It was said that he had refused, it was
whispered about that if the stable had been dissatisfied with his riding at Epsom, the jockey had
been equally dissatisfied with his mount. Report said
that there had been great difficulty about finding a
substitute, and, despite all eager enquiry, even now
there was no ascertaining who was to take Wrench's
place. That the horse had arrived at Doncaster all
right was certain; but this little difficulty about his
rider caused his retrogression in the betting, and
amongst those not altogether pleased with the
aspect of things was Mr. Sam Wargrave. Wargrave,
to use a slang phrase, " knew his way about " on a
racecourse as well as most people. He had been,
too, a little behind the scenes with regard to that
accident at Tattenham Corner; he was a good judge
of racing, and had no doubt in his own mind that
" King of the Huns " ought to have won the Derby.
He had, moreover, the courage to back his convic-
tions, and he and the little clique with which he

was associated had supported " King of the Huns " in a very substantial manner. Now Sam was puzzled : he was wary and cunning in all matters connected with racing; he had been told "King of the Huns" was doing a capital Leger preparation. Could he have been misinformed in this matter ? However, he would have to abide now by what he had done, for he had nothing to guide him as to what he had better do, and there was but little time left to decide. Like himself, his friends did not quite relish the look of things, but they also saw nothing for it but to stand to their guns.

Again and again was the question put to James Praze as to who was going to ride the " King," but the trainer's reply was invariably, " Never mind ; there will be someone to ride him right enough." While, when questioned concerning the chance of his horse, his reply was simply, " He is here and well," but of what part he expected him to play in the race he said never a word. When the numbers went up on the telegraph board, and it was seen that Darley was the jockey for the " King," there was much wonder and enquiry as to who Darley was, for in those days Darley was a name quite unknown to racing men, and the " King " receded still more in the betting. And now Jim, attired in his first racing-jacket, was thrown into the saddle, and sent forth to make his first essay in the profession of his adoption. As he was about to follow his opponents out of the paddocks, Praze checked him. The boy bent down to listen to his master's last words

"Get well away with them, and then lie off. You can take close order at the distance ; but don't be hard upon your horse if you find you can't win. I don't want him cut up; and, remember, I'd as soon you were nowhere as third." And with that Mr. Praze gave Jim a nod and walked off in the direction of the trainer's stand.

Jim felt very serious when he went down to the post ; he had ridden of late in several trials, and learnt a good deal of his profession, but he was now conscious that no amount of rehearsal will prevent one feeling nervous on the first appearance. Again and again he muttered his orders over to himself. "I'll stick to them whatever happens. It would be the making of me to win, and I believe I ought to. You never sulked in your life with me, did you, old man ?" And patting his horse's neck, Jim committed himself to the charge of the starter.

Two or three breaks away, in which Jim keeps his head and behaves with wise discretion, and then down goes the flag, and they are off. Following his instructions, before he has gone a quarter of a mile Jim has pulled his horse back and is lying about ten or a dozen lengths from the leaders, and this position he steadily maintains till nearing the bend of the Red House. By that time, " Chorister " has threaded his way pretty nearly to the front, and Jim thinks it is time to close up and lessen the gap between them. He has lessened it a good bit, but is still four or five lengths behind. He calls upon his horse slightly, and the " King," showing no sign

14

of cowardice, responds gamely to his call. He is
beginning to feel anxious. "But no; not till the
distance, he said. Ah, here it is." And then Jim
calls upon his horse to take close order. Gradually
he creeps up, and already, as at Epsom, rises the
cry " 'King of the Huns' wins!" But half way
up a horrible suspicion shoots athwart Jim's mind.
His horse is faltering slightly in his stride. He is
running game as a bull-dog in his difficulties; but
Jim can disguise from himself no longer that his
horse is in trouble. Still, he thinks, the others,
like himself, may have had pretty near enough of
it, and perseveres. There are only two left in it in
Jim's judgment, " Chorister " and an outsider, who
are racing together close upon two lengths in front
of him, and a third horse that is lying at his girths.
For two or three seconds he rides the " King " hard,
and then recognises that he is beat, that he can
never catch the favourite. He drops the whip-hand,
which he has half-raised, as the bitter thought
comes home to him. " No, don't cut him up if you
can't win, he said, and never mind about being
third." Jim eases his horse, and in another second
or two " Chorister " is hailed winner of the Leger,
while " King of the Huns " is placed fourth.

Defeat is hard to bear at the beginning of life;
as we go on we take it less hardly. It has come to
all of us, aye, even to the greatest amongst us.
Napoleon knew it, and so did the great Turenne;
and there have been retreats, from that of the Ten
Thousand, that have been famous as victories; nay,

was there not one General of the last century who
rendered himself illustrious by defeat ? who the
wags of his nation described " as like a drum, only
heard of when beaten." However, Jim Darley had
yet to acquire equanimity in reverse, and it was
with a grievous feeling of disappointment that he
rode his horse back to the paddock.

It was all over now, there was nothing to do but to
pay and look pleasant ; and to do Mr. Sam Wargrave
justice, he was much too old a hand at a game of
speculation to make much moan over getting the
worst of it, but he did rather wonder how it had all
happened. How was it that " Chorister " had so
decisively beaten " King of the Huns"? a horse
which had so conclusively beaten him over the
Rowley Mile in the Spring. The " King " looked
fit and well; the boy rode him well enough; if it
had come to a case of a close finish, young Darley
would probably have been outridden ; but it wasn't
a case of that. He supposed the " King " must be
a non-stayer, that was the only solution he could
possibly find for his defeat.

14*

CHAPTER XXIII

" PRAZE EXPLAINS HIS TACTICS."

WHEN the account of the race reached Bottlesby there was much sympathy expressed for Tom Bramber—as well there might be. We never sympathise so much with disappointment as when sharing in it ourselves. And was not that garden-party, promised by Mr. Wargrave, dependent on the victory of " King of the Huns " at Doncaster ? As for Bramber, nobody seemed to know what to make of him. This strange whim of his, of giving up his farm, and going away to settle, he apparently didn't know where. What could it all mean ? People tried to dissuade him from it, but he only shook his head, and said he must go. He had been at Bottlesby too long, he wanted change ; he had not a word to say against his landlord ; he held his land at a fair rent, and the Squire was always willing to meet his tenants in any way. No, he had nothing to say against him ; nor for the matter of that anyone in the place, or near it ; but, for all that, he had made up his mind to go. It was no use arguing with him. When he spoke to Mr. Chacewater about giving up his farm that gentleman made no attempt to dissuade him. The fact was, his wife had told him her suspicions, as to how things stood between Bramber and Kate Darley.

And so the Squire had only said—" I shall be very sorry to lose you, Tom. You and yours have been there all my time ; but you're old enough to know your own business ; and as you tell me it is best you should go, you must. I can only say the best wishes of Mrs. Chacewater and myself go with you. One question only. It has nothing to do with ' King of the Huns,' has it ? "

" Nothing whatever, Sir," rejoined Tom. " How it was he cut up so badly in the Leger I don't know as yet. I haven't heard from Praze for some time. He'd be expecting to meet me at Doncaster, you see. And though I've lost a little money, I don't suppose it's very much. I left everything to Praze, as regarded betting ; he's a careful mate, and would take good care not to let me in heavily."

" I'm glad of that," said the Squire. " There was no scrimmage in the race this time. I am afraid the ' King ' is not quite so good a horse as you thought him."

" Perhaps so," returned Tom. " It's possible his victory in the Biennial was all a fluke. However, I am sick to death of it all, and shall tell Praze to dispose of my half of the horse as soon as pos- sible."

" A wise decision," said Mr. Chacewater. " There's no stock so expensive to keep as race-horses."

Two or three days afterwards, Bramber received a letter from the trainer ; and on opening it, was agreeably surprised to see a cheque for a goodly sum flutter out of the envelope ; having glanced at which, he turned to see what Praze had to say for himself. The letter ran as follows:

" DEAR TOM,—
" I hereby enclose your share of the plunder, and now to give you an account of my tactics all through the piece. To begin with, the horse was desperately upset by the collision in the Derby. He was fretful, irritable, and much disposed to show temper at his work. To go on with him in that state was to ruin him; the horse would have turned coward, or a confirmed rogue, and never have been to be relied upon in the future. There was nothing for it but to ease him, and it was soon evident that the stopping his work did him good. At last I began to send him along again, and the horse began to gallop quite in his old form. As you know, I was dying to have it out with Sam Wargrave and his friends, and was much puzzled how the return match was to be played. I told some of my pals at Tattersall's to keep an eye on them, and soon found out that it was they who had introduced the ' King ' into the betting market for the Leger, and that they were quietly appropriating all the long shots about him. At the same time it dawned upon me that there would never be time to thoroughly wind the horse up for Doncaster. He had been eased rather too long. And then it struck me, here was the chance I wanted. I sent a commission to lay into the ring. And as the ' King ' kept galloping day after day in capital style, Sam War-

grave's friends got sweeter and sweeter. The demonstration against the ' King ' at York was my allies opening with the heavy artillery. For the rest, understand, the ' King ' was thoroughly well at Doncaster, and ran a good horse, considering he was rather wanting in condition. I put young Darley up, with orders to win if he could ; but not to cut the horse up if he couldn't. He's a clever lad that, and rode strictly to his orders. I am delighted to hear that Sam Wargrave and his friends napped it very hot indeed.

" Yours sincerely,
" JAMES PRAZE."

The cheque, no doubt, was handy, and Tom really was pleased to find that the " King's " defeat was no real blot on his scutcheon, and was to be fully accounted for. But for all that he did not change his intention, but wrote to the trainer, to tell him he wished to dispose of his share of " King of the Huns " as soon as, with a due regard to himself, Praze could conveniently manage it.

Towards the end of that autumn, there appeared a romance by a new writer, which gradually attracted considerable attention. Neither the press nor the public proclaimed with unnecessary emphasis that a new genius had burst upon the world—new geniuses are apt, by the way, to resemble comets in their very transitory appearance. People talked about it, and what was still more to the point, read it, and when they had done so, recommended their friends to go and do likewise. Gradually the book was a good deal noticed by the reviewers, not altogether for good, for can it be supposed that critics, any more than their fellows, enjoy immunity from derangement of the liver? But upon the whole it was as well reviewed as could be reasonably expected, and better still, some of those who were most appreciative in their judgment, while pointing out faults not unusual especially in a first book, pronounced it to give great promise for the future. Others, whose criticism was marked with more severity, said it was manifestly the work of quite a young man, who had as yet much to learn in the mechanism of his art, but that the book gave them the impression that the writer could do considerably better if he tried, and that they should look forward to his next effort with no little curiosity. In due course, through the medium of the circulating libraries, " A Parthian Flight," as this story was called, found its way down to Chacewater Grange, and was also to be seen on the drawing-room table in Carlingham Park. Miss Wargrave read the book, as Miss Wargrave usually did any light literature that was talked about in Society. It rather struck her fancy, and she held forth so much about it, at a dinner-party at the Grange, to which the Wargraves had been invited, that upon Mrs. Chacewater remarking that it was lying upon the table, Lucy Marton, who was also dining there, forthwith borrowed it and took it home with her. Before Lucy had gone very far into the first volume,

she was so struck with the book that she involun-
tarily turned to the title page to see the name of
the author. " Richard Waters " told her nothing,
but the more she read, the more she felt that she
recognized the writer. Every trick of thought, and
in somes cases even a turn of expression, reminded
her of Reginald. There are very few of us who
have not pet phrases of our own. I am not talking
of slang or anything of that kind, but an expression
in quite ordinary English which has become
habitual to our life. I know one man who constantly
interlards his conversation with, " What you may
call." I don't suppose the majority of people
notice it, it is perfectly inoffensive, and I have no
doubt that he is perfectly unconscious of doing so.
But when you take to putting your thoughts upon
paper, it attracts attention which it usually escapes
in speech.

As soon as she had finished the book, Lucy wrote
to the publishers to demand the address of Mr.
Richard Waters. She received a courteous reply
regretting that they were not at liberty to give it,
but that they should be very happy to forward
any letter she might think fit to send to that
gentleman. She then wrote to Reginald himself,
but received no reply. This was unexpected;
having as she conceived penetrated Reginald's
secret, and discovered his *nom de plume*, she
had anticipated a grateful reply to the pretty letter
of congratulation she had written him, and from
this acknowledgment she would learn where he

now was. This artful young woman had an indefinite idea that, once known, the Rector could then mediate between father and son, that is the way she put it to herself, but, in her heart of hearts, she wished to know the truth of this story about Reginald and Kate Darley. Lucy, as might be conceived, was pretty well up in the gossip of the village to start with, and then her father had made no secret of what he had learnt from Tom Bramber, and in Lucy's eyes an entanglement of that sort was one of the worst things that could possibly befall Reginald Chacewater. She did not know which was the worst view of the question; look at it whichever side you might, she looked upon it as his ruin—whether he was to return to the Grange with a girl who from her position was impossible for a wife, or whether the story should gradually be told through all Bottlesby, of how the young Squire had brought shame upon pretty Kate Darley. It might not be too late, if her father could talk to him now it might transpire that though Reginald had been imprudent he had committed neither folly nor sin. But then, Lucy reflected, the Rector's intervention should be speedy, there was no time to be lost, and yet alas, she was no nearer the discovery of Reginald's whereabouts than before she penetrated his secret. But when Lucy told her father that she felt perfectly sure that "Richard Waters," who had written this clever story, and Reginald were one and the same person, how she had written to the publishers to ask his address, and how it had been refused to her, and why she had been so anxious to obtain it, the Rector replied : " I have thought it all well over, and I have decided to go to Chillingham, and see Kate Darley. We don't know where Reginald is, and I have no reason to think he is there, but we do know Kate is. I shall see her, and must then be guided by circumstances."

Lucy warmly applauded her father's decision ; they would at all events then know precisely how things stood with Reginald and Kate Darley, and she even thought that it was perhaps better, after all, that her old friend should be wedded to Kate, for whom the Rector's daughter had always had a strong liking, than that he should fall a prey to the wiles of that designing minx, Clara Wargrave.

But there is someone else chafing bitterly over the obscurity in which it has pleased the author of " A Parthian Flight " to shroud himself. There has never been the slightest mystery about who " Richard Waters " is with Kate. Not only is it the name under which he has gone during the whole time he has been at Chillingham, but she has also received a copy of the book with his handwriting on the title page ; she is in as complete ignorance of where Reginald is as Lucy herself, very angry with him in consequence, and still more angry with Tom Bramber, whom she looks upon as the cause of it. She had told herself it was all nonsense, and it was high time she put an end to such folly, but now what she had decided was best done has come about without

her intervention, Kate is very far from satisfied.
She knows at last how much she cares for this man,
and she finds that sorrow of parting that she
thought she could bear so bravely a much sharper
experience than she had looked for.   Then she is so
pleased and proud of the book, and recognises here
and there many scenes which they had talked over
together and which she is wild now to talk over
again.

"He might have been here now," she murmurs,
"if it hadn't been for that stupid Mr. Bramber.
What business had he to come worrying down here ?
I'm sure I never gave him any encouragement, he
had no reason to expect anything except 'No' for
an answer.   It's too bad; nobody has any right to
interfere with me, except my own father, and from
all accounts he's quite content that his children
should go their own way, and not trouble him.   I'm
earning my own living honestly, and I won't have
these Bottlesby people prying into my life."   And
Kate stamps her little foot wrathfully on the floor, as
she thinks it is the prying of these Bottlesby people
that is the cause of Reginald's absence.

Poor Tom Bramber !   He had struck a streak of
bad luck with a vengeance did he but know it, and
is playing his cards to boot as badly as it is possible
for a man to play them.   Had he only told his love
a year ago, he would at all events have found Kate
Darley heart-free.   Mr. Praze would have told him
that he owned the best horse of his year in England,
and yet he did not seem able to win a race with

him. He was desirous of selling "King of the Huns," or at all events his half of him, and when he succeeded, the chances were, such tricks does Fortune play with her votaries, that "King of the Huns" would carry all before him.

CHAPTER XXIV.

"A PARTHIAN FLIGHT."

THE more the Reverend James Marton pondered over this thing, the more he thought it behoved him to interfere; he was no meddlesome priest, ever anxious to have a finger in his neighbours' affairs, but he honestly looked upon it as his duty to come to the assistance of his parishioners when he saw his way to doing so. He came to the conclusion, at last, that the first thing to do was to go to Chillingham and see Kate Darley. From Kate he should doubtless ascertain how things stood between her and Reginald. If he was married to her no one was fitter to mediate between Reginald and his father than himself. It was, of course, by no means the match that the Squire would desire for his son; that he should be angry and annoyed at it was only natural, and Reginald's conduct in first allowing that he had perished in the accident in the Regent's Park to be believed, and even yet persistently keeping his whereabouts secret from his family, was still further exasperating to the Squire, no doubt. Clearly the first thing was to see Kate, if it was only the stepping-stone to finding

out where Reginald was. That he had left Chillingham he knew from Tom Bramber, but Tom had no
knowledge of Reginald's proceedings further than
that. This was all clear enough, thought the Rector,
as he took his ticket for Chillingham, but supposing
that other view of the case should present itself,
and that he should find Kate Darley not Reginald's
wife but his mistress, what was he to do then?
He was a man of the world, as well as a clergyman;
he knew well all the misery that such a connection
as this usually entails, yet, loss of caste as it is to
the woman, how often it proves the ruin of a man's
early career. And in the event of there being
children, what a blot it was on their lives. As
Rector of Bottlesby it behoved him to exhort
Reginald to make the one reparation of his fault
left to him, but, as a man of the world and the
Squire's intimate friend, he felt that to counsel and
abet a marriage between his son and the daughter
of one of his tenants might lead to a severance of
their old friendship and render him powerless to
help in bringing about the reconciliation of father
and son. Disagreeable reflections these with which
to beguile his journey to Chillingham, but the
Rector was not of the sort to be deterred from doing
his duty because it might not be pleasant, nor was
he of a kind to hesitate betwixt his duty to God
and man.

Mr. Marton had no occasion to make any enquiries
as to where Miss Darell lived; he had got her
address from Bramber before he left, and at once

proceeded to Kate's modest lodgings. He was shown up to the sitting-room, and informed that Miss Darell would be down in two or three minutes. He glanced round the room, and then, as people do under similar circumstances, began turning over the books and photographs upon the table. There were several of these latter. Kate in hat and habit, more than one inscribed "Miss Darell, on her celebrated horse 'Selim'"; the redoubtable "Beppo," especially, posed in various attitudes; but, much to the Rector's relief, there were none of the artiste in short skirts and fleshings. Suddenly a look of interest flashed across his face as he took up one of the books. It was the first volume of "A Parthian Flight," and strong confirmation of Lucy's opinion that Reginald Chacewater was its author. He turned carelessly to the title-page, on which was written, "Kate Darley, with the Author's love." And this placed it beyond all doubt, for Mr. Marton at once recognised Reginald's handwriting.

At this moment the door opened and Kate made her appearance; though she mastered herself sufficiently to extend her hand and greet the Rector in her accustomed fashion, it was palpable that it was not him she had expected to see. Indeed, no thought of the Reverend James Marton had ever crossed her mind. The popular equestrienne was accustomed to be called upon by people in the way of business, sometimes it was a photographer, sometimes it was a gentleman connected with the Press, a messenger from the Hippodrome;

but what she had hoped for most on this occasion was that it was someone who brought her news of Reginald, for she had heard nothing of him since he left Chillingham. Not a line even had accompanied his book, and she so yearned to see him; she so longed to talk over that book now it was finished as she had talked over and commented on it when it was in course of composition; she had been carried away by it. She thought it immensely clever, and that the author was destined to take a very foremost place in literature. True, critics had spoken well of it; but little wonder there was a glamour around that book for Kate Darley, for she made no disguise to herself of her own feelings as regarded the writer. And if the girl who loves you can see nothing in the outcome of your brain, then, verily, a man requires to have much faith in his own abilities.

There was a pause between them, their first greetings once over, for Kate on her part was marvelling much to what she was indebted for the Rector's visit, while he, on his side, was a little puzzled how best to set to work on his self-imposed mission. It was hard to arraign the quietly-dressed, pretty, ladylike girl who bade him be seated with so much composure, for her backslidings, and at the same time it would be still more awkward should he hint at such shame to Reginald's lawful wife. At last, taking up the book, he said:

"I don't want to be indiscreet, Kate, but I have inadvertently received confirmation of what Lucy and I only suspected, and that is that Reginald Chacewater is the author of this very clever novel."

Kate started ; she knew that was a secret, and for the moment forgot that the inscription on the title-page had probably betrayed it to the Rector.

" Yes, it is very clever. I don't know——" she stammered, " the author has not put his name upon the title-page."

" No," laughed Mr. Marton, "but he has put his handwriting on the title-page, and to one who knows it as well as I do that is quite sufficient. But, Kate, I have come over from Bottlesby on purpose to see you. I have come to see what I can do to put things straight between Reginald and his father."

Kate made no answer, she would guard Reginald's secrets to the last. She would admit nothing concerning the book, she would not even admit that he was living, although she knew from Bramber that had already been discovered. She answered never a word.

" Kate," he continued, " will you not confide in me ? Believe me I am anxious to smooth things both for you and Reginald. It was Tom Bramber that gave me your address and I came——"

" Tom Bramber ! " cried Kate, springing to her feet, while her eyes flashed with anger, and her cheeks flushed at the remembrance of her last interview with Tom. " Mr. Bramber ! " she ex-claimed vehemently, "and what has Mr. Bramber to do with me ? What right has Mr. Bramber to meddle in my affairs ? What business is it of his

15

where I live, and what right has he to hunt me out, and proclaim where I am living, and what I am doing upon the housetops; to spread shameful lies about me? Yes, lies, Mr. Marton," she continued passionately. "What am I doing here? Getting my living by riding in a circus, and who, I should like to know, has any right to interfere with me?"

She looked very pretty as she paused breathless, with quivering lips, her eyes still sparkling with indignation, her slight figure drawn up to its full height, her little head thrown defiantly back, and the Rector thought, as he gazed upon her, if Reginald had lost his head about this girl he had good warrant for doing so. He had known both her and her brother from childhood, and he ought to have remembered that hot Darley temper which had got them into so much trouble in their young days. Kate's blood was thoroughly up now, and it was not likely that anything he could say would pacify it for the present.

"Like Mrs. Chacewater and many other of your best friends," he replied, "I am sorry that you have taken to this mode of life; it may not be wrong, but it is full of temptation for a girl of your age."

"You would mew me up in a school-room," she rejoined sullenly. "I, who love horses and revel in a free life. I have chosen my own path, Mr. Marton, and I intend to adhere to it. My father cares nothing for what I do as long as I am not a burden on him. It is my own affair, and a girl need not be bad, though she is a circus rider."

"But, Kate," he expostulated.

"Let me go my own way," she replied angrily, "you, at all events, have nothing to say to it."

He saw it was no use to pursue the subject further, and reflected somewhat ruefully that so far he had failed signally in his errand, and knew no more what the relations were between her and Reginald than when he started. "If you will not listen to me about yourself," he said at length, "you will at all events tell me where I can find Reginald. His father is very wroth with him, and, in my opinion, every day he persists in keeping them in ignorance at the Grange of where he is and what he is doing makes a reconciliation between him and his father more difficult."

"I will tell you not one word about Reginald Chacewater," she answered. "I do not even acknowledge that he was the author of that book; his secrets and his motives are his own, and, as far as I know them, will never be betrayed by me."

There was a quiet, dogged determination in her tones that recalled to the Rector some of the stormy hours of Kate's school-days. He knew there was nothing to be done with her now; that to make her speak in her present mood was hopeless, and yet, as he rose, he could not refrain from saying, "Reginald Chacewater was in Chillingham, I know."

"He may have been," was Kate's cool reply, with a quiet inclination of her head.

"Do you know where he is now?" he asked abruptly.

15*

"No, Mr. Marton; I do not," replied the girl, "and, as I said before, if I did, I would not tell you."

"Then I can be of no good here," replied the Rector. "I can only hope, Kate, that you will never repent having so rigidly withheld from me your confidence." And with these words, Mr. Marton extended his hand and bade Kate a courteous good-bye, though he confessed to his daughter afterwards that, as he went down the staircase, he felt as if he could have shaken the girl for her obstinate reticence.

Sundry desultory and abortive enquiries after Reginald in Chillingham, and then the Rector betook himself to the railway-station, made the best of his way back to Bottlesby, and was fain to acknowledge on his homeward journey that he might as well have remained at home for all the good which he had accomplished. True, Kate Darley had pronounced all the scandal about her to be an infamous lie, but then he had only her own word for it, and then the Rector sadly reflected that he had known young women assert their innocence under similar circumstances upon more than one occasion, and that the future had far from justified their denial.

Very dissatified was Kate as she thought over her interview with Mr. Marton. She was annoyed beyond measure to hear that her old friends at Bottlesby disapproved of the line of life she had adopted. It was hard that she should be interfered with; she was earning her bread honestly, and in a manner that she took pride and pleasure in. "I was very happy indeed," she mused, "with Mrs. Chacewater,

and I am sorry she should think it of me, but then
I know I was more a companion to her daughter
than a governess; it was not likely that I should
ever get another situation like that, and I have need
of patience and of temper for the course of life they
would have mapped out for me. I never could keep
my temper with anything but horses, and since I have
been in the circus, they have taught me to be still
more patient with them, while Jim writes me word
that it is just the same at Newmarket, and that Mr.
Praze says that three-fourths of the bad-tempered
horses are only what the boys made them. I am
sorry even that Mr. Marton should think ill of me,
but it is done now and I wouldn't change it if I
could. Oh, Reginald, Reginald, if you would only
write to me, I would care little what they said or
thought about me. I so long to see you again, to
congratulate you about your book, and to talk it all
over with you, to know how you are and what you
are doing; if I could but see you again, if it were
only for an afternoon, even if I could only write to
you. It was cruel of you to leave me so hurriedly,
with your kiss on my lips, and no word of where you
were going. Never to let me have a line since;
if you had thirsted for news of me only a tenth as
much as I do to hear of you, I should have had a
letter from you long ago."

Kate Darley, indeed, was getting very restless and
unhappy; she had no idea what had become of
Reginald, nor indeed, as she ascertained by diligent
enquiry, had any one of the troupe. There was

nothing very singular after all, Kate was compelled to admit, in the fact that Reginald should have not confided to any of his small circle of acquaintance whither he was going ; she knew that his ambition was to achieve a great literary success, to clear off his debts with the proceeds thereof, and then to return laurel-crowned and triumphant to his family. Well, the success was accomplished, surely the money must be flowing in now, and there could be no reason for his further concealment, but any way there could be no need of his concealing himself from her.   Ah ! she had told herself all along, again and again had she said that he was only amusing himself with her, that theirs was one of those pleasant flirtations which seem so much and mean so little.

> " And the best and the worst of this is
> That neither is most to blame,
> If you've forgotten my kisses
> And I've forgotten your name."

Lotos eating, she had called it, and vowed that she should take no harm by it.   Fool that she had been, she could not say so now.   She knew, with a sore sting in her heart, that she had toyed with the flames and that they had scorched her; she thought they could be good comrades, but he had taught her to love him, had won her heart, and now she was forgotten.   The sunlight had gone out of her life and Kate clung more closely to her profession than ever as the sole thing that took her out of herself. But it is easy to change all that when one is in love and nineteen.   Coming back one evening from the Hippodrome, Kate found a letter that brought back the smiles to her lips and made her pulses tingle again with delight.

It was from Reginald, and dated from a place called Twybury, distant only some two hours by rail. He spoke with pride of the success of his book. "I should be hard to please," he said, "were I not content with the reviews as a whole. Some hard knocks I was bound to get, did any man ever do anything worth doing that there were not some to rail at it? and on the whole the Press have been very kind to me. I ought to be both proud and pleased, I have succeeded beyond my deserts, and yet I am not contented. Don't think me a sordid creature, Kate, but you know I had hoped to gain money by this. It was not from a mean motive. I hoped by the work of my own hands to pay what I owe, without troubling my relations, but fame alas, is not always accompanied by riches, and it seems the first book, though successful, may bring the writer but small recompense for his labours. Write to me under the old name, but let no one know where I am living, as I must remain a bit longer in obscurity. You have done better with your new life, Kate, than I have. You at all events can earn your living, and it is not quite clear to me as yet that I can.

"Ever dear, most sincerely thine,

"R. W."

Not a very passionate letter this, but for all that it sent Kate to bed happy and contented.

CHAPTER XXV.

" THE SPRING HANDICAPS."

WITH the coming spring the legitimate turf world began to bestir itself, I mean that genuine section of its followers which turns up its nose at all hybrid branches of the sport it loves so well, and is not to be interested by any cross-country business, save perchance the Grand National. For three months it had lived more or less in a state of torpor, beguiling itself by conning the racing records of the past year and vainly exercising its judgment as to what was to turn out the best three-year-old of the coming season. With the publication of the weights of the spring handicaps, pulses quickened and both backers and layers began once more to argue and substantiate their opinions in that manner so dear to all Englishmen. Mr. Praze down at Newmarket studies these weights with a practised eye, and is apparently by no means dissatisfied with something he sees in them. He has made no very strenuous endeavours to carry out Tom Bramber's instructions and has not as yet disposed of Bramber's moiety of "King of the Huns"; that noble animal consequently figures in that gentleman's name in all the spring handicaps. I am writing be it remembered of the old plunging days, before the romance of the turf

had died out, when yearling books were afloat and it
was possible to back a horse to be champion three-
year-old of his year, to win a hundred thousand
pounds before he had ever even seen a race-course ;
when the betting on big handicaps commenced in
heavy fashion, not only the moment the weights for
them were out, but even long before. As Mr. Praze
superintends the work of his string this morning
on the Heath, he eyes the " King of the Huns "
narrowly, watches him stride easily along in his
three-quarter-speed gallop under Jim Darley's hands
and eyes him closely as he pulls up. That the
horse has wintered well and grown into a magni-
ficent specimen of a thorough-bred there can be no
doubt, and the gloss on his coat and the way the
muscles stands out about his thighs and quarters
show him to be very forward in condition.

"Ah," mutters Mr. Praze to himself, " there you
are, the very best of your year I'll swear it, and yet
you ungrateful vagabond, what have you done for
those who brought you up, and fed you, and trained
you ? Nothing but win an ordinary Biennial at
Newmarket, and why? on account of your beastly
temper ; if you hadn't sulked at Epsom last spring
you could have won fast enough, though you were
knocked into. If you hadn't sulked on your own
gallop and made me afraid to go with you, you
would have won the Leger. And now here you are
—a horse that ought to have won the Derby, turned
loose in the City and Suburban with eight stone four
on your worthless back. Win it ?—yes you can win it

the length of a street if you choose to try; I wonder
whether you will. Yes, legs are a trial, roaring is a
sore trouble, but for a downright double-distilled
curse, calculated to ruin a millionaire, give me a real
good horse with a bad temper."

Whatever Mr. Praze might think, the " King of
the Huns " did not at all commend himself to the
general public. The colt made his *début* last year
with a great flourish of trumpets, which he had to
some extent justified by winning the Biennial in
the hollowest of fashions, but since then he had
very much discounted that performance by proving
a disastrous failure; he had started a hot favourite
for the Derby and had finished nowhere; similarly
at Doncaster, although he had been again backed
for a great deal of money, he had not taken any
prominent part in the race. The body of the public
as a rule do not forgive disappointments, and many
who had stuck staunchly to " King of the Huns "
and clever James Praze all last year now renounced
their allegiance, vowed that the " King " was an
immensely over-rated horse, and that for once Praze
had made a mistake, that the Biennial had been all
a fluke, that the horse had made the most of a
capital start, had been more forward in condition
than any of his opponents and so had never been
caught. And not only was this the case with the
general public but even old turfites took this view.
Mr. Sam Wargrave and his friends, for instance, had
come to the conclusion that the starting of " Cockchafer " at Epsom had been a somewhat unnecessary

precaution on their part, that the "King" would
have been beaten upon his own merits precisely as
he was at Doncaster. The consequence was that
much to his satisfaction Mr. Praze saw no disposition on the part of anyone to introduce the
name of "King of the Huns" into the betting
market. But there was one person to whom what
the "King" was to do in the forthcoming season
was a most momentous question, and that was Jim
Darley. That his horse was the best in England
was an article of faith with Jim, and that if he was
only given a chance on the back of the "King"
this spring he would prove that last year's running
was all wrong he believed implicitly; he had been
too long in a racing stable not to feel sure that the
"King" was not at his best when he rode him in
the Leger, and whatever he might do in the hands
of another jockey, Jim felt certain the horse would
run straight enough in his hands. Which of these
handicaps would Mr. Praze run him for and would
he be allowed to ride him? These questions con-
sumed Jim's soul with feverish anxiety; he had not
spent three years on the Heath without having
learnt something about the apportioning of weights,
and he knew that a four year old which ought to have
won the Derby in the preceding year to have got
into three of the Spring Handicaps at the slightly
varying imposts allotted to the "King" was a piece
of great luck. Which would he run for? would he,
Jim Darley, be allowed to ride? He would have
given all he possessed, not that that was much, to

ask the trainer these questions, more especially the latter, but he dared not. Though kind to his boys Mr. Praze was a rigid disciplinarian, requiring unquestioning obedience, and rarely condescending to speak much to them.

Jim literally tingled with excitement to the tips of his fingers when, the work finished one morning, on returning to the stables the trainer said quietly: "Come up to the house, Darley, as soon as you have done your horse, I've got a question or two to ask you."

The "King" conscientiously dressed down, and his clothing replaced, Jim hurried off to hear what Mr. Praze might want with him.

"Now, Darley," said the trainer, "do you remember what I said to you before the Leger?"

"Yes, sir," rejoined the boy, "you said, 'Ride this race exactly as I have told you; remember I'll forgive your not winning, but if you don't ride strictly according to orders, you won't be wanted to ride in public any more.'"

"Just so," replied Mr. Praze. "You did what you were told and I was perfectly satisfied with you. Now did the horse show temper with you any time during that race?"

"No, sir, he ran honest as daylight, until he was beat, but I think—I think——"

"Don't do that, Darley," replied the trainer with a smile, "you're not paid for it. However, just this once let's hear what you do think."

"That the 'King' wasn't the horse he was at

Epsom," blurted out Jim, not a little scared at his own audacity.

"And he's never shown temper with you since?" enquired Mr. Praze, without taking the slightest notice of the opinion he had elicited.

"Never since last summer, sir, he goes as kindly as any horse can."

"That'll do, Darley," replied Mr. Praze; "very likely you'll get a chance of sporting silk before the spring's over. Always stick strictly to orders and don't talk, mind."

It was with a sense of great elation that Jim walked away from his interview with his master. He was to have his chance then this spring and take the second step in the career he had marked out for himself. In his eyes a crack jockey towered far above a leading statesman. Eminent lawyers, actors, artists, were all nobodies compared to the leaders of his own vocation; to have ridden the winner of the Derby was a far greater thing than to have delivered the greatest oration ever heard at Westminster. Now was his chance. "King of the Huns" was himself again, and no more like the horse that he had felt dying away under him on Doncaster Town Moor than a man in rude health is like the same man much below par. His first instinct was to crush his fellows with the intelligence; the dearest aspiration of most of them was that they, in course of time, might be trusted to bestride their charges in public, and in the days of our callow youth to brag of any slight success of this kind is well-nigh irresistible, but Jim clenched his teeth sternly and muttered, "'Don't talk,' he said, and dash it, I won't." Jim Darley had never had much reverence for his betters, nor of those set in authority over him, but if there was any one in this world of whom he did stand really in awe, it was Mr. Praze.

Tom Bramber at Bottlesby in the meantime has been very busy making preparations for giving up his farm and for leaving the place. He is to be quit of the land at Lady Day and all his stock and plant is to be brought to the hammer some two or three weeks before. He pays little attention to what is going on in the racing world and has not even noticed that "King of the Huns" figures in his name amongst the entries of several of the spring handicaps. He has bothered his head nothing about the colt, Praze will sell his half for him, as soon as he finds a favourable opportunity, there can be no difficulty about that, and cruelly disappointing though the "King" has been to them, he is at all events worth a good deal more than they gave for him. Tom has grown somewhat morose of late, and held himself aloof from his old friends and acquaintances, while the gentlemen and farmers round Bottlesby are much of the general opinion and look upon "King of the Huns" as an impostor.

The world is wont to be harsh in its judgment on those who disappoint it; when it is whispered about that great things may be expected from either man or horse, to fail is to become an object of derision. There used to be between the shafts of a hack-cabriolet that plied for hire in the town of Andover a horse whose sire had won the Derby, and whose mother had been hailed winner of the Oaks. Great things had been expected of that high-bred youngster when he made his *entrée* into public life ; and that was how it had all ended.

Neither the Squire nor Mr. Marton thought anything about " King of the Huns " this year ; they had both quite sufficient to occupy their minds in this business of Reginald's and Kate Darley's. Whatever the rest of the village might think, both at the Grange and the Rectory they knew how bitterly Tom Bramber was cut up with Kate's rejection ; that it was the reason why he was leaving the home of his childhood, and that the wound was as yet so sore that it was cruel even to touch upon the subject. That Kate had thrown his honest love on one side, for the sake of a life of shame with Reginald Chacewater, rankled sorely in Tom Bramber's heart, and should opportunity serve of taking vengeance on her seducer he vowed that nothing should stay his hand. All idea that Kate and Reginald were married was now rapidly dying away amongst those it most concerned ; the Rector and Tom Bramber were, we know, of that opinion, and at the Grange, Herbert Chacewater and his wife had come reluctantly to the conclusion that some time must elapse before their son can return to them ; not, indeed, until this unfortunate con-

nection was either put an end to or perchance made
lawful.

But there was one more household in the neighbourhood of Bottlesby to whom this question of
Reginald's entanglement was also of absorbing
interest, and that was the family at Carlingham
Park. If Miss Wargrave had welcomed the news
that Reginald was alive with delight, it was with a
feeling of angry disappointment she received the
further intelligence that Kate Darley was the
companion of his flight and had been the cause of
all this mystification. She had no recollection of
having ever set eyes upon Kate, but she had no
difficulty in finding out who she was, and that the
daughter of a mere Bottlesby farmer should dare to
come between her and her schemes, should have
attracted the notice of the prince whom she herself
condescended to favour, moved Clara's wrath not a
little. Scant mercy would she have shown her rival
had she lived in the feudal times, and old Darley
been one of her father's retainers. Still, after all,
she reflected that things looked better for her than
they had done since the first news of that dreadful
accident. When a man is once dead there is no
more to be done ; he has run his race, and there is
nothing in this world can affect him more ; but as
long as he is alive there is no saying what tact and
perseverance may not persuade him to do. As
before said, Clara Wargrave was a good-looking girl
and accustomed to make the most of every point in
her game. She neglected no adjunct of dress and

millinery; she was quite aware that if she could boast no family, she was, at all events, "a lass wi' a tocher."

"Bah," she said to her father, with a shrug of her shoulders, "it's very provoking of him, but men are such fools. This minx, no doubt, for the present can turn him round her finger; but he'll soon get tired of her dairymaid charms, and be only too glad to have done with his pretty plaything."

"But suppose, Clara, she is married to him?" said her father. "There was a report to that effect some little time back."

"When I said men were such fools, I didn't suppose that even Reginald Chacewater could be such a fool as that; at all events, papa, what you have to do is to find out at once where he is, and as much as you can about their connection. She is dancing or something of that kind in a booth at Chillingham, and wherever she is, depend upon it he is not far off. As he is holding no communication with his father, they are probably in great poverty; so much the better for what I want. Nothing, I should think, brings a deplorable mistake of that kind home to a young man much more quickly than poverty. Find out all about him for me, father. It should be easy, and, remember, the first thing you have to do is to detach him from that girl."

Sam Wargrave readily promised to do as his daughter desired; a clever, successful, unscrupulous

16

man, he had swept greater obstacles from his path than this promised to be, in his day. He was anxious that Clara should marry Reginald Chacewater for many reasons; not perhaps the least that his own peace and quietness depended a good deal on getting the fair Clara satisfactorily settled. If money and unwearied enquiry could do it, Sam Wargrave resolved that he would know all about Reginald Chacewater before a week was done.

CHAPTER XXVI.

" TRACKED DOWN."

WHEN Kate Darley came to re-read Reginald's letter and muse over it, she became conscious of a strain of great depression running through it; his book was a success, and yet it seemed to her that it was also a disappointment; as yet it was evident that the labour of months had produced no monetary results. And it is an old-world story, how often the fruits of their first literary labours have been but dust and ashes to men embarked on that thorny career. But when those who sit in judgment have recognised the merits of the performance, it does seem hard that the more solid guerdon should not also at once reward the craftsman. Reginald had yet to learn that the gathering of the harvest is slow when one's name is as yet unknown. He is indeed a little anxious about his own position; he has come very nearly to the end of his resources; and, economise as he may, it is evident that he must speedily find some way of earning money to enable him to live. He is diffident about writing to his publishers, to ask them if there are no profits due to him on account of " A Parthian Flight," while on their side, they are waiting until the book is doing well, which will enable them to send him a substantial cheque. It is true he can live very cheaply at Twybury, but as for procuring employment, that seems rather difficult. In the first flush of his success, he thought that it would be easy to get something to do in his own line. But one weekly paper is as much as Twybury can support; and its limited staff, which combined other avocations with that of journalism, amply sufficed for its requirements. Placing one's candle under a bushel is a mistake very few of us ever fall into; but what is to be done with a man who, after achieving a literary success, persists in remaining incognito in these days ?

The more Kate pondered over that letter, the more the desire grew upon her to see the writer again ; why should she not ? It was easy enough to run over to Twybury for the day; it was only asking to be taken out of the bill for one afternoon at the Hippodrome. She would do it; she would speak to the manager at once ; run over to Twybury the next morning, and be back again in Chillingham in time to ride "Beppo" at the Hippodrome in the evening. The manager made no difficulties ; and having telegraphed to Reginald to meet her at the station, Kate started in high spirits on her

16*

proposed expedition. As soon as her eye fell upon
Reginald, she recognised that things were not well
with him, there was a worn and weary look upon
his face, and the quick eye of a woman was not
likely to overlook the traces of narrow circumstances which a man's dress is apt to betray when
the shoe begins to pinch hard. Glad as he was to
see her, Reginald, on the whole, would rather that
she had not come. He was somewhat ashamed that
Kate should see him in his present circumstances.
He had never affected to be anything but poor, at
Chillingham, but there are gradations of poverty;
and there he had always had a sufficiency, and been
able to live much as his companions of the Hippodrome did ; but now it had come to that, with him,
that the cost of his dinner was a matter of profound
calculation, and the nice little luncheon that he
gave Kate at the hotel would entail a couple of
days' abstinence. He strove hard to put a cheerful
face on things, but he did not deceive Kate Darley
in the least. He confessed that, as yet, he had
derived no solid results from his book, and laughed,
and said : Well, he had won fame, and that should
be enough for him. Did she not remember Byron's
lines ?

> " For this we spurn Apollo's venal son,
>   And bid a long good-night to Marmion."

Not that his lordship was at all above taking his
dues a little later, filling his pockets, forsooth, in a
fashion that makes one's mouth water.

Then they discussed *the* book again ; and Kate, craftiest of coquettes, quoted some few of the passages that had particularly struck her. She declared that it was a mere question of time ; that good work in this world was always paid for in the end — which showed less knowledge of the world than innocent belief in it — and that, ere many days had passed, she was sure he would hear satisfactorily from his publishers. Then Reginald had to hear about all his old friends of the circus ; to learn how Tom Bramber had called upon her. Kate rather slurred over the account of Bramber's visit, and flushed a good deal as she alluded to it. Then she recounted how Mr. Marton had also been to see her, and had been very urgent that she should give him his, Reginald's, address. " But as I didn't know, I couldn't. Not that there was any need, sir, for you to take such a precaution with me —I told him that I would not tell him, even if I knew ; nor yet betray any other secret of yours. And yet, Reginald, I did ; but, indeed, it wasn't my fault ; your book was lying on the table, he took it up, and at once recognised your hand-writing on the title-page. I would not acknowledge that it was yours, but he only laughed, and said that Miss Marton had recognised it as such, as soon as she read it."

" Then the murder's out," laughed Reginald. " Not that it much matters. Little as I have dabbled with literature in London, I know the name of an author whose book has hit the mark is an open secret in a very short time."

" And now it's getting time I was off," exclaimed
Kate ; " it would never do for Signorina Darell to
disappoint the public. Come and see me off, Reggie,
won't you ? "

So those two walked quietly down to the railway
station, and having ensconced her in a carriage he
stood talking to her at the window till the bell rang.
"Good-bye," she said. "I have hurriedly brought
you a little souvenir which I hope you will find
useful," and as she spoke she slipped a small parcel
into his hand. "Good luck, and God bless you,
don't leave me so long without a letter again."

The train sped rapidly out of the station and
Reginald for two or three minutes stood looking
rather sadly after it. Kate had done him good,
and, as a brave-hearted woman can, made him take
a much more cheerful view of the situation. He
would not give in as yet at all events; nonsense,
he had done by far the most difficult part, had
proved at all events it was not all a mistake,
that there was some good in him, the money would
come eventually ; he would not go home to his
friends with empty pockets, a mere suppliant for
alms, though how on earth he was to live just at
present was, he admitted, an inscrutable mystery.
Then he bethought himself of Kate's present; he
opened the packet and turned over the neat little
silver mounted note-book it contained, half mechani-
cally ; it would come in very useful in his present
vocation, and it was awfully kind of Kate to think
of him. He was turning the leaves of it over idly

when a small pocket in the cover attracted his
attention; another second and he had drawn from
it a bank-note for ten pounds, and realized what the
kind-hearted girl had meant by her souvenir. He
knew this was probably pretty well the whole of
Kate's store, that it was to avoid all possible chance
of refusal on his part that she had thrust it upon
him in this manner. Men don't take money in this
wise, although the papers daily record the doings of
caricatures of them who ask nothing better, and for
a moment Reginald's brow reddened at taking
assistance, sadly though he needed it, at Kate
Darley's hands. Then with a big oath, he muttered,
"She's a girl in a thousand, and if she was born
to wear stuff gowns instead of silk, she's the
brightest, pluckiest, prettiest girl I ever met; I'll
accept her loan, and may I never prosper in this
world if it's not repaid in full before three months
are over." He wrote a very pretty letter of
acknowledgment the next day, and in it he asked
Kate to pledge herself to pay him another visit that
day month.

Kate's note-book seemed to have brought luck
with it, for within a week Reginald received a letter
from his publishers, to whom he was only known
as Richard Waters, congratulating him on his
success, and enclosing him a cheque for £50 as a first
instalment of his share of the profits accruing from
" A Parthian Flight."

It was a very long way off, those waters of Pactolus
that Reginald in his sanguine nature had pictured

to himself as the results when he first read those favourable reviews, still, to borrow a metaphor from the prize-ring, there is much satisfaction in first blood, and even his publishers held out hope that this was but the herald of further remittances, and though Reginald could not but admit that the liquidation of his debts promised to be as slow a process as those of the nation, yet, thanks to the elasticity of youth, they weighed no more upon him now than do Britannia's. He wrote in the highest spirits to Kate Darley, acquitting himself of his debt and promising her a perfect banquet upon her next visit. Kate was delighted to find how speedily her prognostications had been realised, though she did think that he need not have been in such a desperate hurry to return her money. Still she was very pleased at the good news, although she shook her head slightly over Reginald's sanguine views; she did not know what his debts amounted to, but she fancied that fifty pounds would produce no very serious impression on them; that the Squire had discharged all these debts long ago had never occurred to Reginald, and was naturally still less likely to occur to Kate. The same post had brought to her a letter from another equally sanguine young gentleman; Jim had written to her in the most exalted strain; his chance was come.

" Never mind what he did last year, his running was all wrong. I tell you ' King of the Huns ' is a great horse, and is sure to win the City and Suburban, and I am to ride him! Think of that, Kate,

I teil you it's a certainty; if I don't win, well, I can never expect Praze to put me up again; my chance has come, I tell you, and if I don't make an outrageous idiot of myself this time, I shall get a bit of riding before the year's out. It's a ' moral,' I tell you."

" Ah, Jim, my dear," said Kate as she shook her head over this letter, " I'm very glad your chance is coming to you and trust with all my heart you will be successful, but as for those ' morals,' my dear, I don't think I'll meddle with them any more. Didn't I nearly break the whole Hippodrome last May over ' King of the Huns'? Why, I shouldn't even dare to mention his name, the whole troupe would laugh at me, and say that I brought them to penury last spring."

But for all these virtuous resolutions, Kate took much too great an interest in Jim's career not to cast an eye pretty regularly over the betting on the City and Suburban, wherein " King of the Huns " figured every now and then at from twenty-five to thirty to one.

It is usually the most ordinary oversight that leads to the detection of the fugitive criminal, and Reginald Chacewater, because he has so many months baffled all enquiry, has now grown fatuous as the ostrich and does not see that his discovery is imminent. The supposition that he had perished in the accident in the Regent's Park had stopped all search on the part of his family in the first instance. Now it was well known that he was alive, and but a short time ago had been living in

Chillingham ; then again, if he had only reflected, the Rector and Lucy were aware that he was the author of *A Parthian Flight*, and that Richard Waters and Reginald Chacewater were one and the same person, and it was but natural to suppose that his publishers would be in possession of his address. What was still more to the point too, was, there was someone now determined to find him, of a very different calibre from either the Squire or the Reverend James Marton, to wit, Sam Wargrave. Sam in the course of his varied career had been engaged in a good many queer schemes, and an accurate knowledge of what other people were doing had been more than once, in his opinion, conducive to his benefit, both in mercantile transactions and on the turf. Taking up the clue at Chillingham, a sharp detective in Mr. Wargrave's employ had been for some days actively engaged in endeavouring to trace whither Reginald had gone. In possession of all particulars of the case, this man had at once decided to keep a close watch over Kate Darley, and, though she was quite un-aware of it, outside her lodgings or at the theatre, she was never allowed to move without this unseen attendant ; he had been at her heels on the morning that she took her ticket to Twybury, had travelled with her by the same train, seen her meeting with Reginald at the station, had written to Mr. War-grave to inform him that he had found " the lost mutton," and was now keeping sedulous watch and ward over Reginald at Twybury. Mr. Wargrave so far was well pleased with the return he was having for his money; he and Clara kept their surreptitiously acquired knowledge entirely to themselves; other people might think that it was no concern of theirs what Reginald Chacewater chose to do, but Sam Wargrave and his daughter thought it mattered a good deal; their spy reported that Mr. Waters, as he called himself, was apparently very hard up, that Miss Darley was still at Chillingham and had only been once over to see him.

" Hard up, my dear; hard up you see, he says, can't be too hard up; as nothing, Clara, depend upon it, brings home to a young man the folly of that sort of connection like empty pockets. A very little longer and this Darley girl will get tired of supporting him out of her earnings, and then you see, Clara, I'll walk in as a friend of the family, write him a cheque for a thousand or whatever it may be he wants, bring about a reconciliation and generally play the part of the stage uncle. After that, my dear, the game's in your hands."

" Yes, papa," returned the young lady, with a complacent smile, " once disentangle him from the web this artful hussy has woven round him and I think you may leave him pretty safely to me. You'll see he'll be a little penitent and a little ashamed of having made such a fool of himself and so quite willing to do what he's told. Besides, after his late experiences, I think I can say without vanity I count for something. Poor fellow, how glad he'll be to escape from his bondage."

CHAPTER XXVII.

"REGINALD TAKES LONG ODDS."

WHATEVER poverty may compel, one of the first instincts of a man who has been brought up as a gentleman is to repair the ravages in his attire, and to once more dress in accordance with his former station. Marryat in one of his novels relates of the hero who from great indigence was suddenly restored to affluence, that his first impulse was to send out a servant to procure befitting clothes and some Eau de Cologne. Similarly, no sooner had Reginald succeeded in obtaining cash for his publishers' cheque, than he also renovated his wardrobe. Under the pressure of hunger we rapidly revert to the primæval, and are apt to regard as superfluities all clothing that can be converted into food. The change in Reginald's raiment did not escape the eye of Mr. Wargrave's lynx-eyed agent, and, though of course, he did not know whence, he reported to that gentleman that the strain was relaxed, that Mr. Waters had evidently obtained assistance from somewhere, and was once more frequenting respectable hotels and dining-rooms. If Sam Wargrave had been well served all his life it was no more than he deserved ; he always employed good workmen, and, for such service as this, not only the best he could lay hands on, but was no niggard of his gold to boot. His instructions to the detective had been brief, but peremptory: "It won't," he said, " I fancy, be a very long job, but now you've found this Waters, stick to him like a leech; I want to know how he lives, everything he does, everything about him; remember, he oughtn't even to sneeze without your knowing it; enough, you and I know one another and you can depend upon my doing the right thing if I am satisfied." A tedious, tiring, unsavoury commission, but every man to his métier, and this one got his living in this way. Still for once the detective was fairly puzzled; what did it all mean, what was the object of it all? He knew all the preliminary facts of the case. Why did Waters, whose real name was Chacewater, persist in hiding? He had done nothing, he had committed no crime, nobody could possibly interfere with him if he chose to spend the remainder of his life in Twybury, nor was there any law to prevent his calling himself by any name that struck his fancy. Then why was Mr. Sam Wargrave so anxious to find him and know what he did? In the exercise of his profession Mr. Wargrave's detective was wont to be as patient as an Indian on the war-path. Still, he could not but think that a duller and more uninteresting case it had never been his lot to be employed in.

" How the deuce the young gent stands such a life as he leads here, I'm blessed if I know; it's killing me that's what it is, although I'm paid for it and used to carrying on this sort of game. Why, if I'd cleaned out some nobleman's plate cupboard and was keeping dark just till the thing had blown over a bit, hang me if I shouldn't think it a real relief to be 'pinched,' and be done with it."

In his intervals of relaxation the agent discovered that Twybury, though dull, was a sporting little place ; it was a small agricultural town and did a considerable trade in sheep, beeves, etc., and the surrounding farmers who frequented it had much to say about racing affairs. These spring handicaps, for instance, were a subject of much discussion at the ordinary on Saturdays of the " Blue Boar," the most popular inn in Twybury. Indeed the landlord, professedly for the accommodation of his guests, though more, perhaps, for his own aggrandizement, made a book upon all the principal events of the turf, and enjoyed so good custom as to have attained quite a name as a provincial book-maker in those parts. The billiard-room and bar-parlour too at the " Blue Boar " were more affected by the choice spirits of Twybury in the evening than elsewhere, and the consequence was that Mr. Wargrave's man, when he considered himself off duty, sometimes beguiled the weary hours by smoking a pipe or playing a game of billiards there.

Now, close as any one man may watch another, there must of necessity arrive moments when the watcher's eye is off his quarry, and it is during such temporary lapse of vigilance that his opportunity will probably come to him only to escape him.

Life in Twybury, as aforesaid, was monotonous,

and from careful study Sam Wargrave's agent knew
Reginald's habits to a nicety; he knew pretty nearly
at what time he would issue from his lodgings, and
could then pretty well foretell his movements for
the remainder of the day ; from the time he left his
lodgings to the time he returned to them, the
detective considered his duty obliged him to keep
an eye on the *soi-disant* Waters.　One morning
Reginald was late in making his appearance ; hour
after hour slipped by and still his door never opened.
What did it mean, could he be taken ill, or what
had happened ?　He had never yet known him go
out before eleven o'clock, rarely so soon, and here it
was past one ; and though he had been on guard
ever since ten, he could take his oath Waters had
never left his abode.　He waited a little longer and
then determined to enquire if he could see Mr.
Waters on some pretext ; that was not difficult to
find, and in a few minutes he was informed that,
contrary to his usual custom, Mr. Waters had
gone out early in the morning and had not
yet returned.　The agent was an impassive man
and did not waste his time in the use of bad language, but he felt pretty much like those who do,
for he guessed that whatever it might be that
Reginald was now busying himself about, that was the
very matter that he had been sent down there to
discover.　There was only one thing for it, and that
was to, at once, seek in his usual haunts the traces
of this young man.　No! luck was against him that
day ; look where he would, he could see nothing of

Reginald, but in one place he did hear of him and that was at the Railway Station; yes, he had been seen there by one or two of the officials to whom he was well-known by sight, he haunted the book-stall, and though, as the proprietor laughingly observed, he was one of the "read without paying order," he did invest in a penn'orth of newspaper sometimes. Had he left Twybury? thought the agent anxiously, but nobody seemed to think that he had done that, he had been to the station that morning, but nobody seemed to have seen him get into the train. The detective felt there was nothing for it but to go on wandering round Twybury till he once more picked up his man, when at the last moment a porter turned up, to whom in the earlier part of his Twybury time Reginald had been liberal, and he joining the discussion, said decisively that he knew Mr. Waters well, and he had seen him that morning, and that he had left the station with a young woman. "A young woman!" ejaculated the agent to himself, " I see it all now, Miss Darell is the only young woman he's spoken to since he's been here; that's the meaning of it, she's come over from Chillingham; and now it's high time I found them and see what they're up to, they may mean being off together again now he's got hold of money."

But no, search diligently though he might, anxiously as he might enquire for a gentleman and lady for whom he had got a note, which was to be delivered immediately, he failed utterly to come across the pair till late in the afternoon, when he caught sight of them walking leisurely towards the station. Needless to say he followed, but was only rewarded by seeing that Kate Darell was the young woman, and that Reginald embraced her tenderly before putting her into the train for Chillingham. Although disconcerted at having no knowledge of how the pair had passed the day, yet the detective did not suppose that it mattered much ; and though he supposed there was nothing more to be done, resolved not to lose sight of Reginald again until he had seen him safely housed for the night. That being done without further incident, the agent thought he would drop into the " Blue Boar," and smoke a pipe.

He was listening dreamily to the gossip going on in the bar-parlour when a voice smote upon his ear that brought him instantly to his feet. Surely, he thought, those were Waters' tones inquiring at the bar if Mr. Brockles was in.

" Yes, sir, he is," replied the officiating ministress, " he's up in the billiard-room, where, if it's anything about a horse, I was to send word to him."

" Then you'd better do so," rejoined Reginald ; " ask him to step down for two or three minutes."

" Are you the gentleman who's got a fancy ? " enquired the landlord smiling, as he entered the bar in compliance with the summons that had been sent to him. " Pray step inside, and I shall only be too happy to accommodate you if I have not already laid." As he spoke Reginald entered the bar, and

17

the detective who, under the pretence of requiring a cigar, had drawn stealthily to the door of the parlour behind it, busied himself in selecting one from the box that the lady in charge proffered him.

"'King of the Huns' for the City and Sub-urban," was the prompt reply, and the detective's ears were full-cock at the announcement.

"Well, he's come up a bit to-day, so I see by the papers. I can't afford to lay you above twenty-fives; what shall I put it down to, five or ten pounds?"

"I want it to fifty," replied Reginald; "put me down twelve hundred and fifty to fifty."

"Excuse me," said Mr. Brockles, "but that's rather a stiff bet in my way of business, and you must remember I haven't the pleasure of knowing you, sir."

"There's the money," replied young Chacewater, and as he spoke he took from his vest pocket a small note-book and extracting a fifty-pound note proffered it to the landlord.

"No, no," replied Mr. Brockles, "that won't do, the law don't allow us to take money in that way; but no matter, I think I can trust you; twelve hundred and fifty to fifty against 'King of the Huns' for the City and Suburban, it is! You can put it down, sir."

"All right, Mr. Brockles," rejoined Reginald, and with a nod of good-night he at once took his departure.

"It's that young woman who's doing the raven business and feeding him," murmured the detective,

as he returned to his seat. " Here he is one day
so hard up he scarcely knows how to pay for a
dinner, Miss Darell appears, and at once he is in
high feather. Now she appears again, and d—n
me, here he is flashing about and betting in fifties.
But then how does she get it ? that's what beats me.
However, it's for Mr. Wargrave to put things together. He didn't think proper to tell me what his
object was, my business is to find out all I can
about this young Chacewater, *alias* Waters, and
report accordingly."

Mr. Wargrave found much food for reflection
when he received his agent's account of Reginald's
latest doings. That he should be in funds at all was
a matter of disappointment to him, as he conceived
that his own schemes would be easier to carry out
if Reginald could be brought to feel the pressure of
poverty. That he should be the possessor of fifty
pounds, though an unpleasant surprise, did not
trouble him much, and a derisive smile spread over
his face at the thought of a young man seeking to
repair his shattered fortunes by betting on horse
races; but what had induced him to back " King of
the Huns," for the City and Suburban was a thing
to be worked out, and it took an astute man like
Mr. Wargrave but a very short time to put the
puzzle together. According to his informant,
Reginald backed this horse at night after spending
the day with Kate Darell; he remembered that the
name of the lad who had ridden the " King " in the
Leger was Darley, what more likely than that he

17*

was in some way connected, and a very few
enquiries in the village told him that they were
brother and sister. Jim, he knew, was a boy in
Praze's stable, and it was therefore pretty conclusive
that that was the source from which Reginald
derived his information. Now, in his own opinion,
the "King" was a bad horse, and however lightly
weighted he doubted his ability to win the race in
question. But Sam Wargrave was by no means
pig-headed, if Praze thought differently he was not
the man to deny that the trainer might know more
about it than he did.

"They didn't know everything down in Judee,"
as the famous John P. Robinson is reported to
have said, and Sam Wargrave was not at all above
listening to a capable opinion from another, though
it might be diametrically opposed to his own. It
was quite certain that Reginald had backed " King
of the Huns "; it was equally clear that in the event
of the " King's " success he would win a comparatively large sum of money and that that would not
at all suit the ends Mr. Wargrave and his daughter
had in view. Ergo, " King of the Huns " must be
prevented from winning the City and Suburban,
but how ? And though he sat and pondered over it
for some time, Mr. Wargrave could think of no way
in which he could influence the destinies of Mr.
Bramber's colt upon that occasion. At last he
resolved to disembosom himself of his perplexity to
his daughter ; true, he didn't in the least see how
she could help him, but she was a clever girl, and

after all the matter was as much, aye, even more, her business than his own.

Clara listened attentively to her father's account of all Reginald's doings at Twybury. She was not a young woman to be daunted by obstacles, and if she knit her brows, it was more from angry impatience at the idea of her destined husband being still infatuated about that wretched Darley girl, than at the apprehension of the ultimate defeat of her schemes. She thought over it for some minutes, and taking a paper, which lay upon the table, glanced carelessly over a list of the probable starters for the same race, and an attempt on the part of the writer of the article to pick the winner. Suddenly a triumphant smile flashed across her face. "Don't be afraid, papa," she cried, triumphantly. "I think I see my way. I'll bet you a dozen pair of gloves that ' King of the Huns ' is not in the first three for the City and Suburban."

"But, Clara, my dear, I don't understand——"

"No reason you should," she replied gaily. "No need for you to trouble yourself more about it; but you will see it will be as I say."

CHAPTER XXVIII.

"KATE GOES DOWN TO BOTTLESBY."

IF there was a gentleman in his calling who felt tolerably well satisfied with himself, it was Mr. Praze on these bright, breezy April mornings. Day by day he grew more pleased with the "King" as he strode along in the sharp gallops that were now pretty constantly his portion. The day of the race drew near, and no horse could be in better health or in higher heart; he showed, moveover, not a trace of that temper which had so disconcerted the stable the previous summer; on the contrary, Jim assured his master that the horse went as kindly with him as possible, and that, in sporting parlance, he could "put him anywhere." The colt, too, was surely but slowly stealing up in the market, which told the trainer that the somewhat extensive commission which he had given to his emissaries to back him was being quietly and dexterously executed. Jim Darley, also, was in the highest possible spirits, and as confident of sailing in an easy winner for the great Epsom Handicap as if the race was already over. Suddenly the "King" began to decline rather ominously in the betting, in consequence of a rumour, so said the papers, that there was great doubt about his starting. Mr. Praze smiled grimly to himself as he read this, for as far as anything could be deemed certain on the Turf, it was that " King of the Huns " would do his best to win the City and Suburban. With Jim Darley it was different; he naturally had not the calmness which comes to the veteran who has braved the ups and downs of many a campaign. To use his own expression, " he knew it was all right," and yet these adverse rumours made Jim thoroughly uncomfortable. He could not but remember how the clouds had gathered around the " King's " name previous to that disastrous Derby, and feared that once again a conspiracy existed to work him evil.

If Jim Darley was disturbed at the way the horse travels in the betting market, it is easy to understand how anxious his sister is getting at all these adverse reports. Note after note comes to Jim with as urgent enquiries concerning the " King's " health and well-being as if he was in good truth one of the leading rulers of Europe instead of being merely a race-horse who has rather disgraced himself. The girl cannot but remember that it was she who had counselled Reginald to attempt to cut the Gordian knot of his difficulties in this wise; that it was she who had advised the laying out of that second fifty-pound note, which he had received from his publishers not forty-eight hours before, and now it looked as if she might as well have persuaded him to throw his hard-won earnings into the fire; that he is not destined even to have a run for his money, and that if these tales in the papers are true, " King

of the Huns" would be quietly in his stable when
the crowd were cheering for the winner of the City
and Suburban. Although Jim's replies were so far
reassuring, insomuch as he declared that there was
nothing the matter, yet it was easy to perceive from
the tone of his letters that the lad himself was
extremely uneasy. In a different way, bear in
mind, this race was quite as momentous a matter to
him as it was to Reginald Chacewater; it might
almost be said more so ; it was to be his first opening,
a prelude to what to him meant honours, fame and
wealth, and that some indefinable cause should
threaten to deprive him of this naturally perturbed
Jim Darley greatly. Like his sister, he watched the
papers closely, and it looked as if their fears were
distantly realised. "King of the Huns" went from
bad to worse in the betting, retrograding in that
ominous manner that betokens that some of the
fielders are in possession of certain information to his
detriment, and the floating rumours at length even
disturbed the serenity of the imperturbable Mr. Praze.
A prompt man was Mr. Praze when he considered his
intervention called for. The day he came to that
conclusion saw him in Town and in close conference
with his own commissioner. That worthy at once
told him that he had been as much dumbfounded
at the fierce fire opened on the horse as he, the
trainer, could be ; that he had made diligent
enquiry as to what grounds the "King's" opponents
were going on, and that, as far as he could ascertain,
it all originated in a statement which Mr. Bramber

had made during a brief visit to London about ten days ago, to wit, that " King of the Huns " would not run.

" If that's all," rejoined the trainer laughing, " I am sorry for them, because I have entire control of the horse ; he's fit as fiddles, and run he will, as sure as I stand here."

" Well you ought to know," replied the commissioner, " but as he's entered in Bramber's name no wonder some of 'em thought there was something in it."

Mr. Praze made no reply, just nodded and took his leave, but as he walked away he bethought him that Tom Bramber had shown himself just a little bit queer in his ways the last few months, he had never turned up at Doncaster for instance, he was going to give up the farm he had lived on all his life, he was desirous of selling his share of the horse, just at a time when the most ordinary judge of turf matters would have known that it was a far wiser policy to stick to his bargain, that the colt's failures in the preceding year while depreciating his value on the one hand, by reducing his weight in handicaps, gave him a great chance of redeeming his character on the other. It surely never would enter Tom's head to do anything without consulting him, more especially anything so foolish as to strike " King of the Huns " out of a big race, which he would in all probability win, but at the same time the trainer was perfectly aware that he had the power to do so, as nominator of the horse ; it was also in his hands whether he should run or decline the engagement. It was almost preposterous to think that Tom Bramber could even dream of such a thing, but Mr. Praze stood to win a very good stake over the "King," and looked upon this handicap to compensate him for all previous disappointments. Mr. Praze was not the man to leave more than he could possibly help to chance under such circumstances, and rapidly came to the conclusion that, to obviate all mistakes or foolishness, it would be better that he should run down to Bottlesby and see Tom Bramber himself. " Sam Wargrave and his friends can't have anything to do with it this time anyhow," muttered Mr. Praze as he drove straight to the station, and then he bethought him that Sam Wargrave lived somewhere near Bottlesby, and in another moment a singular idea flashed across his mind. " It would be a queer start," he muttered, " but, hang me if I don't think old Sam's in it again, only this time he's got at the man instead of the horse."

Having taken his ticket, the trainer leisurely paced the platform till such time as the Bottlesby train should start. He soon became aware of a slight, pretty, lady-like girl who was like himself awaiting her train. I have heard it remarked that a man who is a good judge of a horse has also a keen eye for a pretty woman; be that as it may, Mr. Praze was decidedly struck by the young lady in question, and not only looked upon her with admiring eyes, but took rather more notice of her than is customary. The fact was, that the trainer not only thought it a very pretty face, but was haunted with the idea that he had seen it before, and so he had, although it was three years ago, and he had but a glimpse of it then; still it was not that recollection that was now puzzling Praze, but Kate Darley bore, if not a striking yet a strong resemblance to her brother, and that it was which troubled the trainer's mind.

It was not long before Kate became aware of her admirer, and no sooner had she succeeded in stealing a good look at him than she at once knew him ; she had never set eyes upon him but on that one occasion when Jim had nearly jumped the pony on the top of him in the Hampshire lane ; but the three years had made no change in the trainer, while it had changed the girl from an untidy romp of seventeen to a self-possessed, lady-like young woman ; if it hadn't been for her brother being in his employ, it was not likely that even a shadow of her face would have lived in Mr. Praze's memory. As the spring advanced, Mr. Slater, according to his usual custom, had sent his branch establishments on their travels, the Chillingham troupe had started on tour, and Mr. Slater was so impressed with the reports sent him of Miss Darell's success in the Hippodrome there that he had ordered her up to head-quarters, and she was now advertised to make her first appearance in a few days at the Royal Hippodrome in Argyle Street. Feverishly anxious at Jim's despondent notes, to say nothing of all the

newspaper *canards* concerning " King of the Huns,'
Kate has come to the same resolution as Mr. Praze,
and resolved to run down to Bottlesby and see Tom
Bramber herself. She had hesitated a great deal
over taking this step, for she had a vivid recollection
of their last stormy interview, and she knew the
light-o'-love Tom Bramber held her. Her brows knit
and her eyes flashed angrily even yet, as she
thought of it, but there was so much at stake, not
only for Reginald but for Jim, that she had resolved
to humble herself, to put her pride in her pocket,
and in the belief Tom Bramber had really loved her,
to beg this favour at his hands, to implore him for
Jim's sake, for Reginald's sake, not to stand in the
way of the " King's " running at Epsom. The sight
of the horse's trainer at the station was a surprise for
Kate ; she could hardly suppose that Mr. Praze would
recollect her, and yet from the way he noticed her,
it really seemed as if he did. She debated much
with herself whether she should acknowledge him ;
she had not that fear of putting direct questions
to him which her brother had, but then it was no
use her speaking to him unless she plunged *in
medias res*, and that might work mischief to Jim.
She was sorely puzzled what to do, and before she
had made up her mind the sharp cry of, " Take your
places," compelled her to jump into the train, and
the opportunity was lost.

Bottlesby Station, as is often the case in these
country places, was some little distance from
Bottlesby itself, and moreover Tom Bramber's farm

was a couple of miles or so on the other side of the village. Hack carriages were scarce, and in reply to Kate's enquiry as to whether he could get her a conveyance to take her to Mr. Bramber's, the porter speedily came back with the information that the only two flys were taken, that one of them had been engaged by a gentleman who was going to Mr. Bramber's.

"He's got no luggage, Miss," continued the man, who knew her well, "he could give you a lift."

Upon the porter preferring the request to Mr. Praze, that gentleman replied he would be only too pleased to give Miss Darley a seat, and the result was that Kate and the trainer drove off together to see Tom Bramber. Praze, by this time, was perfectly aware who his fellow passenger was, but for all that the errand that had brought them both to Bottlesby was not mentioned between them, nor was there any reference to racing matters further than that Kate alluded to her brother being in Mr. Praze's employ, and the trainer in reply remarked that Jim was a good, steady lad, and safe to do well in the profession he had chosen.

On their arrival at the house, in answer to their enquiries, Bramber's old housekeeper said that her master was at home, at least, he wasn't in the house just that moment, but he was only somewhere about the farm, and if they would just step into the parlour and wait for him, she would send some one to look for him, anyway he wouldn't be long; and with that she ushered them into the room, which it

was evident Tom habitually used, excusing herself
for doing so by the intimation that there was no fire
in the best parlour, and that the days were a bit
chill as yet.

"Now, Miss Darley," said the trainer as they
seated themselves, "I don't know what your business with Bramber may be, but as soon as he makes
his appearance, I'll take a turn outside and leave you
here to have a talk with him."

Kate had accidentally taken her seat near the
writing-table which stood in one of the windows,
and as Mr. Praze spoke her eyes fell upon two
letters which were lying upon it. One was addressed
in Tom's own hand to Messrs. Weatherby and Son,
Old Burlington Street; the other was addressed to
Mr. Thomas Bramber, and the handwriting was
apparently that of a woman. Kate had not a
brother in a racing stable without having acquired
considerable racing knowledge; she knew very well
that Messrs. Weatherby were the officials appointed
by the Jockey Club to whom entries for great races
were made, and equally to whom the striking out
of horses so entered was notified. The quick-witted
girl divined what had happened in a moment, and
turning to the trainer exclaimed:

"It strikes me, Mr. Praze, that we're both here
upon the same business, and if so, should my appeal
be successful, you will be spared further trouble,
we are only just in time; there," she said, rising
and pointing to the table, "lies the order to scratch
'King of the Huns' for the City and Suburban,

and there also lies the letter of the woman at whose instigation Mr. Bramber has done so."

Mr. Praze cast one glance at the writing-table, and then threw a glance of admiration on his companion; he understood at once what that letter to Old Burlington Street meant, but that Kate should have divined it so quickly certainly was astonishing; whether she was right about a woman being at the bottom of it, there was now no time to speculate.

" You are quite right, Miss Darley," he replied, " that's exactly what I wish to prevent. I feel sure I cannot do better than leave the matter in your hands, and that after you have seen Bramber, you will tell me that letter has been destroyed," and with that Mr. Praze left the room and betook himself to the fireless best parlour, feeling quite convinced that his policy at present was to keep out of the way.

CHAPTER XXIX.

CLARA'S LETTER.

CLARA WARGRAVE was not only a clever woman, but she possessed many of the ingredients that go to compose a great conspirator, cool-headed, with unflinching nerve, and showing an undaunted front under difficulties, to say nothing of great fertility of resource, she was no light antagonist to have pitted against one. She was determined to marry Reginald Chacewater, and not the less likely to carry her point because her feelings were so little involved in the matter. Her father was both fidgetty and uncomfortable; Clara, like all notable plotters, refused to show her cards; she declined to let him know how she intended to proceed, and merely replied when he pressed her, " Never mind, Papa, you leave it to me, and you'll see that ' King of the Huns ' will play a very minor part in the City and Suburban."

Sam Wargrave waxed quite irritable over the subject; what did she want to make such a confounded mystery of the affair for; was he not as much interested in it as she ? Sam Wargrave indeed was as wild with vexation as a man of his buccaneering instincts is wont to become, when he is conscious of a big robbery going on without his being in it. Strictly speaking, it was a duel between these two girls; Clara, relying for success upon the vengeful feelings of a disappointed lover; Kate, on the other hand, trusting that Tom's had been too honest a love not to induce him to refrain from harming those near and dear to her.

" Only give me vanity, and you may take all the other passions," saith Sheridan. And, taking all in all, it is probably the most powerful factor that sways mankind. Miss Wargrave, at all events, had the most implicit faith in its influence, when she penned the letter that had attracted Kate's attention, and which she recognised as a woman's, though in a hand unknown to her. If her father chafed over the mystery in which it pleased Clara to veil her proceedings, he, at all events, comforted himself by the reflection that the ominous decline of the horse in the betting went far to show that, whatever her plan might be, it promised to be successful, and but for knowing it was hardly worth his while, Sam Wargrave would have been sorely tempted to field heavily against the horse himself, but there was so little inclination to back the " King " now, that there would be little to gain by doing so. He and his daughter little thought, as they read in their morning paper that " King of the Huns " was friendless, at the proffered odds of fifty to one, that the battle of the City and Suburban was being fought out at a farm-house within a few miles of them.

Kate had not long to wait before she heard Bramber's step outside. He stopped at the front-door for a moment to speak to his housekeeper, who was waiting there to receive him. Both visitors were well-known to her; Mr. Praze had, upon more than one occasion, stayed at the farm; and as for Kate Darley, she had known her ever since she was a child. The good lady indeed was so wroth with Kate just at present that it is doubtful whether she would have gained such easy admittance to the house had she not been accompanied by the trainer. Mrs. Stephens was of course not ignorant of Bottlesby gossip. She not only looked upon Kate as no better than she should be, but she also knew that her master was said to have been rather sweet upon the girl; and that anybody who had the chance should think twice about marrying Tom

18

Bramber, amounted to positive impertinence in the housekeeper's eyes. There was nobody good enough for Master Tom, she thought, for miles round; he had had a narrow escape, he was well out of it; and now, what did the brazen little baggage want with him? Mr. Praze's arrival with Kate had outwardly stifled all these reflections. The trainer, she knew, had always been an honoured guest; and as she knew Jim Darley was apprenticed to Mr. Praze, she came to the hasty conclusion that his sister also might be in some way muddled up in the racing business. That Praze should have come over to see him did not surprise Tom much; but what on earth Kate Darley could want with him Tom could not conjecture. That, after their last interview, she should even wish to see him again, he should have thought improbable, and why accompanied by the trainer? Another moment and he had thrown open the door, and found himself face to face with this false love of his.

He made no attempt to offer her his hand, but with a rather brusque bow, said :

" I don't know of what use I can be to you, Miss Darley, but I suppose you have something to ask of me, or else I should have scarce seen you here. I can only trust old Stephens has done her duty, and asked what she shall get for you after your journey ? "

Kate's eyes flashed ominously for a moment, and then regaining her self-control, she replied—" It would scarcely be a question of meat and drink that brought me to your house, Mr. Bramber. I have come, not so much to beg a favour at your hands, as to ask you not to inflict an undeserved disappointment on two who are near and dear to me, to ask you only to do what is right, to act in the honest, straightforward manner that all who know you are justified in expecting at your hands."

" You are talking riddles to me," he rejoined

" A mere quibble," she returned hotly. " You know, as well as I do, to what I am alluding."

" And suppose I do ; I have only to say I see no necessity for disclosing my intentions."

" You have done so already," she cried. " That letter to Messrs. Weatherby tells me what you have done ; and that other tells me that it is at woman's dictation that you have done it."

" Yes," he said, with an uglier smile than had ever been seen across Tom Bramber's face. " Stephens should have known better than to have left you alone with my letters ; it was not likely that one of your sex should resist such temptation."

It was an ungenerous retort, and he felt that it was so the minute the words had escaped his lips. But this girl was very dear to him ; and though he would hurt no hair of her head, he was determined to wreak what vengeance he might upon her seducer.

" You closed *your* letter yourself, look at it, you will find it still unopened ; as for that other, I haven't touched it ; I don't know who wrote it—but I can tell you what she says. What her object may

18*

be, I don't know. But she urges you to wreak vengeance on me, because I had no love to give you; to strike at me through my brother, looking anxiously forward to the winning of his first race."

"It is nothing of the kind," replied Bramber fiercely. "The writer urges me to inflict such punishment as I may on the scoundrel who not only stole my love from me, but brought her to shame besides; who snatched from me the woman I loved with all my heart and soul, to make her the plaything of his idle moments. I swore Reginald Chacewater should, if it ever were in my power, pay dearly for the wrong he had done you, and I'll keep my word."

Kate coloured, and for a moment gazed defiantly into his face; it was set hard, and she saw that he meant what he said.

"Your informant lies," she said at length in a low tone, "you might have known me better, Tom Bramber, than to believe that of me, however appearances may be against me."

"Do you dare to tell me," he exclaimed excitedly, "that it is not true, that you are not—— ?"

"Reginald Chacewater never said a word to me that any girl need have been ashamed to listen to," replied Kate proudly.

"And what is he then to you, that, regardless of your good name, you mix yourself up with him in this manner?"

"My husband," replied Kate quietly.

"Your husband?" replied Tom incredulously,

" then why did you deny it when I went to see you at Chillingham—why did you refuse to admit that he was so to Mr. Marton, why did you allow Bottlesby and all the country to think that you were his mistress ? God knows, Kate, that no man was ever more unwilling to believe that of you than me."

The look of indignation with which she heard him softened as he finished speaking.

"I am trusting you with a great secret, and you must promise that it shall go no further until I give you leave. Now listen to me. Reginald and I met by the merest chance at Chillingham; it had never entered either of our heads that anyone would suppose we had gone off together; when you saw me there I was neither married to him nor pledged to him ; I had only just awoke to the fact that I was in love with him, and hoped that he loved me. Your coming caused him to leave Chillingham and go to Twybury, and there I went over twice to see him; the second time he asked me to marry him, and," she continued, blushing a little, "he was so confident of my answer that he had made every preparation, and we were quietly married that very morning."

Sam Wargrave's agent had no idea even yet of what a mistake his want of vigilance had been that eventful morning at Twybury. It would have saved his employer and Miss Wargrave much trouble and anxiety.

" That you couldn't fancy me, Kate, will be a

sore disappointment to me for many a long day,"
rejoined Tom Bramber slowly, " but it lightens it a
deal to know that you are the young Squire's
lawful wife. When Mr. Reginald offered you an
honest love and you had to decide between us, well,
it could only end one way, and, Kate," he continued,
extending his hand, "as far as a beaten man can do,
I congratulate you."

A warm hand-shake was exchanged between
them, and after a little consideration Tom said, " I
don't think this will be wanted now," and as he
spoke he took up the letter addressed to Messrs.
Weatherby and tossed it into the fire. " But there
is something about this that I don't understand,"
and as he spoke he took up the letter addressed to
himself in a woman's hand. " The writer urges me
to take vengeance on Reginald Chacewater, and points
out that striking ' King of the Huns ' out of the City
and Suburban will go far to ruin him. I don't know
who she is or how she knows this, but is it true ?
Has the young Squire backed my horse heavily, and
if so how came he to do it ? "

" He did it because I told him," replied Kate, " he
did it for fifty pounds, which means a lot of money
to him just now."

" And you got your inspiration from Jim, I suppose ? That I understand, but who is this woman
and what is she driving at ? "

" Let me see the letter," replied Kate quietly,
" No," she continued after she had read it, " it is
written by a woman, but I have no idea who; its

object, I should say, is to injure Reginald, I doubt otherwise if she much cares whether your horse runs or not. May I keep it? I shall perhaps meet the handwriting again some day."

"If you like; and now I must really go and shake hands with Praze, and see what he wants, though I daresay you know."

"That letter to Weatherby burnt, and something to eat," replied Kate laughing, "but don't forget I'm Miss Darley yet for a little while."

Tom found the trainer smoking a cigar outside, and one glance at his face informed Mr. Praze that his mission was accomplished. But during all this time the latter had been turning things over in his mind and had come to the conclusion that Sam Wargrave had a finger in the pie after all. He had no grounds for this suspicion, but, shrewd man as he was, he had, so to speak, got Wargrave on the brain—all he knew for certain was that Tom had written a letter to Weatherby. But Sam Wargrave or his friends had conspired against the horse for the Derby last year, and, though he could not understand why, he believed he had done so again, and upon this point he could not help questioning Tom. Bramber willingly told him all he knew about it, passing over the false charge against Kate, as was only natural; he owned that the letter to Weatherby had been what the trainer suspected, said that he had written it in a moment of extreme exasperation caused by a hideous calumny against people he both loved and respected; who their

calumniator was he honestly didn't know, but that
it was all a lie he was now thoroughly convinced.

Mr. Praze was silent for a little after Tom
finished, and then said, " Has Wargrave any spite
against you?　Have you ever done anything to
offend him ? "

" No," replied Tom; " how could I ?　I'm no
tenant of his, you know ; we exchange a few words
when we meet ; that is all."

" Well, you see," continued the trainer, " Sam
Wargrave, to say the least of it, had a pretty shrewd
idea that 'King of the Huns' wouldn't win at
Epsom last Spring, and I thought he might be
interfering again."

" Interfering ! " cried Tom.　" Why you told me
yourself it was the horse's temper lost him the
Derby.　Wargrave, I know, didn't fancy him for the
race ; neither did many other people.　What do you
mean ? "

" I've no more to say than this," rejoined Mr.
Praze.　" Have you shown Miss Darley that letter ?
she's a clever girl that, and more likely to read the
riddle than either you or I.　Whoever wrote you
the letter had reason for it."

Tom nodded assent, and Mr. Praze, being in a
hurry to get back to Town, declined to partake of
anything further than a glass of sherry, and Kate
took advantage of his fly to return under the
trainer's escort.

CHAPTER XXX.

"GAME AND RUBBER."

THE effects of that scene in Tom Bramber's parlour showed themselves rapidly in two or three different directions; Jim Darley, for one, was made jubilant by a few reassuring lines from his sister, and also by the way his horse strode along with him morning after morning; in the betting market, too, there was a marked difference, in the language of Tattersall's the "'King' had come again," and those very liberal odds of a few days ago were no longer proffered. On the contrary, it seemed to have dawned at last upon the public that though the "King" might not be so good a horse as he had been at one time considered, still that in the forthcoming race he had been very leniently treated, and must, at all events, have a fair outside chance. Sam Wargrave viewed with apprehension the shortening price quoted about Mr. Bramber's "King of the Huns," and nervously questioned his daughter as to whether she was quite certain the means she had taken to prevent the horse's winning were sure and efficacious. Miss Wargrave had faith in her own cleverness; she had no belief in Kate's marriage, and she deemed herself an excellent judge of human nature and of the motives that swayed it.

That a man like Bramber should hesitate to revenge himself upon one who had bereft him of the woman he loved never entered her calculations, and that she had not been so very much out in her reckoning we have already seen. But on one point she had been mistaken, and that was in being utterly in-credulous that Kate could be a wife. She was not so very far out in the first instance, for Kate was not married when Clara devised her scheme; but then neither was she what Miss Wargrave deemed her. It is true it might be more satisfactory to learn that the horse's doom was already sealed; but then Clara comforted herself with the reflection that a man in Bramber's position would gloat over such vengeance as he could take, and prolong it till the last moment to make it sweeter. On another point her father had unwittingly led her astray; although his agent had correctly reported to Sam Wargrave the exact amount of Reginald's bet, yet Sam thought it highly improbable that the presumptive heir to Chacewater Grange had confined himself to such betting in sugar plums as this was. Clara, there-fore, looked upon the result of this race as a much more serious thing to Reginald than it really was.

But the day has arrived, and, to Mr. Wargrave's disgust, when he opens his daily paper he reads that hundreds to six are taken freely about "King of the Huns." He is so excited on the subject that he seizes a Bradshaw, and, thanks to his habits of early rising, discovers that he has time to catch a train which will land him in London, and enable him to

proceed thence to Epsom, and see the City and
Suburban run for. He announces his intention to
his daughter, and further points out to her in the
racing intelligence that the horse is spoken of as
having arrived at Epsom. It is not a question of
money with Mr. Wargrave ; strong as is his belief
in that, he recognises that this is something more ;
that his future peace and comfort depend materially
upon the fair Clara being settled in life. Clara
herself is still serenely confident in the success of
her scheme, and adheres blindly to her opinion
as to why Bramber still stays his hand. She
obstinately declines to tell her father why she is
so confident, and, not sharing in her belief, Mr.
Wargrave starts on his journey. On arriving at
Epsom, Sam pushes his way at once into the betting
ring. There is no particular change in the situation ;
although by no means first favourite, " King of the
Huns " is still firm at the odds quoted in the
morning paper ; there seems to be no doubt in anybody's mind that the horse is going to start, and
Mr. Wargrave is still more mystified than ever as
to his daughter's proceedings. He remembers now
that, though he had always supposed it was in consequence of some occult influence of hers that Tom
Bramber had been led to contemplate scratching
the horse as was rumoured in the papers, yet Clara
had never said that the " King " would not start,
but only that he would not finish in the first three.
About his starting there could be now no question,
for his number was up on the telegraph board, and

Jim Darley announced as his rider. Had Clara
been with him and seen this, she would have
clapped her hands, and pronounced it the refinement of revenge, and worth waiting for. To deal
such a blow at Kate's lover at the hands of her own
brother, Clara would have looked upon as a conception which did Bramber infinite credit. But her
father understood no such subtleties. Mr. Wargrave was a practical man, and it did not take him
long to read the cards aright when they were once
down on the table. He remembered at once who
Jim Darley was; it had not occurred to him before
that it was no doubt through this boy's sister that
Reginald derived the information which had caused
him to back "King of the Huns"; and it was
hardly to be supposed that Jim Darley had gone out
of his way to mislead Kate about the race. He
recollected the boy had ridden the horse in the
Leger, and, beaten though he was, Sam Wargrave
attributed it to no fault of horsemanship. "No,"
he muttered; "he's meant this time, and it's too
late to interfere now; if he's only fit, he'll win
to-day. I'll just walk round to the Paddock, and
have a look at him."

The process of weighing-out had been completed,
sheets were stripped, saddles adjusted, and riders
thrown on to the backs of their respective mounts,
when Wargrave got to the Paddock. His quick
eye speedily caught sight of the colours he wanted,
and Wargrave walked over to take stock of "King
of the Huns." Like many a racing man, although

he knew nothing of hunting, he was a judge of a horse, and knew when he had undergone a thorough preparation. Two or three minutes sufficed to show that "King of the Huns" had done all that was necessary in that line, and that, if beaten to-day, it would be from no fault of his trainer. Jim Darley, having settled himself in the saddle, was walking his horse slowly away to join his brother jockeys as they filed out of the Paddock; for a moment he was alone. Sam Wargrave threw a quick glance around to where he had seen Praze and Bramber in earnest conversation two or three minutes before; they were still there, near the gate of the enclosure. Quick as thought, he stepped forward, as if to have one more look at the "King" before he went out, on to the course.

"That's a beautiful colt of yours, my lad," he said, addressing Jim. "Odds against; why it's a thousand to ten *on* him. I'll lay it," he continued with a meaning glance at young Darley.

For a moment Jim seemed about to speak, his eyes sparkled, with greed as Wargrave deemed, at the offer; but he apparently thought better of it, and, confining his reply to a glance of intelligence and a slight nod, continued his way. As he neared the gate, Praze stepped forward, and, in a low voice, asked him what that fellow said to him.

"I will tell you after the race, sir," replied Jim quietly.

The trainer looked keenly at him for a moment, and then said, "Remember what I told you; the old orders; get comfortably round Tattenham Corner and then " cut their throats."

As for Wargrave, he walked back to the stand, with the proud consciousness of having done his duty to himself and his family. That any boy brought up in a racing stable could fail to understand his villainous offer, Sam never doubted, and, at all events in the present instance, he was right. It was no time to say much, but he thought more highly of Jim than ever for his tacit acceptance of his infamous bet. A more deliberate bribe to a jockey to prevent his horse winning it would have been impossible to offer, and Wargrave felt a little uncomfortable as this occurred to him. It was a good many years since he took part in a fraud of this kind, and he winced a little as he thought of it. If the boy should tell, what would men say of it? as a respectable country gentleman he could not afford to have stories of this sort flying about to his detriment. However, he consoled himself with the thought that if Jim Darley won his wager, he would probably hold his tongue for his own sake, and if on the contrary " King of the Huns" was returned successful the boy could not possibly know who he was, and if he kept away from race-courses for some few months the whole thing would be forgotten.

It's a queer assertion to make perhaps, but it is at all events not more foolish than on speculating how many cycles longer this world of ours is going

to exist, but I never see a big race won without
thinking how many far-away dramas may be concerned in the result. It is, of course, the same in
all matters by which money may be possibly lost or
won, and though one often hears the stern dictum
that nobody ever made money by horse racing, yet
where there are losers there must be winners; and
a successful Derby may mean a season of temporary
affluence. To have won the Club Sweep would
hardly seem to justify matrimony and increased
expenditure, and yet to Reginald Chacewater and
his pretty wife, seated on the box of a brougham
opposite the Grand Stand, the race they have come
to witness represents a kind of equivalent to this. A
still further remittance from his publishers has put
Reginald in funds, and he has come up to London
and brought his wife down to Epsom to see, as
he says, their fate decided. If "King of the
Huns" should prove victorious, then, as Reginald
expresses it, "they will go to the Grange, he with
gold galore in his pockets, laurels round his brow
and such penitence as he can muster in his heart for
his past behaviour. ("But it gave you to me, Kate,
all the same," he interpolates). "If that noble
animal fails us, then we must go all the same,
though penniless, and trust to fame to cover our
impecuniosity. For, you know, Kate, my wife can't
go on riding in a circus; there'll be a row, I
suppose, at first, but they always liked you at the
Grange, and they'll come round in a little." And
though liking, and not in the least ashamed of her

profession, Kate, who had been brought up in the fitting reverence of the Grange family, knew that it was not in accordance with things socially, that Mrs. Reginald Chacewater should be figuring as a star artiste at the Royal Hippodrome.

Their modest luncheon was over, and standing on the box-seat of the brougham steadying herself with one hand placed upon her husband's shoulder, Kate is anxiously waiting the clang of the bell that shall proclaim the competitors for the City and Suburban are away. Will Jim win? His last letter was very confident; it is only his second race, and there are so many crack horsemen against him; it means so much to him, and it will make it so much easier for *her*. She dreads this going home to the Grange, she knows that the old Squire will look upon his son's marriage as a terrible *mésalliance;* it is not much, but surely it would soften things a little if Reginald could go home with full pockets, it would at all events be better. She is terribly afraid that this marriage may cause a fatal rupture between Reginald and his parents, and though she knows she should still be guilty of marrying him, if it were yet to do, it would cause much bitterness to her if she had come between him and his father and mother.

" Another false start," she gasped wearily.

" Not a bit of it," cried Reginald,, " the flag's down in earnest this time, and Jim's well away on the far side," and as he spoke the bell pealed out loudly, though, unlike the " Bells of Shandon,"

by no means musically. If not leading, Jim was
well in the front rank, and the "King," coming
down the hill in grand style, showed prominently
in the race, as they neared the Corner, making
Kate's heart beat high with exultation, and bringing
a curse at his rider's stupidity to Mr. Wargrave's
lips. At the turn, Jim steadied his horse, and going
wide round it, lost two or three lengths, but once
in the straight and young Darley lost no time in
taking the "King" up to his horses, and in another
few strides came along with the lead. From this
out, it was the Biennial over again. Once in front
the black and scarlet hoops stalled off every challenge, were never caught, and finally won with the
greatest ease by three lengths.

"Oh, Reginald, isn't it glorious, it's quite delightful, and wasn't it worth coming all the way
to see?"

"Yes, it is rather a *coup* for all of us," rejoined
her husband, as he helped her off the box seat,
"we've come off all round to-day; but sit down
now, while I get hold of our fellow and the horse,
and that done, we may as well go home before the
rush comes; the play's over as far as we're concerned."

Jim Darley had thoroughly understood Mr. Wargrave's infamous proposition, and his first impulse
had been to reply in that strongly vituperative
language which never failed a stable-boy in time of
need; but he had learnt a good deal since he had
been in Mr Praze's stable, and, mastering his

19

temper, he decided it would be better to deceive
him, his own expression would have been "sell
him." Jim really was angry, but putting aside all
moral feeling on the subject, and he was a
thoroughly honest lad, he was indignant to think
that anyone should think him such a fool as to
throw away the first opening that had come to him
in his profession, and it was aditional sugar in the
cup to Jim as he "weighed-in" and heard the "All
right" pronounced, to think how he had sold the
stranger. When he got back to the Paddock, and
the trainer had thrown a critical eye over "King of
the Huns" to satisfy himself that the horse was
none the worse for his race, he said:

"Well, my lad, he ran very kind with you, and
you'd no trouble to win this time; you'll do,
never fear; you've got a head on your shoulders, and
don't forget what you're told."

Jim's face flushed with gratification, for the
trainer was chary of commendation, and from him
this was high praise.

"I hope you'll give me another chance, sir, before
long," replied the lad.

"I shall bear you in mind; but now, tell me,
what was it Mr.——" and here Mr. Praze stopped
abruptly, "I mean the gentleman who spoke to you
just before you left the Paddock, said?"

Tom Bramber stared enquiringly, for he had not
noticed the little incident to which Mr. Praze
referred.

Jim grinned, as he replied, "He laid me a

thousand to ten that the ' King ' won. Do you know his name, sir ? because I think I'll just look round and enquire for him. I should like to pay him that ten pound."

" Confounded scoundrel!" cried Tom, "I only wish I knew who he was ! "

Mr. Praze was not much given to merriment, he was indeed rather of a sardonic disposition, but he fairly chuckled in response to Jim's grin. " No, my boy," he said at last, " I can't tell you his name, but I don't think he'll ask you for that tenner even if you *should* happen to see him."

The trainer kept his discovery to himself, but as he walked away, he murmured to himself:

" Done again, Sam Wargrave, that's game, the rubber and the long odds."

CHAPTER XXXI.

FORGIVEN.

THE first thing Reginald Chacewater did, consequent on the victory of " King of the Huns," was to write to his father, explain the mystery of his disappearance, announce his marriage with Kate Darley, and ask for forgiveness and leave to bring his wife to the Grange. That he was the author of that brilliant masterpiece " A Parthian Flight," he prudently kept in reserve ; it was an extenuating circumstance to be made use of, should the home authorities threaten to be obdurate. Reginald had not much fear of their being reconciled to his marriage in the long

19*

run; but he was conscious that the Squire had just grounds for resentment, and could hardly be expected, in the first instance, to approve of his choice. He was far more sanguine of "things being all right" than Kate; the girl knew Mrs. Chacewater had been very fond of her, and had treated her with great kindness; she was conscious of not having behaved loyally to her benefactors, and suffered pangs of remorse upon that account. She had not ventured to tell Reginald of what scandal there had been about their relations at Bottlesby, and had little doubt that this not only had reached the ears of Mrs. Chacewater, but been accepted as a fact besides. She was nervously anxious to see what reply the Squire would make to her husband's appeal. Some few days slipped by and Reginald's letter remained unanswered; it was in vain he pointed out to her that he could hardly hope to be welcomed with effusion. It was only natural that his father should be angry and not hurry himself to forgive. Kate fretted a good deal over the ominous silence. The following week brought a discovery, which considerably disconcerted Reginald; upon receiving his winnings from the Twybury book-maker, true to his purpose, he at once set to work to pay off his debts, and then discovered the uselessness of his brilliant manœuvre, and that, upon the supposition of his death, these had been already settled by his father, and that one plea he counted on for forgiveness was consequently wanting.

At last Reginald got tired of the Squire's persistent silence, and wrote a strong appeal to his mother, telling her, that not liking to ask his father to pay the residue of his college debts, the accident of the Regent's Park had suggested to him the wily scheme of disappearing, and setting to work with his pen, to earn money to satisfy his creditors. That "A Parthian Flight" was the result of his exertions, and that he could claim a very fair success for a first essay; that while down at Chillingham, he had come across Kate Darley, with whom by the merest accident he had escaped from the ice, "and, thank Heaven, mother dearest, I've persuaded her to be my wife; you know what a sweet, good girl she is, as well as I do, and I assure you that I only want my father's forgiveness and yours to be thoroughly happy. I was wrong not to think of all the pain and anxiety the report of my death would naturally cause you, but it was the impulse of a moment, my creditors were clamorous, and, once committed, I was ashamed to go back—save the deception I have practised upon both of you, I have nothing to be ashamed of."

Fond as Mrs. Chacewater was of Kate, she most certainly would not have picked her out as a daughter-in-law, but she was a practical woman, and it was no use thinking about that now; the thing was done, and there was nothing for it but to make the best of it. Kate was his inferior by birth, but, thank goodness, she had been brought up a lady, and then the lady of the Grange fell back upon that great consolatory reflection that it might have been worse ; she knew as well as her husband did, that they must forgive Reginald at last, he had made submission, he was their only son, and his offending was not such as to justify perpetual feud between him and his father. Then he was the author of " A Parthian Flight," the story of which everyone was talking, and Mrs. Chacewater felt extremely proud of her son's first literary offspring. So that evening she pleaded Reginald's cause with her husband, and the Squire, who, in reality, only wanted a decent pretence to be reconciled, gladly yielded to his wife's entreaties. A letter of forgiveness was therefore despatched to the culprit, tempered, as was to be expected, with some rebuke, and an almost conditionally expressed desire that Kate should at once retire from her present calling ; and that, at some considerable pecuniary sacrifice, had been already arranged with Mr. Slater.

While these negotiations were going on between the reigning monarch at the Grange and his exiled heir, the Wargraves were in a state of extreme bewilderment. Neither father nor daughter could at all make out what had happened; Clara was aghast at the complete failure of her scheme, and her father was repenting that he had laid those liberal odds at Epsom. That " King of the Huns " had won, and that Reginald consequently was now in funds, they of course knew, and Mr. Wargrave's agent had made them acquainted with the fact that Reginald had left Twybury, and that he and Kate

Darley were now living openly together as man and wife in the vicinity of the Oxford Circus.

Clara was more disgusted than ever at the defeat of her machinations and still flouted the idea of their being actually married. But all doubt on this point was speedily dissipated—once Mr. Chacewater had despatched his message of peace he saw no reason for any further concealment, and, as a preliminary, at once announced to the Rector that Reginald was about to return to the Grange and bring a wife with him. "As for saying, Marton, that I am altogether pleased with the marriage and that he has chosen as I could wish, I can't, but the thing is now done."

"Then he is married to Kate!" ejaculated the Rector in great astonishment.

Mr. Chacewater nodded in the affirmative.

"No, Squire, it's not to be supposed that you would like the match, no father in your place could; from a worldly point of view he might have done much better, but for a girl that'll stick to him through the wear and tear of life I'm not quite sure he could. It required no doubt in the first instance an effort to forgive them, but we must remember, that we have wronged these young people in believing them to be wicked when they were only foolish."

The Rector spoke bravely, and in accordance not only with his belief, but his Christian character. Though a man of the world, he was a conscientious priest, and, grasping the situation at once, was desirous for the reconciliation between father and son to be thoroughly cordial. Still, as he carried the news homewards, he could not but regret the extinction of a day-dream in which he had sometimes indulged. He had never breathed a word of it to Lucy, but she and Reginald were great friends, and he could not help thinking that if they could take a fancy to one another, it would be a great satisfaction before he died to see her installed as future chatelaine to Chacewater Grange. He was not a rich man, and, apart from his preferment, had but a modest income. It would have been pleasant to have thought of his little Lucy reigning eventually as the great lady of the parish in which they were. However, there was an end to all that now, and he could only hope that Lucy's affections were still under her own control. That his daughter should receive the news unmoved, though a source of satisfaction to the Rector, was not to be wondered at. To begin with, she was not an emotional damsel, and in the next place, she by no means possessed the callous worldly wisdom of Clara Wargrave. Such transgression as Reginald had been held guilty of, would have made any love affair between her and the man who committed it impossible, at least for a time. She was no believer in such transitory affections, and moreover, like Parson Wilber's parishioners, possessed "Old-fashioned ideas of what's wrong and what ain't," and had schooled herself for some little time now, to crush all feeling she had originally had for him. The girl honestly strove to persuade herself that she was glad that Reginald's conduct had been shamefully misrepresented, they could still be all honestly proud of the successful author, and made up her mind to call upon Mrs. Reginald as soon as she should arrive, and be great friends, if Kate would only allow her to be so.

The Rector thoroughly understood that the news had been given him expressly for publication; it was, further, only common justice that the scandal current in Bottlesby against Kate should be at once strongly refuted; and the consequence was that before twenty-four hours were over the tidings reached Carlingham Park, and were received there in the first instance with much incredulity, but enquiry soon convinced Sam Wargrave of the truth, and that Reginald and Kate were really married. When at length convinced that her designs were finally overthrown, the fair Clara exhibited the snappish side of her disposition, to which allusion has already been made. She was not such a fool as to dream of showing her disappointment outside her own family; but it is quite certain that Reginald's marriage was much more earnestly deplored by her father and mother than it was by his own people. Miss Wargrave's dictum on the situation was that they should at once call and offer frigid congratulations on the event.

" It will never do, papa," she said, " to be the least backward in the matter, and as soon as the happy couple arrive, we must of course call upon them, and ask them to dinner. They are our nearest neighbours, and are likely to be rather touchy about the bride being properly welcomed. It's a terrible thing for them, of course, and poor Reginald will no doubt be sick to death of the baby-faced chit before six months are over."

Miss Wargrave had never taken very much notice of Kate, although she had of course seen her in the days when she was governess at the Grange. A tall, showy young woman herself, she had regarded Kate as an insignificant little thing, undervaluing her good looks, as women are apt to do their opposites. Although she kept it to herself, she was as angry as she ever permitted herself to be; but she had great powers of self-control and, save her increased acerbity towards her father and mother, gave no sign of her wrath; nevertheless her scheming brain was already plotting revenge against her successful rival. A vain, good-looking girl, she had certainly, before his disappearance, believed Reginald by no means indifferent to her personal attractions. With her consummate taste in dress and knowledge of the world, the fair Clara thought, the glamour of his passion once over, she should speedily eclipse the circus girl, as she had contemptuously called Kate, in Reginald's eyes. Men are weak, and if she could inflict the pangs of jealousy upon Kate, Miss Wargrave had no intention of denying herself that gratification.

There was one person, however, to whom the announcement of Reginald's marriage gave unqualified satisfaction, and that was his sister Jessie. That her brother should marry her dearest friend was, as she said, delightful, and she so expatiated upon the subject to her mother, that, on their arrival a few days later, Mrs. Chacewater was almost as enthusiastic in welcoming her new daughter as Jessie herself. There was a long talk between Reginald and the Squire that night, in which he went frankly into the details of the whole of the last year of his life; told how he had backed " King of the Huns" out of the proceeds of his book, at his wife's suggestion, and had won money enough to have paid all his debts, and had found they were already settled. "Nevertheless, father," he said, "the money came in very handy, for Kate had apprenticed herself to the Royal Hippodrome, and was such a success there, that old Slater, the proprietor, made me pay five hundred to cancel her indentures. And though, perhaps, in your eyes, I have made a foolish choice, I don't think so; and, after all said and done, it's my mother's fault. If she hadn't brought up Kate to be a lady it would never have happened."

CONCLUSION.

THERE might be a little hesitation, but that the neighbourhood generally would welcome Mrs. Reginald was pretty certain to be the case; and the neighbourhood was then most agreeably disappointed. From the position she had formerly held at the Grange, Kate was unknown to most of them; and, as the daughter of a farmer, and one

who had been a professional circus-rider, callers were
prepared to meet a bold-eyed, masculine woman,
and were fairly astounded at the slight, pretty, lady-
like girl that Mrs. Chacewater presented to them as
" my new daughter." In short, Kate was a great
success, and, as one old friend of the Squire's
remarked to his wife, driving home from their first
call on Mrs. Reginald: " I tell you what, Emily, if
that's the way they bring them up in the Royal
Hippodrome, I only wish our girls had gone there
instead of to that school at Brighton." Mrs.
Wilbraham laughed at her liege lord's joke, as she
replied : " A risky experiment ; but, I confess, one
would never guess that Mrs. Reginald had ever done
anything of that kind."

The Wargraves, in particular, were amongst the
earliest to welcome them ; as neighbours living only
five or six miles away, it was only natural they
should be. He was habitually hospitable, but, at
his daughter's instigation, Sam Wargrave was
profuse in his attentions to the new married couple.
Miss Wargrave declared that it was indispensable,
as she could not bear it to be supposed that she had
been left to wear the willow, a matter that had
occurred to few of the people round about. True,
here and there old ladies remembered that there
had been a bit of flirtation between the two, and
had wondered whether anything would come of it ;
but it had pretty well faded out of recollection, and
Clara knew as well as anybody that it had done so.
But she had always cared for Reginald, as far as it

was in her to care for anyone. The country was dull, and if she could amuse herself by producing a misunderstanding between husband and wife it would be no unpleasing addition to Miss Wargrave's enjoyment. The consequence was that, when the shooting season came round, Reginald was often asked over to Carlingham Park for a day or two as a bachelor. Kate was not suspicious; but from the first she had conceived an instinctive dislike to Clara. She had implicit trust in her husband, but she could not help thinking that he was more at Carlingham Park than there was any occasion for. Still, she did not trouble her head very much about it.

The dropping a stitch in knitting, I believe, is likely to unravel the whole work, and circumstances they could not have anticipated, were about to drag the machinations of the Wargraves into broad daylight. It must be borne in mind, in the first place, that both father and daughter had no belief in Reginald's marriage, until some few weeks after the City and Suburban was decided. Mrs. Wargrave, although somewhat afraid of her daughter, was an energetic, managing woman, generally wrote her invitations herself, and had hitherto invariably penned those so lavished on Reginald and his wife. But when, one morning, Clara suggested that Reginald Chacewater should be asked to join a shooting-party, which had been organised for the ensuing week, she willingly assented, but pleaded being very busy and asked her daughter to write it for her. Miss Wargrave, without giving the matter a thought, did so at once; if anyone had suggested to her that she had better not, she would have asked with unfeigned curiosity, why not? That anonymous letter she had penned some six months ago had, by this, pretty well faded from her memory, and, even had it not, she would have failed to see that writing an invitation to Reginald Chacewater to come and shoot could have any possible connection with the subject. The note arrived at the Grange during breakfast, and after opening it Reginald tossed it on the table, remarking as he did so, "An invitation to shoot at Carlingham; I think I'll go."

" Wargrave must have a lot of birds this year," said the Squire. "How long is it for, Reggie? Remember I want you at home on Friday."

" All right, I shall be back by then, it's only for two days," and so saying, he lounged out of the room.

When Kate rose, she passed her husband's seat on her way to the door, and as she did so, noticed Clara's note, and picked it up in purposeless fashion; but as her eye fell upon it, the handwriting struck her; where had she seen that hand before? It was not Mrs. Wargrave's, of that she was quite sure, and as she glanced through the note and came to the signature of Clara Wargrave she recollected. Surely it was the same handwriting as that in the note that Tom Bramber had given her. That note was in her dressing-case still, and it would be easy to compare the two. If so, Clara Wargrave was the

woman who had instigated Tom Bramber to strike
" King of the Huns" out of the City and Suburban.
But why had she done so ?   The reasons she gave in
that letter were merely arguments to induce Bramber
to do what she wished.   But why did she wish it ?
It must have been in her father's interest.   Kate had
heard of the successful *fête* that Mr. Wargrave had
given on the strength of his " Chorister " winnings.
She knew also of the mishap that had befallen
" King of the Huns " in the Derby from her brother,
and Jim had darkly hinted, at the time, that the
collision which had destroyed ¦the horse's chance,
had been deliberately planned.   Mr. Wargrave must
have betted heavily against the " King " at the City
and Suburban, and at his suggestion Clara must
have written that letter to Tom Bramber.   By this
time Kate had reached her bed-room and was com-
paring the two notes ; yes, there could be little doubt
about it, the hand that had penned the one had most
assuredly penned the other.   What a disgraceful
thing; she did not like Miss Wargrave, but she
would never have believed that she would have
stooped to do a thing of this kind.   Then her eye
fell on the shameful aspersion of her own honour,
and the blood flew to her temples, and her eyes
sparkled, and a bit of the old leaven flashed out, as
she said to herself, she would know this woman no
more.   She felt sure, when Reginald and the Squire
were made aware of it, that they also would be of
opinion that neither Clara Wargrave nor her father
were fit to associate with honest folks.

When Reginald was shown the two notes he was furious: that a man pretending to be a gentleman should behave in this wise, was disgraceful, for that Clara had written at her father's dictation, he had no doubt; but the thing that angered him chiefly, was the attack upon his wife's fair fame. When the Squire was informed of the discovery he took a more rational view of the matter. "Decline that invitation, by all means, and we'll drop the Wargraves; that letter of his daughter's is quite justification for doing so, but now you must look at the whole thing from his point of view. Wargrave can give a very specious explanation of his conduct to the world generally. To begin with, my boy, by keeping your marriage secret, you gave a handle for the report that it had not taken place, and he will argue that Miss Wargrave only wrote what all Bottlesby believed; and in the next place he will admit that he had his own reason for " King of the Huns " not winning the City and Suburban, and that he did his best, in consequence, to induce Bramber to strike him out. Sharp practice, if you will, but hardly sufficient to ostracise a man altogether. As far as we go, the acquaintance must cease, but I don't see what more you can do."

Reginald saw that it was not desirable to revive all the scandal current about Kate and himself before they were married, and it was also true that Sam Wargrave could give a tolerably plausible account of the matter; but for all that, the idea that the Wargraves were not to be called to account for their villainy was a bitter pill to swallow. What could have made them so bitter against him ? What had made Clara attempt so malignantly to blacken his wife's character? And that was rather a puzzle to Kate herself; but when the Squire's view of the case was put before her, she utterly refused to pass the thing over in the placid manner that he suggested.

" No," she exclaimed, " I'll have it out with this woman face to face. I will show her her own letter, and tell her it's a lie. Why she has uttered it, I don't know, but I will. She never thought that note would fall into my hands, but it has, and so will her motive for writing it come to my knowledge. It is war to the knife between us. And I will make no terms with Clara Wargrave." Kate had of course told both the Squire and her husband of her visit to Bramber's farm, her accidental encounter with Praze, and how she became possessed of the note. That she should let the trainer know she had discovered the writer of it, was natural ; as also it would have been to acquaint Bramber of the discovery, but Tom had left Bottlesby and gone off to settle nobody exactly knew where. A few days brought Praze's reply, in which he could only attribute the whole affair to the evil machinations of his old enemies the " Wargrave lot," and chuckled much at having once again got the better of his opponents. He also narrated how, at the last moment, Wargrave himself had actually attempted to bribe Jim Darley to pull his horse, and so lose the race.

20

" We have him now," cried Reginald, when he had read the letter. " We can have him up before the Stewards of the Jockey Club for fraudulent practices, and I should think if they please they could warn him off the Turf, at all events the exposure would be sufficient to cause his ostracism by all decent people," and the Squire thoroughly endorsed his son's view of the case. In Reginald's eyes the trainer's was the right reading of things, a mere ordinary attempt to make money, by betting against " King of the Huns " and then insuring his defeat. But Kate adhered to her opinion that Clara had some other motive to serve when she penned that note to Bramber, and as to what that was, she was speedily enlightened. She had become very great friends with Lucy Marton, and in the course of a confidential chat one afternoon gave her a somewhat sketchy account of the transaction, and said that what puzzled her about the business was Miss Wargrave's inter-fering in it at all.

" She has always struck me as a very independent young lady, and by no means given to pay much attention to the wishes of her father or mother."

" Yes," replied Lucy, " she is not much given to ask guidance from anyone, and what her object can have been upon this occasion I can't see. She couldn't even have known that the horse's success or defeat would concern Reginald, but I can give you one hint that may throw some light upon it. I am convinced that before he disappeared she intended to marry him, and I think till your marriage was announced the probability is that she had not quite given up that hope."

Lucy did not think it judicious to say so, or she might have added that the fair Clara had of late manifested a decided inclination to annex Reginald as an admirer, and that she thought it behoved Kate to take care of her " own " even now, but wisely held her tongue ; still her speech let a flood of light into Mrs. Reginald's mind, and she resolved that reckoning between her and Miss Wargrave should not only come, but come quickly.

It must not be supposed that when Kate Chace-water decided on " bearding the lion in his den," and confronting Miss Wargrave with the slander and treachery of which she believed her guilty, that no feelings of anxiety or trepidation assailed her. On the contrary, as she stood before her glass, and set her neat little felt hat rather defiantly on her dark curls, and proceeded to otherwise prepare herself for the encounter, a half doubt crossed her mind if, after all, it might not have been well to abide by the Squire's advice, and, as everything had after all come right, " let sleeping dogs lie."

" Would it be better," she murmured to herself, as she buttoned her close fitting jacket, " to do this ? " and not to rake up the story of her marriage, and so give her rival the chance of insulting her with that old slander, which through the kind reception of her husband's parents, had almost completely died away. Then class prejudice runs very strongly in

20*

small country places, and a girl brought up as was Kate Darley is apt to regard the inhabitants of such houses as Carlingham Park as a somewhat superior order of beings, whom it is difficult to approach on terms of equality.

But Kate was possessed of considerable nerve and pluck, and besides this, love and anger, which will make the most patient Griselda brave, entered considerably into the feelings which induced her at length to decide on going at once to the Park and demanding an interview.

Loving Reginald as dearly as she did, and feeling herself to be scarcely worthy of the devotion which her husband gave her, what to her mind seemed the highest honour any girl might look for, that of being his wife and the future mistress of the Grange, Kate also felt that (if only for his sake) it behoved her to face Miss Wargrave at once, and to make her acknowledge her perfidy, apologise for her impertinence, and in fact to generally bite the dust.

So young Mrs. Chacewater found herself walking up the long drive which led to the hall door of Carlingham Park, inwardly considering how she should commence the attack and what she should do if, as was quite likely, Clara Wargrave should coolly disclaim all knowledge of the anonymous letter.

"For," thought Kate to herself, as she walked rapidly along, "although I feel sure the handwriting is the same, and that moreover she *had*

designs on Reggie, and would have sacrificed me or
anyone to have secured him for herself, yet I have
no absolute proof, and, if she denies it, where can I
obtain any ? "

At last she decided to let things take their chance
and be guided by circumstances as to how she should
bring the accusation home to the sinner.

On arriving at the house, she was informed by
the butler that Miss Wargrave was at home, and
would be with her immediately.

During the interval which elapsed between the
exit of that functionary and Clara's entrance, Kate
" pulled herself together," as it were, for the coming
battle. Looking round the big handsome room,
which bore more evidences of wealth than the more
faded beauty of the reception rooms at the Grange,
Kate took heart, and told herself that if she had
been deemed good enough to be wooed and won by
Reginald Chacewater, and to be accepted by his
mother as her daughter, she was indeed quite equal
to upholding her position with people like the
Wargraves, of whom their money might be said to
be their strongest claim to distinction. She was still
thinking when the door opened and Miss Wargrave
entered the room.

Now it often happens that when we have laid our
plans with great care and subtlety, some little and
quite unexpected circumstance will throw all our
strategy to one side, and we shall after all take an
entirely different line of action to what we had
arranged. So it was in the present instance that

Kate, who had meant elaborately and by degrees to introduce the subject of the anonymous letter, was surprised, as will be seen, into a movement which made its authorship a thing beyond dispute, while it is probable that had she quietly proceeded, as she at first intended, Clara's *aplomb* would have stood to her and she might for ever have evaded the possibility of detection. But there undoubtedly is, deep underlying the thin veneer of civilization and the superficial polish which it gives, a certain vein of natural savagery in our natures, which some unlooked-for incident will force out, and never is this more strongly marked than in a quarrel between two women who have been rivals.

In this case jealousy was predominant in the hearts of both, and there is no stronger factor in the gamut of human passions, or one more warranted to bring out bitterness, in its raw state.

Kate looked long and steadily at the woman who, perfectly dressed and with a careless, half-contemptuous air of intimacy, now approached her. Womanlike, she closely observed, without appearing to do so, the exquisite get-up, and stately figure of the girl who had, she believed, cruelly maligned her in times past, and who now tried to alienate her husband. Probably at that moment, although she herself was unaware of it, Miss Wargrave's undoubted beauty and extremely becoming morning toilette added gall to bitterness, for it is wonderful how much more forgiving one woman is likely to be to another, however deeply sinning, if she meets her in an ill-fitting gown.

Clara Wargrave's *insouciance* meanwhile was entirely assumed. She too had, or thought she had, bitter reasons of dislike towards young Mrs. Chacewater. Such love as Clara had to spare for anyone but herself she had given long ago to Reginald, she had, so to speak, marked him for her own, long before he or anyone had thought of little Kate Darley as anything but a child — old Farmer Darley's neglected daughter, as she contemptuously described her. But for this little upstart, this nursery governess, this circus rider! Miss Wargrave believed she would ere this have been Reginald Chacewater's wife, a position which, apart from the real affection she had for him, would have suited her exactly. As has been shown, Clara Wargrave greatly exaggerated the feelings which Mr. Chacewater had entertained for her. He thought her indeed a handsome woman, with whom he was quite willing to flirt, but he had no fixed idea of falling in love with her to any extent, still less of asking her to be his wife; but a spoiled, handsome, self-willed girl like Clara Wargrave, who was also an heiress to boot, would have found this difficult to credit, and that his admiration went no further than this limit never entered her mind, on the contrary she regarded Kate as one who had unfairly robbed her of her legitimate lover, and whom therefore she justly hated. As a matter of fact Reginald had never cared for anyone but the girl he married, whose sympathy and regard had been so innocently and affectionately displayed towards himself during the dark days of his adversity.

And now as Clara looked at the pretty girlish face and figure of the woman who stood, as she believed, in her place, a great hatred for her rival seized her, and so far from regretting any previous attempt to injure her, she resolved that if it were to be done, she would—although no one was better aware than herself how useless and detrimental is a flirtation between a girl and a married man—make Reginald Chacewater love her, and so revenge herself on his wife.

" I hope," said she, coolly offering her hand to Mrs. Chacewater, " you have not been here long ? I have been interviewing my dressmaker, and as she comes from town to fit me — a thing I believe she will do for no one else—I always consider her visit as too solemn for interruption. In fact I give orders that no one is to disturb me while Madame Leroux is here."

Kate Chacewater took no notice of the extended hand, except by a slight gesture of her own, implying that she rejected this usual salutation, and fixing her large eyes on the other's face said :

" Had I been obliged to wait far longer I should still have done so, for I meant to see you."

" Indeed," said Miss Wargrave with assumed cool- ness, while she inwardly raged at the " insolence of this girl," in declining her proffered hand, " I can hardly imagine that anything that you could have to say to me would be of much importance. Something about the new golf club, I suppose? but really I have not much to do with that. Such a number of *odd* persons get into all our clubs now, that it is useless to attempt to keep them at all *nice !* It's really better to resign oneself at once to the inevitable, and keep to one's private ground."

" I agree with you," said Kate, " that it is difficult to keep a club, or even a neighbourhood, at all ' *nice* ' when persons are admitted whose education at any rate should have made them conduct themselves as ladies, but who are, like yourself, too innately bad to be influenced by any training."

" Training ! " sneered Miss Wargrave. " You speak as if you were still in your circus ! "

" No," said Kate, " I do not. The poor girls in the circus were simply ignorant, they were not—as I knew them—either traducers or slanderers. Not one of them but would have been ashamed to act as you have acted. Not one would have tried to blacken my character, or have made love to my husband ! "

" Blacken *your* character ? " cried Clara, beside herself with rage, at this last thrust. " *Your* character ! What character have you to speak of ?—you who were Mr. Chacewater's mistress, as we all know, and lured him into marrying you out of pity. Ask the man Bramber, who would have married you, but for your disgraceful conduct ! "

" Ah ! " cried Kate, producing the two letters, and thrusting them before the angry woman. " I have asked Mr. Bramber, and he has shown me your letter in which you dare to say——"

"Dare! yes, and I dare it again," said Clara, interrupting her furiously. "You to speak of character! you to dare to come here! a common circus girl! and worse than even we know, I daresay. I might easily have said worse of you, and yet not have said too much."

"Ah!" cried Kate, "then it *was* you who wrote these shameful letters? I knew it! I knew it, but you have confessed. And now all 'the neighbourhood' which you are so anxious to keep ' *nice*' shall know what sort of woman Miss Clara Wargrave really is, and what sort of man her father is also, to permit his daughter to act thus; and my husband! any gentleman in the county will see that Mr. Wargrave's attempt to tamper with the jockey who rode 'The King' is brought before the Jockey Club. There will be punishment for such a cruel plot as you and he had prepared for us—for me and my dear husband—who have never injured you."

Clara, who in her fury had almost forgotten the anonymous letter which she had written to Tom Bramber (more than six months ago), now saw too late that she had betrayed herself, and, as the consequences of this mistake, both to herself and her father, crowded on her mind, felt almost overwhelmed.

"I—did not see!" she began stammering, "I did not recognise the handwriting! I have admitted nothing, I deny——"

"It is all useless now," said Kate, who, feeling mistress of the situation, could afford to be calm again. "I know all, and what is more, all Bottlesby shall know it also. I wish you good morning, Miss Wargrave, and I think it will be long before I—or anyone who hears this story—will care to enter Carlingham Park again."

Then drawing her slim figure to its full height, young Mrs. Chacewater swept past her prostrate rival, who made no attempt to stop her, and with the very slightest inclination of her head, left the room, and the house—it is needless to say for ever.

Clara Wargrave sat still for a long time, feeling absolutely crushed by the situation into which her own spite and folly had led her. Furious with the girl who had just left her—bitterly angry with Reginald for preferring another to herself—she was still more angry with her own conduct in the affair. That she, who prided herself on her tact, should have neglected the commonest precaution of sufficiently disguising the addresses of the two letters!

"That I should have been such a fool," she murmured to herself, as she watched Kate's vanishing figure in the distance, going down the long curves of the drive, "as to have such an admission surprised out of me by that girl. Why had I not *aplomb* enough to coolly deny it?—there was no proof."

Then, too, Kate's last words, uttered at hazard as they were, filled her soul with terror! What if really it were possible to drag this affair—which

Clara more than suspected was true—before the Jockey Club, of her father's tampering with the jockey—Kate's own brother, she recollected—who was to ride the "King of the Huns" in the great race !

"Well," she thought, "after all, there is one comfort, there were no witnesses to this scene ! it is but her word against mine. And if it comes to the worst, I must deny the whole thing. As to father, he must do the best he can, and I can trust him to get out of it somehow."

After a storm, there generally comes calm, and so, when Kate had, to her own mind and to her husband's, satisfactorily proved that the spiteful writer of the anonymous letter and Clara Wargrave were one and the same person, they decided after the first burst of indignation to let the matter drop. Kate was satisfied to see that the discovery had thoroughly disgusted Reginald with the fair Clara, and that he had no longer any wish to go to the shootings at Carlingham Park. She had never been at all jealous of her husband, feeling indeed too secure of his love, but still no woman likes to have her husband continually asked to a house in the neighbourhood without her, and as a bride Kate had especially resented this in the Wargrave invitation.

Reginald, who was deeply angered by the inso-lence of the remarks in the letter anent his wife, yet felt that it was difficult to expose Clara's base-ness to any good end. It would merely rake up the foolish scandal about their marriage, and now as they were becoming popular in the neighbourhood, they both felt it better to let the Wargraves alone. Reginald contented himself with writing a sharp letter to Clara's father, in which he expressed himself strongly on the subject of both his and his daughter's behaviour.

This letter, received as it was just as they were going to dinner, made Mr. Wargrave exceedingly uncomfortable, and certainly deprived him of his usual appetite.

After dinner, he called Clara into the library, and they had a long talk, during which they exchanged several uncomplimentary opinions of each other's tactics, but on one point they were quite agreed, namely to keep the matter to themselves, if they were permitted to do so by the enemy.

"Fact is, Clara," said old Wargrave, "you and me have made a mistake, the worst mistake of all, my girl—we have *gone and got found out !*"

"Yes, papa," said Miss Clara, "and if we all went up to town a little earlier than usual, it would be as well!—and give things here time to shake into their places again."

And so it was decided, and for a time Bottlesby knew them no more.

There is little more to add ere saying good-bye to the *dramatis personæ* of this story. Miss Wargrave did go to town, and feeling that her credit in the neighbourhood of Bottlesby was somewhat insecure, and perhaps—who knows?—wishing to show Reginald that she would not wear the willow for him eventually married one of her father's friends, a City man, whose fortune at any rate left nothing to be desired, and if her husband was not quite the aristocratic hero of her early dreams, he was, at any rate, a good honest fellow, and indeed—as Kate said on meeting Mr. and Mrs. Josephson long afterwards at a local party—"a great deal too good for her."

As for Reginald and his impulsive, warm-hearted little wife, they settled down most happily at the Grange, and—when, in the fulness of time the old Squire and his wife were laid at rest in the quiet churchyard, where so many dead and gone Chace-waters already slept—had become thoroughly dear to those amongst whom they lived, and popular alike with rich and poor.

Reginald's literary work occupied much of his time, and if in his latter days of prosperity he never achieved such a brilliant success as in his first novel—written under the clouds of adversity and poverty—he yet held his own amongst his compeers. And Kate, at any rate, believed there never were such stories written before or since.

Theirs is indeed a most happy household, and as time goes on and children come to the Grange, old Mrs. Darley—released at length from her long bondage by the death of her husband—takes up her abode near them, and I think likes the honour and glory of the big house almost as well as the super-vision of the grandchildren—although to her dying day she never admitted that she did.

Even the feud between the Wargraves and themselves seemed likely to heal when Lucy Marston at
length decided to accept the eldest son of the house,
Captain Horace Wargrave, whose military experiences had much improved him already, and
whose love for Lucy went still further to make him
a very decent fellow, with nothing of his father's
vulgarity or his sister's ostentation.

Mr. Praze continues to prosper, and often
when he can spare the time he runs down to see
Tom Bramber, who—his first love-troubles well got
over and forgotten—has married the pretty daughter
of a neighbouring farmer, who, albeit she knows of
her Tom's early infatuation, likes and admires Mrs.
Chacewater of the Grange with all her heart.

Praze's prophecy comes off to the letter. Jim
Darley, ere many months have passed, does indeed
sport silk! and becomes one of the first jockeys of
the day, to the great joy and pride of his old patron.

As to the famous "King of the Huns," his
racing triumphs over—and are they not written
in the chronicles of his day?—he finds a luxurious
home in the breezy paddocks near his old master's
house, and in the comfortable clover pasture and
good sleeping quarters which are his lot passes the
honourable remainder of his days. And so with
him—not the least important personage in it—our
little story ends.

Kate and Reginald never forget that on him had
once hung their fate and happiness, and are pro-
portionately grateful

" Ah, Reggie," said Kate, one Sunday afternoon, as she and her husband stood looking at their old friend, " we had better luck than we deserved. If I had not run away from school! if you had not got into debt! if the ' King ' had not *run fast enough !* "

" Well," said her husband, " in that case I should never have written my book—and perhaps never have met you—and certainly the ' King ' would not have won the Rubber—but there is much virtue in an ' if.' "

THE END.